KATE

CHRIS REMBERT

PAGE PUBLISHING, INC.
Conneaut Lake, PA

First originally published by Page Publishing 2021

ISBN 978-1-6624-1098-7 (pbk)
ISBN 978-1-6624-1099-4 (digital)

Printed in the United States of America

PROLOGUE

Have you ever been in love? No, I mean *really* in love? That's what I asked myself as I watched my wife's face disappear beneath the cold black dirt.

"Shit, it's fucking cold out here!" I said to myself, rubbing my hands together, looking for some semblance of warmth.

I continued to cover her up. Now with a little more desperation. In part because I wanted this over and done with. But the real reason I guess, was because I couldn't stand the look on her face. Her laying there, looking up at me, judging me with her cold, smug, lifeless eyes.

I know what you're thinking though. *This guy's an asshole.* Yeah, and if I were you, I would probably be thinking the same thing. But I'm not you, so frankly, I don't give a fuck about your opinion. Because the sooner I bury this bitch, the sooner my problems become nonexistent.

"Whew, almost done." I panted.

And you wanna know the funny part in all this? The more dirt I threw on her, the freer I became. It was absolutely liberating.

The air was cold, damp, and still. And here I was blowing plumes of smoke into it in a feeble attempt to calm myself down. After all, this *was* the first time I had killed someone. And I had not mastered the unfeeling easiness of a veteran killer. But the more dirt I shoveled into the hole, the more unfeeling I became. And the fact that it was only thirty-nine degrees had nothing to do with it.

"Fuck, I should have gotten some gloves from the barn."

Again I found myself panting heavily while inspecting my hands for the calluses that would be there tomorrow. Fuck it! Calluses were a small price to pay to get rid of this problem.

The dirt was hard, and every time I struck it with the spade, the *ting* sounded like it had wafted across the entire ridge line. But I was determined to finish, and an hour and ten minutes later, I was packing the dirt tightly before going to forage for leaves and branches to camouflage my dirty deed.

"That should just about do it."

I looked at the job I had done and felt my chest and soul swell with pride.

"It's finally over," I said, trying to convince myself that what I had done here was for the greater good. But there was just one more thing I needed to do. So I unzipped my pants, pulled out my penis, and told my crazy-ass *ex*-wife to drink deep. And with a final shake I was relieved, in more ways than one.

I zipped up my pants and grabbed the shovel. Then I looked around to make sure that no proof of me being here ever existed. And as for the dead detective in the barn, I would leave it to his colleagues to find him. My job was done, and all I wanted to do was go home. So I did.

"Okay," I said, exhaling while heading for the car, trying as best as I could not to agitate my wounds.

CHAPTER 1

Peter ~ October 27, 2001, the world was in chaos. I sat in front of the television enveloped in the pain of a nation. Although it had been over a month since the planes crashed into the World Trade Center, I still felt the need to get out and do something. So I went to my computer to look for a place to volunteer.

"Let's see here… Nope, not there," I said, scrolling past the link to help load trucks at a local donation center.

"Okay, here we go."

I clicked the Red Cross icon at the top right of the screen, read the page, and clicked on the volunteer link. I had planned to go down and sign up the following day to do my part.

And that day was *beautiful*. The sun felt good on my face, and today, I was going to go and make a difference in my life. And maybe in someone else's.

"My keys, my phone, and my wallet," I said, patting my pockets to confirm my personal inventory.

I got in the car, and twenty minutes later, I was at the Red Cross field office pushing the alarm button on my key chain to listen for the double chirp. I walked toward the office, and to my surprise, the end of the line almost tailed out the door.

"Excuse me, is this the line to volunteer?"

The thin man I tapped verified my inquiry with a slight nod.

Now I don't believe in destiny, but today, at this moment in time, it just felt like what happened next could not have been avoided. No way, no how.

There she was walking toward me. She was gorgeous, and her complexion glowed in the sunlight. She was with a guy, so right there, I didn't think I had a snowball's chance in hell of getting to know her. Boy, was I wrong. No sooner than the thought had crossed my mind, here she was saying, "Excuse me."

I was so caught up in my thoughts and her looks that I didn't even hear her talking to me.

"Excuse me," she said again, this time with a small tug at my sleeve.

"Is this the line to volunteer?"

"Um yes, yes it is." I said with the biggest frog in my throat.

She stood there with an anxious uneasiness, like she wanted to say something else but couldn't come up with the words. So I thought it was my duty to initiate the conversation.

"What made you want to volunteer?" I asked.

Corny, I know.

"When I saw what happened in New York, I just wanted to help and sooo… I thought there was no time like the present. And here I am. What about you?"

"Pretty much the same reason," I said.

We both shared a light chuckle before she turned and said, "This is my cousin Jeremy."

I don't even think he looked up from his phone long enough to see who I was. But that didn't matter because his was not the attention I wanted.

"Kate."

"Peter."

"Nice to meet you Peter."

"The pleasure is mine, Kate."

The line started to move, and with every step toward the table, I felt that this would be the last opportunity I would have to seal the deal.

"So…do you want to catch a movie or go have drinks sometime?" I asked nervously.

"Wow, you move fast. But okay, yes, I would." She laughed.

She pulled out her phone and scrolled to the keyboard.

"What's your number?"

"562-633-2968," I said.

"I'll call you when I'm ready."

"Ma'am!" the lady at the table yelled.

I watched her walk away, longing for the time when I would see her walking toward me again.

It had been two weeks, and she still hadn't called. I didn't really think about it too much because I had taken a leave of absence from work and was on my way to New York to help feed the first responders.

I was super excited because I had never been to New York. And at the same time, I was nervous. What if another attack happened while I was there? Or what if I saw something that I couldn't handle? It was too late to turn back now, and besides, I didn't want to. An hour later, I was walking through the terminal at LAX when my phone rang.

"Hello?"

"Hey there, going somewhere?"

It was Kate.

I put my bag down and looked around the terminal. How did she know where I was?

"So you just planned to leave and not say anything?" she continued.

I was stumped. So I just stood quietly, searching the terminal with my eyes.

She laughed and said, "Nothing to say? That's okay. I forgive you anyway."

I leaned over to pick up my bag, and that was when I noticed her standing there. Just as beautiful as the last time I saw her.

"Hey, what are you doing here? How did you…?"

"Relax. I'm not stalking you. I'm on my way to New York, and this is my gate."

The smile on my face was literally from ear to ear.

"Well, I'm also going to New York, and this is also my gate," I gloated.

"If I didn't know better Peter, I would have thought you planned this."

"And if I *had* planned this, it could not have gone any better."

"Let me get that for you."

I reached for her carry-on.

"What a gentleman. Thank you. So, Peter, tell me a little bit about yourself."

"Well, I'm a real estate investor, fairly new to the game. I had just closed a strip mall deal in Long Beach when one day, while watching TV, I decided to get off my ass and give back. And that's the day I went to the Red Cross office."

"So I met you in your time of inspiration?" She chuckled.

"Yeah, I guess you could say that," I said sheepishly.

She was very outgoing, which I liked because I was not, and that kept the conversation going.

"So continue," she said.

"Well, I was born and raised here in Los Angeles. Let's see, I graduated from Benton High School before receiving my BA in business from Wharton. Um, I have one sibling, Lilly, who lives in Echo Park not too far from my mother. And then there's Jose, but he's something different altogether. That's pretty much it, nothing too exciting. So what about you?"

"Well, as for me, it's just me. My parents died when I was young, and I was pretty much raised by my aunt. Jeremy is my cousin."

"So what made you get into real estate?"

"It's not something I had planned to do. But four years ago, I was laid of my job as an investment analyst and needed some money. Sooooo…my friend calls me and asks for a loan. He tells me he had his eye on some property in Boyle Heights that he's turning into a commercial housing property, and he needed investors."

"So how did that turn out?"

"Well, I went down and looked at the lot. And as he was talking, the place just seemed to transform right in front of my eyes. And the more he talked, the more excited I became."

"I hope it was a worthwhile investment," she said, offering me a piece of gum.

"Well, not at first," I said.

She looked confused.

"What I mean is that, although I was excited about the project, I wasn't exactly confident in it succeeding. So I backed out."

"Was your friend upset?"

"He said he wasn't, but I could tell it bothered him."

"So what happened then?"

"As luck would have it, one of his other investors backed out, and I decided to take a chance and…"

"And…?"

"It all worked out. We opened Cityscape two years later and—"

"Wait a minute! You own Cityscape?"

"I don't own it outright." I chuckled.

"But you *are* one of its owners, right?"

"I guess you could say that."

I was so caught up in the conversation that I hadn't noticed that we were already at the breezeway about to board the plane. When we boarded, I was hoping she would sit next to me, and when she did, I was ecstatic.

After five hours, eight drinks, and a layover, we finally landed at JFK and were walking through the terminal on our way to the baggage carousel.

"Man, I can't wait to go and lie down at the hotel," I said.

"What, you're tired? I was hoping we could hang out for a while."

I was tired, but here was the girl I had waited two weeks to talk to. And I liked everything about her. So I said okay.

"Where are you staying?" I asked.

"I'm at the Wellington."

"Me too!" I said, almost too giddy.

That was a relief because now I didn't have to travel to see her. And I liked that.

The cab ride over was pretty quiet, and I think we were both pretty beat. But I told myself that I would muster up the energy to go out with her tonight.

*****

After checking in, we walked over to the elevator lobby and entered an open car.

"What floor?" I asked before I pushed 15.

"Ten, please," she said.

The ride up was quick, and within seconds, the doors were opening on her floor.

"Well, this is me," she said with a slight sigh.

"What time did you want to meet up?" I asked.

"You know what? Can I get a rain check?" she asked, nervously waiting for my answer.

"Yeah, that's fine. In fact, I was thinking of a way to tell *you* the same thing," I said relieved.

She leaned over and gave me a kiss on the cheek, which I was not expecting at all, but I liked it.

I watched her walk away, hoping that the elevator doors would close slower than usual. Suddenly, I had found a new energy and wasn't so tired anymore. I wanted to push 10 and go knock on her door to let her know that I didn't want the night to end. But for now, I would just have to wait until tomorrow to see her again. A few minutes later, I was at my door trying to figure out what I was going to do with this newfound energy.

"I think I'll go get a bottle and watch some football," I told myself.

I turned on the TV and went in the bathroom to hop in the shower. The warm water felt good running across my face, and it seemed to soothe every muscle in my body. And believe it or not, the thought of staying in with a bottle became more appealing as time passed.

I got out, got dressed, put my room key in my pocket, and grabbed the ice bucket when somebody knocked at the door.

"Yes?" I said curiously from inside.

Nobody answered, so I walked over and looked through the peephole. No one was there.

I opened the door, and what I saw blew my mind. It was Kate standing there in an overcoat and not too much else.

"Are you busy?" she asked seductively.

Now come on. What was I going to say?

"No, no, not at all!" was what I did say overanxiously.

She walked in, and by the time I closed the door, she had pulled a bottle of scotch out of her pocket, looking for the glasses.

"Do you have ice?"

I looked at the bucket like I expected it to be there.

"Um no… I was just going to go get some."

"Okay. We're gonna need it." She chuckled.

I felt for my key and walked out the door.

While walking down the hall, I had that newfound energy, which came to form in a dance. And when I returned, seeing her in her bra and panties turned it into something else.

I closed the door to begin one of the best nights of my life.

CHAPTER 2

Peter ~ July 4, 2003. The past couple of years were incredible, and today marked a milestone in our relationship. We were engaged and moving in together.

"Here, let me get that for you," she said, grabbing one of the boxes I was carrying.

I couldn't believe how lucky I was. Something like this just never seemed to happen to a guy like me. But don't get me wrong. I liked it, and I liked her.

Just the thought of moving in made me eager for the next step—yep, marriage.

Wait a minute. Was I really thinking about marrying this woman? I watched her walk up the stairs and told myself, "Hell yeah!"

That evening we were sitting at the table about to eat.

"Babe, do you want some cheese on your broccoli?" I asked.

"Oh no baby, I can't eat cheese. It just turns my stomach inside out. Believe me, you don't want any part of that." She chuckled. But she *was* right. I didn't.

"But babe, there is something I want to know."

"What's that?" I asked.

"What were you talking to the downstairs neighbor about?"

I stopped chewing.

"She asked me about the mail," I answered swallowing.

"What about the mail?"

I stopped chewing again.

"She said that someone had broken into her mailbox and asked if we were missing any mail."

"So you like this woman?" she asked seriously.

Yep, you guessed it. I stopped chewing *again*.

"Babe what are you saying?"

"I'm not saying anything. I'm asking. It just seems to me like *you* were doing all the talking with Ms. Apartment Four."

I didn't even know what apartment she lived in. So how did she know?

"I don't understand baby. What are you getting at?" I asked, wiping my mouth.

"Nothing baby, nothing at all." she said looking down.

I didn't know what to think. This was the first time I had ever seen any kind of jealousy from her, and I didn't like it. I decided to overlook it, hoping it would never happen again. At least no time soon.

After that one incident, we really didn't have any more problems. The lady in 4 moved out shortly after our last conversation (thank God), and everything seemed to be going well until...

"Honey, how was work today?"

"It was okay. It was work." I said.

I didn't see the sneak attack because she caught me in the middle of a Lakers game.

"Just okay?"

Commercial.

"Yeah, just okay baby."

"So nothing out of the ordinary happened today at work?"

Game back on.

"Huh?"

She turned off the television.

"Baby, what you are doing?" I asked.

"YOU'RE A FUCKING LIAR!" she screamed before she threw the remote at me.

Now I was completely lost. I sat there with the look of an idiot, completely oblivious, trying to recap my day.

"Baby, what are you talking about?" I asked again.

"I came to your office to surprise you for lunch, but I saw that you were busy."

"Why didn't you just tell Carol to call me?"

"I didn't want to spoil your fun."

Kate had a look on her face that I had never seen before. It was twisted, like she had just eaten something so bitter that she despised even putting it into her mouth.

"Kate, baby, what are you talking about?"

"Do you like her?"

"I don't know what you're talking about. I love *you*."

"Only when she's not around. Who is she Peter?"

"Who?"

"Stop playing with me! The woman I saw you with! The woman in the red dress!"

"Her name is Gail, Gail Chamberlain. She's a potential investor for Delaney Place."

"What else is she investing in Peter?"

She stormed into the bathroom and slammed the door.

"Come on baby, don't be like that. She's just a potential business partner." I said walking after her.

She came out a few minutes later and didn't say another word to me the rest of the night.

Three days had passed since the incident, and most of the tension in the house had died down. And I was hoping things would get back to normal soon. To tell you the truth, they were just about to; that was until I got to work.

"Pete?"

"What's up Jose?"

"I need a really big favor."

"No, you can't sleep on our couch anymore." I joked.

"It's not that... Huh? What? I thought you guys liked when I visited?"

"Visited, not lived."

"You mean to tell me you didn't like my game night nachos?"

"Not every night bro. And certainly not using the ones from the night before under fresh cheese."

"Waste not want not dude."

"Well, I want not." I laughed.

"Anyway, that's not what I came in here for."

"And what would that be?"

"I need you to take Gail out and schmooze the shit outta her tomorrow night."

"I thought you were supposed to be schmoozing the shit outta her tomorrow night."

"I was, but something came up." he said smiling.

"You mean *someone* came up."

He knew I knew he was blowing this business dinner off because he had a date.

But I still made it hard for him though.

"Man, you know that Kate has been on me because of her, don't you? And now you want me to shred our fragile truce so that you can get between somebody's legs?"

"Yes." he said deadpan.

I exhaled heavily and rolled my eyes. How was I gonna tell Kate?

All the way home I was on edge. On a whole, Kate was a wonderful woman, but when she got mad, there was hell to pay. And right now, I was dead broke.

I walked into the house, and surprisingly, Kate was in a good mood. The first in a while.

"Hey handsome. How was work?"

"Okay."

"Just okay?"

Uh-oh.

"Yeah, pretty much the same as any day."

"Well, good, I'm glad you had a good day. Come sit down. I made your favorite."

"Okay, let me go wash up first, and I'll be right down."

I went upstairs more nervous than ever, wondering what I would say to Kate about Gail. My uncle used to always say, "Bad news goes down better over dinner."

I didn't know what in the hell he meant by that, but there was a reason why he said it. So tonight at dinner, I would tell her about Gail.

I went into the bathroom and ran the water cold to cool my face, which seemed to be getting hotter by the moment.

"HONEY, COME ON DOWN BEFORE YOUR FOOD GETS COLD!" she yelled upstairs.

Great! Now she was cutting into my procrastination.

I wiped my face off and loosened my tie before throwing it on the bed to head downstairs. When I walked into the dining room, she was already at the table looking at her phone, sipping wine.

"Hey baby, ready to eat?" she asked.

I nodded nervously and sat down.

"I got some new red at BevMo! Try it and see if you like it."

I picked up the glass and took a sip. I was a wimp. If I hadn't let Jose talk me into this, I wouldn't be in this position right now. She was my wife. So I should be able to tell her anything, right?

"Kate, I need to tell you something," I began nervously.

She looked at me and then at her phone without saying a word.

"We're almost ready to start on Delaney Place. We just need a few more things, and it's a go."

"Things like what?"

"Things like Gail Chamberlain's money."

Suddenly I couldn't breathe, and the air in the room seemed to get dense almost instantly.

"Okay, so what about it?" she asked, crossing her arms.

"We need to go over some final planning, and Jose wants to take her to dinner."

"Okay, so let Jose take her to dinner."

"He would, but something else came up."

Damn, it was getting hot.

"So what are you telling me Peter?"

"I'm telling you I have to take her to dinner to close the deal. You know, try and schmooze the money out of her."

I can't believe I said *schmooze* again.

"Go ahead. Do what you need to do Peter." She said calmly.

The fact that she *was* calm scared the shit outta me. Right then, I think I would rather have had her yelling her brains out. At least then I would have known how she felt about it.

She just sat there sipping her wine and looking at her phone.

After dinner, I thought I was in for it, but Kate was still calm and acting rather normal.

"Baby?"

I turned around and saw her standing there in a skin-tone camisole.

"Don't you wanna come give me some love?"

She closed the door, and I don't need to tell you what happened next. Okay, I'll tell you. I *killed* it!

The next morning, I woke up feeling like a champion. And tonight after I sealed the deal with Gail, I would be king.

That morning was like any other. Kate was on the phone with her assistant scheduling the day's events as I got dressed. I shoved a piece of toast down my throat and grabbed my coffee before kissing my wife and walking to the garage.

Throughout the day, I kept in touch with Kate to assure her that she was on my mind. I even called her from the restaurant just before Gail arrived.

"I thought I was meeting Jose tonight?"

"Yeah, you were supposed to, but he had something else he needed to handle that could not wait."

I opened the door for her and led her to the hostess table.

"Reservation for two under Flores." I said.

The hostess looked confused, and I didn't say anything.

"Right this way, Mr. Flores." she said with a sarcastic swipe.

Again I said nothing.

"So what do you think about our proposal Gail?"

"I thought it was very well planned and thought out."

"So does it look like something that you would be interested in being a part of?"

"It does."

I flagged the waiter and said, "A bottle of your finest champagne please."

"I hope that I'm not being too forward in ordering the champagne."

"No, not all." She chuckled.

"I think Delaney Place will see dividends inside of six months because when we looked at our cost analysis, we were way under budget, which puts money back into your pocket." I said.

The waiter brought the chiller and placed it on the table before opening it to pour our drinks.

"A toast to a new partnership." I said, holding up my glass.

"To a new partnership." she said, doing the same.

An hour later, I was on my way home happy about my schmoozing and anxious to get back to my wife.

*****

On the way home, my phone pinged, so I pulled it out to see who it was.

It was Jose.

"Hey bro, how did it go?"

"Okay." I said.

"So we're in business then?"

"Yes."

"Good job bro! I knew I sent the right man for the job! We should go out and celebrate."

"Not tonight bro. I have to get home to Kate. You do remember that I'm married, don't you?"

"Yeah, and I feel sorry for you every day."

"Good night Jose."

"Good night Pete. Good job bro."

About twenty minutes later, I was exiting the freeway when my phone pinged again.

"Baby Margie needs me to okay some contracts. I should be home shortly."

I had no reason to doubt Kate because this was not the first time her assistant had called after hours, so I didn't think much about it. I just wanted to get home and catch the end of Thursday Night Football.

CHAPTER 3

Kate - I told Peter that I had business at the office tonight. But the only business I had involved showing Ms. Chamberlain who Mrs. Galvan was. So I found out where she worked so that I could case the place out. You know, hiding spots and all that.

And to my surprise, I saw her pulling into the lot.

I checked my phone to see if it was her. It was. Could my luck have been any better?

"Yeah, I think so. I really like the owners. They seem like they will work with me." she said into her phone.

"I didn't see him in the booth. Maybe he's making his rounds."

I walked not too far behind her, pretending to be entranced by what was on my phone.

"Charlie, I'll be all right." she said.

She stuck the keys in the door and walked into the small office. I walked past the door and looked in before going to sit on the bench in front of the laundromat.

A few minutes later, she came out, still on the phone.

"Okay babe, I got what I needed, and I'm on my way to the car. I'll call you in a bit."

She hung up the phone and started to fumble through her purse for her keys. Now was the time, and I had to act quickly. The guard was on the far side of the parking lot, dealing with a woman and her flat tire, which gave me enough time to teach this bitch a lesson.

I walked up behind her and pulled out my knife.

"Shit, I gotta get this door fixed." she told herself before I jammed the blade into her back.

She threw her arms into the air and screamed. I reached around and put my hand over her mouth while I pushed the blade in and out.

"Do you know who I am?" I asked.

She collapsed, which actually helped.

So I plunged the knife into her stomach as she crumbled from the immense pain.

"Frank!" she called out from the ground.

"Why did you do this? What have I done to you?" she asked, wailing.

"You needed to learn to stay away from other people's husbands, you home-wrecking whore! He was supposed to be with me tonight...*not you!*"

I knew she could see the evilness in my smile, and I liked it. I looked down and saw the blood begin to pool around her body as I reached down to remove the knife from it. But before I left, I put it back in seventeen more times so that I could watch her die a slow and painful death. It felt kinda strange though because I actually enjoyed it. And from that moment on, I *knew* I could kill again if I had to, or if I wanted to.

I decided to call Peter and see if he was still at home. If he was, that would give me enough time to change and get back to him before he got suspicious.

"*Hey baby.*"

"Hey. What are you doing?"

"*Nothing. Just having a beer, watching the game.*"

"Okay. I just wanted to let you know I'll be home in a bit. Marcie and I are just finishing up."

"Okay, I'll see you then. Be careful baby."

I hung up the phone and began to take off the bloody clothes. It was everywhere.

"Gotta get clean. Can't let Peter know what I've done."

I looked around to make sure no one had seen me. Then I ran back to the car to place the soiled clothes in the trash bag I had hidden in the trunk.

It was cold, and I was shivering in the night air.

"Gotta get home." I told myself again.

I opened the gallon of water I had and poured it over my arms and legs to rinse whatever leftover blood there was from my body.

"Okay, hurry up Kate. You gotta get outta here." I told myself, looking into the darkness with wide eyes, hoping to leave before the guard came back.

I was shaking and barely able to slip on the T-shirt and sweats I had. But after about ten minutes, I was finally ready to leave before...

"Ma'am, do you need some help?"

Shit, it was the security guard.

"No, I'm all right."

He walked closer.

"Are you sure there's nothing I can help you with?"

"No, I'm okay."

I closed the trunk and walked toward the door.

"What's this?" he asked.

I walked back toward the trunk. In my haste, I had left the sleeve of my bloody blouse hanging out.

"Oh, that's nothing. Don't worry about that. I was going to take it to the laundromat but decided not to."

He grabbed his radio and said, "Yeah, this is Thompkins. I'm going to need another officer over here near This Suds For You."

"Officer, really, this is not necessary."

"I'm going to need you to calm down and take a seat ma'am."

"Officer..."

He pulled out his taser and said, "Take a seat ma'am."

I pulled my knife from my pocket and collapsed on the trunk.

"Ma'am, are you okay?"

He walked over and put his hand on my shoulder.

"I'll be okay. Just as soon as I get rid of you."

"What?"

I turned quickly and stabbed him in the stomach before I took the blade and pushed it up under his chin and through his mouth.

He fell back in pain and pulled the knife out before I ran to rip it from his hand.

"I told you I was all right. But you just didn't listen, did you? If you had, you'd be living right now. But instead, you're going to die out here in the cold alone."

I hurried into the car and sped off, hoping that no one else saw me.

*****

Peter ~ At about 9:30 p.m., I heard the garage door open, and a few minutes later, Kate walked in.

"Hey honey, I'm home safe and sound." she joked.

It seemed as though she was in a hurry because usually she would come in and give me a kiss. Tonight she headed straight upstairs.

"WHAT? NO KISS?" I yelled up from the couch.

"I stink baby. I just finished working out!" she yelled down.

"I thought you and Margie were working on some contracts?"

"We did. We finished early and decided to do some cardio!"

I didn't say anything and really didn't think about it because the Giants were coming back on New Orleans. And besides, she was home, so it really didn't matter at this point.

After the game, I poured her a glass of wine and took it upstairs.

"I've got something for you."

She came out the bathroom after wrapping her hair.

"Good, I needed this. It's the perfect nightcap baby."

Now my wife enjoyed her wine, and in the years I had known her, I never saw her guzzle it like she had tonight.

"Are you okay?"

She stopped drinking.

"Yes, why do you ask?"

"It's just that you're going to town on that wine. I've never seen you do that before."

"Look, I've just had a busy day is all, and this glass of wine really hit the spot."

"Okay." I said.

"Where's the bottle?" she asked.

"Downstairs." I chuckled.

She didn't find it funny. She just hurried out of the room and down the stairs. And when she came back, what had been a full bottle of wine was now almost gone.

"Baby, what's going on? You're acting strange."

"Nothing baby, really. It's just been a long day. To tell you the truth, I just got rid of a problem I had. So actually, it turned out okay."

"Are you sure?"

"I'm sure baby," she said, walking over to kiss me.

"Okay, then I'm going to get another bottle."

The next morning came quick, and I woke up to the repeated ringing of my phone.

I opened my eyes and felt the heaviness of my hangover when I reached for it.

"Hello."

"Peter, where are you?!"

"I'm at home. What's going on man?"

"What happened last night dude?" Jose asked seriously.

"What do you mean what happened? I told you. I closed the deal with Gail and came home. What's going on Jose?"

"Dude, have you seen the news?"

"Man tell me what the fuck is going on!"

"Gail is dead man! That's what's going on!"

"What! What do you mean Gail is dead?"

"What do you think I mean?"

"What happened?"

"Somebody stabbed her like twenty times outside her office last night."

"Huh, how in the fuck did that happen?"

"I don't know. All I know is that the police were at my door at six a.m. asking me questions about me having dinner with her last night."

"You didn't have dinner with her, so why would they…? The reservation!"

Just as I had had that revelation, I heard someone at the door knocking like the police. I ran to the window and saw that it *was* the police.

"Jose, I gotta call you back."

"Pete, what happened last night?"

"I told you what happened. Look, I gotta go. I'll call you back."

I went downstairs and opened the door.

"Sir, are you Peter Galvan?"

"Yes I am."

"Do you mind if we come in and ask you some questions about your whereabouts last night?"

"Do I need my lawyer officer?" I joked halfheartedly.

"That's your prerogative sir, but I don't think that's necessary right now. We're just trying to find out what happened last night."

"What *did* happen last night officer?"

"May we come in sir?"

When I looked out the door, it looked like there were a hundred cops outside, but only two came in.

"Mr. Galvan, is your wife at home?"

It was funny because for the first time this morning, I was wondering the same thing.

"I don't know officer. I just woke up."

He reached into his pocket and pulled out his card.

"Well, when you see her again, give her this and tell her we would very much like to talk to her."

I took the card and sat down.

"What's going on officer?"

"We have a witnesses that said they saw you and Mrs. Chamberlain out last night. Is that true?"

"Yeah, that's true. We had dinner."

"May I ask when you left her?"

"A little after eight thirty or so."

"And what happened after dinner sir?"

"I came home."

"Was your wife at home when you got here?"

"No she wasn't officer."

"Do you know where she was?"

"At her office, I think. At least that's what she told me."

"You think?"

I knew what he was doing. He was trying to trip me up by making me nervous.

"I spoke with her earlier that evening, and that's where she told me she was."

"Do you know if anybody was there with her?"

"Her assistant, I think."

"You think?"

"Yes, I think."

"You wouldn't happen to know her assistant's name, would you?"

"Her name is Margie. Margie Chapman."

He flipped his notepad open and scribbled something down before saying, "Okay Mr. Galvan, I think we're finished here."

I didn't say anything because *I* wanted to know where my wife was. And the quicker they left, the quicker I could find out. There *was* something I wanted to know though, so I asked.

"Officer, what happened last night?"

"Mrs. Chamberlain was murdered last night along with a security guard outside of her office."

"Oh my god!"

"God had nothing to do with this Mr. Galvan."

He turned to walk out before saying, "I do have one more question though."

I put my hands up and said, "Shoot."

"Okay then. Why was the reservation made in your business partner's name?"

"Because he was originally supposed to take her to dinner, but then he had something to attend to. So I took her."

"Okay, I guess that's all then. I'll be in touch."

As soon as they walked out, I ran upstairs and grabbed my phone to call my wife. The phone rang two times before she picked up.

"Where are you?" I shouted into the phone.

"I'm at the market baby. What's wrong?"

"Somebody killed Gail Chamberlain last night!"

"The same Gail you went to dinner with?"

"Yeah, and I think the police think I did it!"

"What? Why would they think you did it? You were with me last night. Are you okay baby?"

"No, I'm not okay. I'm a suspect in a murder investigation."

"You're not a suspect. They would have arrested you if you were."

"Well, they want to talk to you too."

"That's fine."

At that moment, her steadiness calmed me, and I felt grateful for that.

"I'll be home in a bit. I'll make you breakfast, and we'll talk about it some more, okay?"

"Okay." I said, hanging up.

I lay back down with my head spinning from more than my hangover.

A while later, I was awakened by a light push on my shoulder.

"Wake up baby. Breakfast is ready."

"Okay, give me a minute, and I'll be down." I said, yawning and rolling over.

I walked downstairs not hungry at all. As a matter of fact, the smell of the eggs turned my stomach.

"Baby, I'm not hungry." I finally confessed.

"You need something on your stomach. So you need to eat. At least eat some toast."

"Okay, then just give me a piece of toast and some bacon then."

"You want coffee?"

"Yes, please."

"So what did the cops want?"

"They wanted to know where you were, first of all. Where were you?"

"I told you I got up and went to the market. I must have just left before they came."

"I wonder why somebody would want to kill Gail?" I asked in deep thought.

Kate had nothing to say. She just sat there eating her breakfast.

"Did you hear me baby?" I asked.

"Yes, I heard you baby, and it is a terrible thing. Our one consolation is that the police are on the case. And I'm sure that they will find the killer."

"How do you know?"

"How do I know what?"

"How do you know it was only one killer?"

"I don't. But do you think two people stabbed her at the same time? There may have been multiple people there, but I think only one person actually killed her. Don't you?"

That was a strange and creepy thing to say, don't you think?

"Well, whoever did it, I hope they rot in hell!" I said because I couldn't think of anything better to say.

"Me too baby. Me too." she said, coming over to rub my head and console me with kisses.

I felt bad about what had happened to Gail, but I was happy that I had an alibi in my wife. And that was all I needed for now.

CHAPTER 4

Peter ~ The police had talked to Margie, and the story my wife told seemed to check out. And after talking to me several more times, things were finally coming back to normal. Or so I thought.

You see, the thing about living in California is that we have a wealth of beautiful days, and this was one of them. I decided to walk down to the village and get a cup of coffee before coming home to look over the schematics for Delaney Place.

"Hey Mr. Galvan, what can I get for you today?"

"What's up Keith? Can I get a caramel frappe with a double shot please?"

"Wow a double huh?"

I laughed.

"Yeah, I've been busy lately, so I really needed this."

I paid him and walked out.

I took my phone out and took a sip from my coffee when…

"What are you doing?"

Shit! I spilled my coffee.

"Kate? You startled me."

"And why would you be startled Peter?"

"Because you came out of nowhere. Why are you in the village anyway?"

"I have to pick up my dry cleaning." she said dismissively.

I put my coffee on one of the tables outside the shop and grabbed some napkins.

"Can you pick up my shirts for me baby?" I asked.

She snatched the ticket.

"I'll see you back at the house." she said, fuming off.

I walked about fifty feet before I turned around. It felt like somebody was watching me. No one was.

I crossed the street, and when I stepped on the curb, my phone fell out of my hand. I leaned down to pick it up, and when I looked up, I saw Kate standing across the street looking at me. I waved; she did not. And so I turned around and continued my walk home confused by what had just happened.

That was strange. I thought.

Was she following me? Because that would also be strange, wouldn't it?

About an hour later, she walked in.

"Hey baby."

"Hey." she said, dropping her keys.

"Where's the dry cleaning?"

"Give me a break Pete. I'm only one person!"

I was confused. What had I done to illicit this behavior? Nothing was the answer. And where in the hell was the dry cleaning she was so worried about?

I grabbed her arm and said, "Baby, what's going on with you? You've been acting strange lately."

"Me?" she asked. "I'm surprised you noticed me at all!"

I *had* been busy lately but no busier than usual. And anyway, Kate almost always had something to do. So the fact that I was busy never bothered her before, until today.

"You're right baby. I have been busy. What do you say we go out tonight, get away from it all for a while?" I offered.

That seemed to calm her down. And just like that, the old Kate was back. At least for the moment.

That night at dinner, we were seemingly having a good time, or so I thought.

"Hello guys, my name is Rachel, and I'll be your server tonight. Can I start you off with a couple of drinks? Maybe an appetizer?"

Kate said, "I'll have an appletini."

"Can I get a scotch with a water back please?"

"Oh, I just love a single malt. It goes great with dinner." the woman said.

"That's true." I said smiling.

Kate got up, dropped her napkin on the table, and said, "I'm going to the bathroom."

She did go to the bathroom but not to use it. She waited until the waitress came to the drink station and approached her.

*****

Kate ~ "Excuse me." I said.

She turned to me with that annoying-ass smile on her face and asked, "Yes, can I get you anything?"

"Yes, you can. My husband and I would like another server please."

"I'm sorry ma'am. Was there something I did wrong?"

"No, it's just that we don't like you."

She stood there looking at me confused.

"But ma'am, you're seated in my station."

"Either move us or get someone else to serve us. When our meal comes, it will not be delivered by you. Do you understand?"

"Is there a problem Rachel?" asked the manager, who was standing nearby.

"Warren she says she's not happy with my service and would like another server."

"And what seems to be the problem ma'am?"

"The problem is how slow you are to accommodate your customers. How many times are customary to ask for another server?"

"I'll get someone else to serve you right away ma'am."

"Thank you."

The manager called over another server as if it were an inconvenience to satisfy my request.

"This is Carl."

I looked him up and down and said, "He'll do."

Peter was sitting at the table, totally oblivious to all this when I returned.

30

"You must have really had to go?"

"Well, you know how ladies are baby. We have to make sure everything is still right before we leave. I just had to wait for my turn at the mirror."

He took a sip of his drink when his phone rang.

"Hey Mom."

"Hey baby, how are you?"

"I'm good Mom. How are you and Lilly?"

"We're good. You know we miss you."

"I know Mom."

*****

Peter ~ It was true I hadn't seen my mother and sister in a while. But that was because Kate and my mother didn't get along at all. So to avoid the conflict, I would visit them alone when I could get away.

"So when are you coming to visit?"

"Soon Mom."

"You could even bring that wife of yours. I just want to see you. You know you haven't been to the new place since I moved."

I felt ashamed because my mother only lived twenty minutes away, and I should have visited her more. But I was in between a rock and a hard place, and that space seemed to be getting smaller by the day.

"I know Mom. It's just that I've been busy trying to close this deal. I promise I'll make time to come out and see the new place soon." I said.

"Sound's loud. Where are you?"

"At the Carrousel with Kate."

"I should have known."

"She's my wife. Who else would I be with?"

There was silence. I think my mother knew I was getting irritated and that I didn't want to have this conversation in front of my wife.

"Okay, come see me whenever you can get away then."

Ouch, one final stab.

"Okay Mom, I will. I love—"

Click.

"So how is the wicked witch of West Covina?" Kate asked jokingly.

"Leave my mother alone." I snapped.

"That's right. Take up for her like you always do."

"SHE'S MY MOTHER!" I yelled.

Kate looked around and said quietly, "*Your* mother, I know."

"What is that supposed to mean?"

"Nothing baby. Look, I'm sorry I upset you. And I'm sorry I talked about your mother. Can we just enjoy the evening and have a peaceful dinner?"

"Yes." I agreed reluctantly, still confused by her new demeanor.

But I was not about to let it go. I would just table it for now.

"Good. I wanted to tell you that the Daniel's deal came through, and I think that will allow us to cut our operating costs by 40 percent next quarter. And with all that new money coming in, I just have to prep Margie for the meeting on Wednesday and tie up the loose ends."

"So you're not going tomorrow?" I asked.

"No baby, that's our date night, and I need to spend some time with you. Margie is more than capable to stand in for me."

I had no problem with that. After all, she was still as sexy as the day we met, and I was no fool, at least in my own mind.

The rest of the week went by in a flash. I was walking upstairs to grab my briefcase when I walked into the room and heard Kate on the phone.

"You know, that would be great. I really want to try and make this work because it's been too long." she said.

I got my case and walked over to give her a kiss.

"See you tonight baby. Go get 'em." she said.

Now who leaves for work in the morning thinking that their wife is a killer? And at this particular time I had no reason to believe that of mine.

KATE

I just went to work like always. What I didn't know was that my wife did not.

*****

Kate ~ "Hey, Edie, how are you?" I said, walking in.

"I'm glad you took the time to see me. You know, we both love your son, and we need to come to a resolution so that we can all be a family for once."

"Well, have a seat. I was just about to pour a cup of coffee."

I walked into the living room and sat on the couch.

"I love the new furniture. This is my first time being here since you've had it."

"Yes, I love it too. It all really just came together when I moved. I usually take my coffee black, but I brought out the cream and sugar for you."

"Thank you, Edie."

"So what can I do for you Kate? What did you wanna talk about?"

"Well, like I said on the phone"—I took a sip of coffee—"this needs something else."

I reached into my purse and pulled out a half pint of brandy and offered some to my mother-in-law.

"It takes the edge off for me. Do you want some?"

"I'll take a bit." she said, holding out her cup.

I poured her a generous helping before pouring myself an even more generous portion.

Edie picked up her cup and drank half of it when my phone rang.

"Excuse me, I have to take this. Help yourself to some more brandy if you like."

A few minutes later, I was walking back into the room.

"Okay, I'll be there shortly." I said into my phone.

"You have to leave?"

"No, not just yet. I wanted to just pretty much tell you what I told you over the phone. I really want us to be friends because I think

33

we're too old to be acting like children. We both have to share Peter until you die."

She stopped drinking, which tickled me inside. It was nice to see the befuddlement on her decrepit face.

"Excuse me?"

"What I mean is that we are *all* getting older, and eventually you will pass on. So until that day, I just want us to be one big happy family."

We both took another sip of coffee.

"That's a lovely statue. Where did you get it?" I asked.

"A friend of Peter's made it for me. She's really a good sculptor. Don't you think?"

"That she is." I said, taking another sip.

I needed it because it was making me feel easier about what I was about to do.

"Can I offer you something else before you go?"

"No thanks Edie, I really do have to go. I just wanted to make sure we had an understanding. Thanksgiving is coming up. And we'd really love to have you and Lilly there."

"We will be there. Thank you for coming. And I'm glad we had this conversation."

She got up, picked up the serving tray, and walked back into the kitchen, unaware that I had picked up the statue and was right behind her.

"You know what I like most about this sculpture Edie?" I said, bouncing its weight in my hand.

"What's that?" she said, startled at seeing me so close.

"Is that it's just heavy enough to kill you with, you miserable bitch!"

I hit her in the head as hard as I could, sending her crashing to the floor. The thud of her body hitting the tile exhilarated me.

"I just love the grip you can get on this piece. I mean, I can really get a *good* grip on it."

I wiped my face with my sleeve and hit her again. I mean, this was hard work. Or at least harder than I thought it would be. She was a tough old bag, so I had to repeatedly raise the sculpture to pound and crush her skull. And after it was over, I stood over her with a smug arrogance and said, "Turns out this really *was* my favorite piece. To beat your ass with."

I walked over and pulled a plastic bag from under the counter to put the sculpture in. After wrapping it in one of Edie's hand towels, of course.

"I know what I'll be thankful for this year. No fucking in-laws!" I laughed, wiping my hair from my face.

"Damn, I'm starting to sweat." I said through a pant.

I took off my blouse and saw that my sleeve was soaked in blood. So I reached into my purse and pulled out the spare. I needed to get out of there and get rid of the evidence. I didn't know how I was going to do it, just that I was.

I walked over to the mirror to inspect my clothing for any more evidence before I walked out the door.

"Okay Edie, it was nice to see you again. Get some rest okay," I said, closing the door behind me.

I guess I knew in some strange way that Edie's death would cause suspicion. But at that moment in time, I really didn't care.

I took a deep breath and got into my car to hear one of my favorite songs playing.

"That's my jam!" I said, backing out the driveway.

I wanted to celebrate, and that meant stopping by the store for another bottle of wine.

CHAPTER 5

Peter ~ Kate got home about six and found me sitting on the couch in the dark drinking whiskey. She turned on the light.

"Damn, baby, you scared me. Are you all right?"

I took another gulp of my drink and stared into the distance.

"I should've been there more." I mumbled.

She ran to my side like the dutiful wife I thought she was.

"Baby, now you really are scaring me. What's wrong?!"

"My mother…"

"Your mother what?"

"My mother is dead!" I wailed.

She sat back flabbergasted, playing the part.

"What happened?"

"They found her in the kitchen with her head bashed in."

"Oh my god!" She gasped.

I looked at her.

"Baby, who would do this to my mother? She never hurt anybody. Sure she could be gruff at times, but she wouldn't hurt a fly. Who would do this to her?"

"Awww baby, I'm so sorry." she consoled.

I took another drink.

"Did the police call you?" she asked.

"No, it was Lilly."

"So where is she now?"

"At the house."

"Well, then why are we still here? We should be there with your sister."

"I was waiting for you so that I wouldn't have to go alone."

"Let's go baby. We need to be there."

When we got to the house, it was surreal. It looked just like what you would see in the movies. People were everywhere doing their individual duties to secure and read the crime scene. Complete with yellow tape and all.

I didn't want to get out the car. But with Kate's urging, I was able to.

We walked up to the house as two uniformed officers stopped us on the walk.

"This is an active crime scene. I'm going to ask you to step back behind the tape please."

"That's my mother in there!" I began.

"I am sorry for your loss, but you are still not allowed inside."

Another man walked toward us and told the officer, "Let them in."

The cop lifted the tape so that we could get to the detective.

"Mr. Galvan, I'm Detective Trask. I'll be the lead investigator on this case. First I would like to offer my condolences for your loss. I just have some questions I need you to answer. Can we step over here please?"

We walked to a place in the yard where we wouldn't be interrupted by the foot traffic.

"Sir, when was the last time you saw your mother?"

"About three weeks ago. We had dinner."

Kate looked at me out the corner of her eye. It was subtle, but I felt it.

"And you ma'am?"

"I don't know, maybe a month ago."

"Sir, do you know why someone would want to do harm to your mother? Did she have any problems with anybody?"

"No, no, not that I know of. Everybody loved my mother."

There was an awkward silence. Clearly everyone did *not* love her. Because if they did, we would not be here, and she would not be dead.

"Okay, thank you. Here's my card. I'll be in touch."

Kate grabbed my arm and said, "Come on baby. Let's go home. It's nothing we can do here now. We need to let the police do their job."

What I didn't notice at the time was the lack of emotion in Kate. I mean, I knew they didn't like each other. But was she really that callous? And as I sit here remembering that night, I can't recall an instance when I saw true sorrow on her face. She just kind of went about things in her normal way.

"Babe, can I get you anything?"

I was caught up in my thoughts, still wondering why someone would do this to my mother.

"Babe, did you hear me?" she asked, walking into the room.

I snapped out of my self-induced coma and looked at her. By the time I realized it, she was already heading back into the kitchen.

Two weeks had passed since my mother was murdered, and the coroner had finally released her body. Kate had taken care of everything, right down to what color the napkins would be at the repast. Teal—that was my mother's favorite color. I literally did nothing, and I was grateful for it. And after it was all over, I depended on Kate's care to get me through. And I was grateful for that too.

About six months after that, I had begun to doubt my wife. I know I wasn't supposed to do that, but this particular day gave me good reason to.

I was lying on the couch when I heard Kate come home. She was on the phone.

"She deserved it, that evil bitch! She deserved everything she got!"

I had left work early because I had a headache that only a couple of Advil and peace and quiet could cure. Kate had no idea I was there.

"Shit with her pretending to be all holier than thou and telling everybody how to act. Somebody probably got tired of her high and mighty ass and killed her for all of our sakes."

Usually, I try not to eavesdrop, but whoever she was talking to, it was about my mother.

"I tell you I could *not* stand that bitch!" she said, laughing.

I sat up and looked at my wife, who still didn't notice me until a couple of moments later.

"Hey, let me call you back."

"It sounds like you're happy my mother's gone."

"Babe, that wasn't about your mother."

I stood up.

"Don't fucking treat me like I'm stupid! I know who you were talking about!"

"Well, it's no secret that we didn't like each other." she said, emotionless.

"So you go and tell people how much of a bitch she was after taking care of her funeral arrangements and saying all that shit *at* the funeral?"

"Baby, people dislike each other all the time. Me and your mom just happened to be two of those people. You're my husband. So why wouldn't I be involved if it meant making things easier for you?"

I sat back down and looked her straight in the eye.

"Did you have something to do with my mother's death? Tell me the truth Kate."

She stopped instantly and looked at me, horrified, gasping.

"How could you even think that I had anything to with the death of your mother? What kind of a monster do you think I am? It's true, I didn't like her because of how she treated me. But I could never take anyone's life! Besides, you are one to talk with the investigation of Gail Chamberlain still going on!"

Ouch, low blow! I guess I deserved it though. In truth, that was part of the stress I had been feeling over the last month. The police had never said outright that I was a suspect, but everybody knew that I was the last one to see Gail alive. And although it was said or not, I *was* the prime suspect in her murder.

What could I say after that? She was right. How could I charge her with my mother's murder, and I was the suspect in someone else's? And although I was still upset *and* suspicious, she had won this round. So I pouted and laid back down.

Kate walked into the kitchen to answer her phone.

"Hello? Okay, I'll be right there."

She grabbed her purse and left.

*****

Kate ~ Twenty minutes later, I was pulling up to the apartment Lilly had rented after the sale of Edie's house.

"Who is it?" she called out from behind the door.

"Kate."

She opened the door with an attitude.

"I thought you told the detectives you hadn't seen my mother in a month?"

I put my purse on the counter and asked, "Lilly, what's this all about?"

"It's about this, you trifling bitch!"

She held up one of the two-karat diamond earrings Peter had given me for my birthday.

"I found this when I found my mother lying in the kitchen in her own blood. I picked it up before I called the police. I wanted to give it to them."

"So why didn't you?"

"Because I wanted to hear you say it."

"Say what?"

"Don't play dumb with me bitch! You might have my brother fooled, but not me!"

Lilly really didn't know how much danger she was in. And I suppose she didn't care. All she wanted to do was find out who killed her mother. Or to hear me say I did.

"Okay, I was there, but I didn't kill her."

"So why did you lie?"

"I was scared, okay? I didn't know what to do. With the police hounding your brother about that other woman's death. I mean, what would that look like?"

"The truth, Kate! It looks like the truth! I think you didn't want anyone to know because you had something to do with both of them being killed."

I laughed.

"You're delusional, you know that? I could never kill another human being! I swear you and your brother—"

"What about my brother? He thinks you did it too, huh?"

I held out my hand and said, "Lilly, give me the earring."

"I'm not giving you shit! You had something to do with my mother's murder, and I'm going to prove it so you can rot in jail, you crazy bitch!"

Lilly ran to her purse and pulled out the .38-caliber pistol she had and pointed it at me.

She nervously pulled out her cell phone and began to dial.

"Lilly, what are you doing?"

"I'm going to turn you in, you demented psycho."

"Do you think your cockamamie story will hold up with your fingerprints all over what you call evidence? You think the police will want to hear anything you say, knowing you removed credible evidence from a murder scene?"

Lilly was nervous because what I said made sense.

As she dialed, the phone slipped from her hand. And when she went to pick it up, I kicked her in the face. She flew backwards and hit her head on the kitchen counter. She had almost lost consciousness, dropping the gun as soon as she hit the floor. My opportunity was here now, and so I took it. As she lay there trying desperately to regain her bearings, I dug into my purse and removed a pair of rubber gloves to slip on. She rolled over, attempting to locate and retrieve the gun. I couldn't believe this bitch was still trying to shoot me. I stepped on her wrist and picked it up before kneeling down to whisper in her ear.

"You know what? I did kill your whore of a mother, just like I'm going to kill you. So our little secret will die here with you today. Isn't that great?"

Lilly began to flail, trying to fight me in her altered state.

I slapped her three times before hitting her with the pistol and putting it to her head.

"Goodbye Lilly," I said, smiling.

I pulled the trigger, killing any threat I had of being found out.

I carefully placed the gun in her hand and gently put them both on the floor.

There was a knock at the door.

"Lilly, are you all right? Lilly!" they said, pounding.

I got up, grabbed my purse from the counter, and went quickly into the bedroom. I walked out onto the balcony and slid the door closed quietly behind me. Whoever was outside burst in and found Lilly lying there.

"Oh my god! Call an ambulance!"

I stood outside hoping I had not been seen. At the moment, there was no one in front of the building, but when the police arrived, that would all change. And I needed to be gone.

"Shit, my earring!"

I slid the door back open and tiptoed back into the apartment. When I peeked through the bedroom door, I could see Lilly's neighbor kneeling over her.

I took off my shoes to creep into the kitchen so that I could swipe the evidence from the counter.

From there, I could see the woman sobbing over Lilly, and the last thing I needed was somebody knowing I was there. And so I decided that she would join Lilly in hell.

I eased open the silverware drawer and slid the biggest knife I could find from it.

"Is anybody there?"

I stood straight up and gripped the handle.

"Hello?"

The woman walked into the kitchen just as I snuck back into the bedroom.

Through the sliver in the door, I could see her staring at the silverware drawer.

"Come on." I urged under my breath.

"Hello?" she said again as she pushed open the bedroom door.

"Is anybody in here?"

"Jess?"

"In here Tom."

The man came in and turned on the light.

"What are you doing in here?"

"I thought I heard something."

From behind the door, I could see them searching the room with their eyes.

"Let's go. There's nobody in here." he said.

"Just let me close the patio door."

"Okay, I'm going back outside to wait for the cops."

She walked over to the sliding glass door and looked out.

I reached over and switched off the light.

"Hello? Tom, is that you?"

I closed the door and walked toward her.

"Who are you?"

"Oh baby, that is something that you really shouldn't concern yourself with."

"What?"

By the time she started to talk, I was already pushing the blade into her stomach. She grabbed my arm to try to stop me. So I head-butted her, which immediately made her let go.

"Don't touch me bitch," I said, disgusted by her quivering.

When she fell to her knees, I could feel an insatiable tingling between my legs.

"This is new." I told myself.

"Please, please don't kill me." she begged.

"Are you still alive?" I asked, kneeling.

"Please…" she begged, barely able to stay conscious from the pain.

I rubbed her head and said, "I'm sorry, but I just can't do that."

I pulled the knife from her stomach and plunged it into her throat twice.

"Fuck," I said as her blood sprayed across my face into my mouth.

I stood up and spat on her before I felt something running down my legs.

I couldn't believe it. I had a fucking orgasm. But I had no time to enjoy it now.

I had to get out of there before the cops came. So I started my escape.

When I returned to the balcony, I threw my purse and shoes into the bushes below and climbed over the thin black rail.

I dropped one foot, then the other before I dropped the fifteen or so feet to the ground. When I landed, I felt my left ankle buckle beneath me, causing me to collapse in pain. And while I was lying there, I could hear the sirens in the distance racing in my direction.

I rolled over and tried to put weight on it, but the pain shot up my leg, and I almost cried. I got up, hopped over to the bushes, and fell to my knees, because if the cops pulled up, I would need some cover. I pushed my hands beneath the bushes to try to find my purse. I found the strap and pulled it toward me before I pushed myself from the ground to limp to the car.

I barely made it. And as soon as I closed the door, the first cop car sped into the parking lot.

"Be cool Kate," I told myself.

I started the engine and drove as calmly as I could past the commotion of sirens and flashing lights.

When I got home, Peter was in the bedroom watching TV.

"Hey."

"Hey." he said.

"Are you okay? I just wanted to apologize for what I said earlier. It was insensitive of me to speak about your mother like that."

*****

Peter ~ I wasn't going to tell her not to worry about it, but I did let her know that I forgave her.

"What happened to your leg?"

"It's my ankle."

"What happened?"

"I broke a heel." she said, holding up her shoe.

I got out of bed to help her to it.

"Here, just lean on me baby."

44

I sat her on the edge and said, "I'm going to get you some ice for that ankle and then run you a nice warm bath."

I ran downstairs and shoveled a handful of ice into a freezer bag before I ran back up to find Kate sprawled across the bed. I grabbed two pillows and gently placed her ankle on them before placing the ice on top.

"You just lay there baby. I'm going to take care of you tonight. How did this happen?"

She lifted her head from the pillow as if she were agitated by the question but decided to answer it anyway.

"I was walking, and when I reached into my purse for my car keys, I must have miss-stepped, and my heel broke."

"Where did you go?"

Again, she seemed irritated by the question.

"I was coming from your sister's."

"My sister's? Why would you be coming from my sister's?"

"Because she called me, that's why."

"What did she want?"

"She sounded upset and said she needed to talk to me."

"About what?"

"About your mother."

"Why would she want to talk to you about my mother?"

"I don't know. When I got there, she didn't answer the door. And as I was walking back to the car, I broke my heel."

I walked into the bathroom and turned on a bath for her. I sat on the edge of the tub and called my sister. There was no answer. I called again… And again, there was no answer.

"Was she at home when you went by?" I yelled from the bathroom.

"I saw her car there, but I didn't hear anything inside when I knocked at the door."

I took out my phone and called again, and yep, you guessed it, no answer.

"I'm going to put you to bed, and then I'm going to go and see if Lilly's all right."

"I'm sure she's okay."

45

"Why would she call you and not answer the door? I know my sister, and she wouldn't ask you to come over there unless she had a good reason."

She put her head back on to the pillow while I went to check on her bathwater.

Shortly after her bath, I put her to bed and made sure she was comfortable. Then I grabbed my jacket and left.

When I got to my sister's, it was the same scene there as the night my mother died. And seeing all the emergency personnel there made my heart race. I pulled into the visitor's parking spot and called my sister again. This time, the call went straight to voice mail.

I sat in the car contemplating going in when my phone rang. It was Lilly.

"Lilly, where are you? Why haven't you answered your phone?"

"Who is this?" asked the man with the burly voice.

"This is Lilly's brother. Who is this?"

"This is Detective Bryce Garrett, LAPD homicide. Where are you now sir?"

I hesitated to tell him because I thought he might know something about Gail's case. And here I was at the scene of another murder. I decided to tell him anyway.

"I'm in the parking lot."

"I'm coming down. I need to ask you some questions."

I already knew that.

About five minutes later, we were walking toward each other.

"Mr. Galvan?"

"Officer Garrett?"

We shook hands, and he began his inquiry.

"First I would like to offer my condolences for the loss of your sister."

This was too much. Did all the homicide detectives lead with that?

"What happened?" I asked, sobbing.

"Well, it looks like she shot herself."

"Are you telling me my sister committed suicide?"

"At the moment yes, that's what it looks like sir. When was the last time you saw or spoke with your sister?"

"Just a couple of days ago."

"Your mother was murdered not long ago, right?"

I nodded yes.

"Do you think that maybe your mom's death caused her to go into depression? Or was somebody after her too?"

"My sister was not depressed! And what do you mean *too*? Nobody was after my sister!" I defended.

"And how do you know this sir?"

"Because I know my sister!"

"Well, can you tell me why she's lying on her kitchen floor with a revolver in her hand and a bullet wound to the side of the head? And why was her neighbor also found dead in her bedroom?"

I could not.

"Do you know if she had any visitors prior to tonight?" he continued.

She did, and I knew exactly who it was, but I didn't say anything. "No sir, I don't."

He reached into his pocket and gave me my third detective's card over the course of half a year. I took it and told him I'd be in touch if I thought of anything else.

On the way home, I didn't cry. Not because I didn't love or miss my sister, but because I was trying to figure out what, if anything, my wife had to do with it. She was there, and my sister was dead, and I wanted to know why. And why was the neighbor killed? What did she have, if anything, to do with it?"

Twenty minutes later, I was pulling into the driveway steaming from the thoughts that ran through my mind. When I got into the house, I ran upstairs, ready to give Kate a piece of that same mind. I pushed the door open and saw her sitting up, waiting for me.

"So is Lilly okay? You were gone a long time, and I was beginning to get worried."

I sat on the edge of the bed and slumped down.

"Honey, what's wrong?"

"Lilly is dead Kate," I said, studying her face.

"Oh no honey, what happened?"

"They said she shot herself, but I don't believe that to be true. They also said they found her neighbor dead in the bedroom."

"It's no way Lilly killed herself baby. Do you think her neighbor killed her and then killed herself?"

"I know she didn't kill herself. We just have to find out who did. And I don't have a clue why her neighbor was there."

I looked long and hard at her. But she gave no inkling of knowing what happened to my sister. I mean, could she be such a cold and calculating killer that she could look me in my eye and persuade me to think she had nothing to do with it? Because if this were so, she was in the middle of an Oscar-worthy performance. And for whatever reason, I believed her. So that piece of my mind I was going to give her. I kept to myself...for now.

I needed to know what was going on. So I couldn't let anyone know what I was thinking. I just kept the pieces of the puzzle to myself.

CHAPTER 6

Peter ~ Ever since Lily died, what seemed to be a chasm of emotion walled itself between me and my wife. Partly because I loved her, and I didn't want to lose her for something I could not prove. Not yet anyway. And two, it was because I had no tangible proof she actually did it.

It was also hard to talk to her because I wanted to ask her so many things. I could just never bring myself to doing it.

I knew I needed to get away from Kate, if just for a little while. So I put my plan in motion to leave. I just couldn't deal with anybody else around me dying. So I felt that I had to leave, and soon. And that meant starting over somewhere else without Kate.

I know I should have just told her what was on my mind, but I just couldn't bring myself to do it without blaming her. I just needed to be alone to sort things out. Selfish, I know.

It had been a while since I buried my sister, and I was still highly depressed about it. I hadn't been to work in three weeks, and Jose didn't like that at all.

"Hello."

"Hey bro, what's going on? Do you still work here or what?"

"What's up Jose? I just needed some time to get caught up on some things and get my mind together."

"And so…?"

"And so what?"

"Did you get it together?"

"You're funny bro. I'll be in tomorrow, I promise."

"Yeah yeah, I heard that before."

"I'll be there, I promise."

I hung up the phone with all intentions to be there the next day.

I picked it up again and started to call my lawyer but thought better of it. I didn't want Kate to walk in on me or see me getting off the call abruptly when she came in. That would surely cause suspicion.

The next morning came with me eager to get to work. But not for work purposes though. It was to get things going. And the first thing I did when I got to the office was call my lawyer and ask him for the number of his best private investigator.

"Ron Johnson's office." said the lady on the other end.

"May I speak to Mr. Johnson please?"

"Who may I ask is calling sir?"

"My name is Peter Galvan. I'm a client of Seth Holstein."

"Hold, please."

Just a second later.

"Ron Johnson."

"Hello, Mr. Johnson. I'm Peter Galvan. I believe Mr. Holstein spoke to you about me?"

"Yes he did. How may I help you Mr. Galvan?"

"I think my wife has been killing people, and I need to find out."

There was silence, and then…

"Sir, this seems to be a very sensitive issue. Do you think you can come down so that we can talk about it in person and in private?"

"Are you available now?"

"Hold on, let me see. You're lucky Mr. Galvan. I just had an opening."

"I'll be right down."

Now all I had to do was sneak out without Jose seeing me. I grabbed my jacket and looked across the hall. Good he wasn't in yet, so I plotted my escape.

"You just got here. Leaving already?" Jose asked, walking up behind me.

Damn it!

"I was just going to see a client."

"Oh yeah, who?"

"Somebody I've been working on since I've been gone."

"Well, I hope so because it's your job to bring in the money, and we haven't had any coming in lately."

"Don't worry. We're good, you'll see."

"Okay then. We'll see." Jose said sarcastically.

I got to the car and put on my seat belt before rushing out of the parking lot to see Mr. Johnson.

Soon after, I was walking into the lobby of Johnson and Associates.

"Good morning. I'm here to see Mr. Johnson."

"Can I have your name sir?"

"Peter Galvan."

"Okay, Mr. Galvan. Have a seat, and I'll let him know you're here."

"Thank you."

It had only been a minute before Mr. Johnson was walking out to greet me.

"Mr. Galvan, I'm Ron. Can you follow me please?"

When we walked back into his office, I was so anxious to tell my story that I started before we even sat down.

"I don't know if I'm being paranoid or what, but over the last eight months, people have been dying. It all started with a client of mines the night we went to dinner. And the next day, I found out she was dead. And then my mother and my sister…"

It was all too much, and I began to break down. I just couldn't talk anymore, and that was when he started asking me questions.

"Besides yourself, was there anyone else that had been in contact with the deceased?"

"Yes, my wife. Everyone except Gail, I think."

"Was she the only one?"

"That I know of."

"Okay, then I'll need the payment we discussed, and we'll get started."

I handed him my credit card, and to my surprise, he scanned it right there. He gave me a receipt and said, "Have a good day Mr. Galvan."

It had been a month since I had seen Mr. Johnson, and I was beginning to get anxious for some answers. Kate was back to normal. And to tell you the truth, life did seem to be getting back to or as close to normalcy as it had been. But I was still anxious to see what Ron had come up with, if he came up with anything at all.

I was at work sitting in my office when I got the call.

"Mr. Galvan? This is Ron Johnson."

"Hey Ron, what's going on?"

"I'm just calling to give you an update."

"Okay, go ahead."

It was just my luck that when he started to talk, Kate walked in.

"I've followed your wife, and I'm sorry to report that she hasn't done anything unusual. Really nothing out of the ordinary."

"Uh-huh" was all I could say.

"Excuse me?"

"Look, I'm sorry. I have to call you back."

I hung up the phone and said, "Hey honey, what are you doing here?"

"Well, I was in the neighborhood, and I thought I'd stop by and see if you were free for lunch."

"Um, no, no baby, I'm not busy. Let me go and freshen up, and I'll be right back."

I should have known not to leave her alone in my office, but hindsight is twenty-twenty. No sooner than I had left, she walked around my desk and pushed the last call button on my phone.

"Ron Johnson's office."

"I'm sorry, who did I call?"

"Ron Johnson and Associates."

"And what is that?"

"Ma'am, how may I help you?"

Dial tone.

When I came back, she was standing by the mirror applying her lip gloss.

"You ready?" I asked anxiously.

And while we were at lunch, she acted as if nothing had happened, engaging in her usual small talk. And after we ate, she gave me a kiss and rushed off. If I had known what she was up to, I would've left town that very moment. After calling the police, of course.

*****

Kate ~ I left Peter and went straight back to my office to see who exactly Ron Johnson was.

"Margie, give me about forty minutes before you let any calls through, okay?"

When I was finished, I sat back in my chair.

"What is he up to? And why did he need a private investigator?" I asked myself.

Why was he having me followed? Did he know or suspect that I was the one doing all the killing? Didn't he trust me?

I didn't know, but you could bet your last dollar I was going to find out.

I looked out the window to see if anyone was watching the building. And on my way out, I looked at every stranger's face, wondering if they worked for Johnson and Associates.

When I left the office, I went to Santa Monica and sat across the street from Ron's office. I waited for him to come out, and after only thirty minutes, he did just that.

"Okay, time to see why you are so interested in following me."

He pulled out of the garage and made a right on Bundy with me not far behind.

After driving four blocks or so, he stopped at a small coffee shop. And to my surprise, he didn't get back in his car. He just took the short walk to Rankin Park and sat at a picnic table.

"Okay, what are you up to asshole?" I said aloud.

"I know you just didn't come here to drink coffee."

*****

Peter ~ I got out of my car and looked around before joining Ron at a nearby picnic table.

"I'm sorry about earlier. My wife walked in, and I couldn't talk without letting her know what was going on."

"I figured that. In the future, just be a little bit more careful. We don't want to jeopardize the investigation."

What I thought was going to be a casual meeting soon turned into something much more.

Ron was a tall guy, around 6'4" or so, and stocky. By no means was he a small man. And for whatever reason, his size gave me solace.

"So I'll let you know if I find anything out. I plan to put another tail on her tonight."

He stood up and blocked the sun from my eyes. And when I stood up to shake his hand, I heard a deafening boom. And it felt like someone had thrown warm water all over me. I wiped the liquid from my eyes so that I could see what had happened. Ron had fallen lifeless to the ground. And standing there was Kate, holding a smoking pistol.

"Kate, what the fuck are you doing?"

She had a cold steely look in her eye, and right then, I knew that she meant business. And that she also knew what she was doing. Suddenly, it all made sense. The look on her face tied everything together. She *had* done this before.

"Let's go Pete," she said, deadpan.

"Go where?" I asked, spitting blood from my mouth.

"You'll know when we get there."

She cocked the gun again. And I thought better about trying her, so I started to walk toward her car. When we got there, she threw me the keys and said, "You drive."

She made me open the passenger door and crawl across the seat. Can you believe that shit?

"Take me home."

"Kate, what's going on? We can get you help if you need it."

I tried to stay calm, wondering how I missed the signs. Coming to the conclusion that I just didn't want to see them in the first place.

"Help? You think I need help? You think I'm crazy?"

"I never said that baby. You know I love you!"

"Really? Did you love that whore Gail like you *love* me?"

"Gail? She's just a business partner, that's all baby."

"*Was* a business partner!" she corrected.

We were not far from home, and my curiosity was soaring. What was she going to do to me when we got there? Were these *my* last moments of life—finding out that my wife was indeed a killer with someone else's blood all over me?

I pulled into the garage and let the door down.

"Get out!" she said, waving the gun to urge me to go into the house.

And plus the look in her eyes now, was more psychotic than before.

"Baby, why did you make me do this?"

"Do what?"

"Don't play with me asshole. You know what!"

"I don't know what you're talking about." I said, trying to stall her as best I could, because I really was not ready to die today.

She started to cry uncontrollably.

"Why was he following me, huh Peter? Don't you trust me?"

I didn't answer the questions. I simply diverted the conversation. Besides, she had just killed Ron and was holding *me* hostage. Would you trust her?

"Baby, let me help you. We can beat this together."

She let her hand drop to her side, and I reached carefully for the pistol. But she didn't let it go.

"Don't leave me!" she insisted as we walked into the house.

I tried to grab the gun again and said, "Baby, I'm not going anywhere."

She buried her head in my chest and pulled me close, while she pushed the gun barrel into my stomach to ensure that I wouldn't try anything.

"What am I going to do now?" She sobbed.

"We'll get through it baby," I said, rubbing her back, trying to put her at ease.

I let go so that I could go and get her a couple of Valium I had left over from a previous prescription.

"Take these baby, and get some rest. We'll sort this out in the morning."

She sat down, swallowed the pills, and rolled over, still clutching the pistol. I walked into the bathroom and turned off the light before grabbing the remote to turn on the TV. I cuddled up beside her wide awake, wondering how in the hell I was going to end all this without her getting hurt. Or me, for that matter.

And yeah, I knew I should have called the police right then and there, but…it's funny what love makes you do. Or what you might think is love anyway.

So here I was, lying in bed, covered in blood next to my wife who had just committed murder in broad daylight.

Who was *really* the crazy one?

CHAPTER 7

Peter ~ The next morning, I woke up to discover that Kate was gone.

"Kate?"

I looked around the room and saw that she had emptied out all her drawers. I ran into the bathroom and saw that she had cleaned out the medicine cabinet too, including the Valium. I ran downstairs to the garage and saw that her car was gone too.

"Shit! Shit, shit, shit!"

I was really scared now because I knew that I would eventually be hunted. Kate was a cold, calculating killer apparently. And it was clear to me now that whoever got in her way would pay in blood. And I couldn't afford to pay that price. So I called the police.

"911 emergency, how can I help you?"

I just sat there, unable to speak.

"Hello? Is anyone there?"

I hung up the phone.

A minute later, the phone rang.

"Hello."

"Sir, are you in need of emergency assistance?"

"What? No, my son got to my phone and I walked in on him pushing the buttons. It was an accident. I'm sorry."

"Okay, we'll be more careful in the future sir."

"I will. Thank you."

I hung up the phone, mad at myself because I didn't have the nerve to tell them that my wife killed someone in front of me and that I thought she had killed my mother and sister too. But at the same time, I knew they would ask me why I hadn't called them earlier. I *was* a hostage, right? She did hold me at gunpoint, didn't she? Would that be enough to clear me of harboring her? I wasn't ready to find out. And I really wasn't going to tell them that we slept in the same bed, with her bloody and a pistol in her hand. But what I needed to know was where my wife was now. And was she plotting to kill me like she did the others?

I went to the closet and pulled out my lockbox to quickly flip through the combination to get my gun. I shoved it, along with two extra clips into my pocket.

"I have to find Kate before she comes after me." I said to myself, rushing out the door.

*****

Kate ~ I had been driving all night before I pulled into an out-of-the-way motel just outside of Bakersfield.

"Good morning. How may I help you?"

"I need a room. Do you have any available?"

"Yeah I have one. Are you alone?"

"Yes."

The man behind the desk reached over and pulled a room key from the board and asked, "Will this be cash or card?"

"Cash."

"How long will you be staying with us?"

"Not long."

"Well, if you are staying day-to-day, your room payment is due by noon each day. If you choose to extend your stay, then we do have weekly and monthly rates available. Breakfast is served at seven a.m., lunch at twelve, and dinner at six in the dining room."

I nodded and walked out.

"Moving in?" asked a young brunette, looking down at me from the second-floor walkway.

"No, just passing through." I said.

"From where?"

I looked up and asked her, "Why?"

"I didn't mean any harm. I was just trying to be neighborly, that's all."

"I won't be here long enough to be your neighbor. So don't worry about it."

I could tell she was embarrassed when she saw my frustration.

"Well, if you need anything, just let me know. I'm June by the way."

"Thank you June, but that won't be necessary."

I stuck my key in the door and walked into the room. And when I got inside, I peeked out the window to see if anybody had followed me.

*****

Peter ~ Meanwhile, I was back at home going crazy, wondering where she was. So I decided to call Seth.

"Hey Pete, what can I do for you?"

"Seth, can I come see you?"

"I'm on the back nine now Pete. Can we—"

"Seth, this is important. I wouldn't bother you if it wasn't."

After a few seconds, he said, "Okay, I'll be home at three. You can come by then."

I hung up the phone and looked at the clock—12:15 p.m., shit. What was I supposed to do until then?

Stay right where I was. And that was exactly what I did.

I had fallen asleep on the couch and was startled awake by a knock at the door. I sat there wondering if I was dreaming; I wasn't. Somebody *was* at the door.

I got up, pulled the gun from my waistband, and cocked it while I walked cautiously to see who it was. It was a man standing there. I unlocked the door and opened it slowly.

"Pete?"

And when I looked out and saw Seth standing there, I was relieved.

I opened the door to invite him in. When he passed me, he looked down and saw the gun.

"Pete what's going on? Are you okay? Why do you have a gun?"

I put the pistol back in my waistband.

"Come in Seth, please."

He walked cautiously into the living room and turned to face me.

"Peter, why do you have a gun?" he asked again.

"For protection."

"Protection from what?"

"You mean from who?"

"Okay, from who?"

"Kate."

He chuckled in disbelief.

"Come on Peter, Kate?"

It was easy to see his befuddlement. Kate was only 5'6", 125 pounds, and here I was a good 6'2", 230 pounds, barricaded in my home, shaking like a wet puppy.

"I know how this might look Seth, but she is a dangerous woman, I promise you. You know that guy Ron who you referred me to? The private detective? Well, they found him in Rankin Park shot in the head?"

"What? Are you trying to tell me that Kate killed Ron?"

"I was there Seth, and it *was* Kate who killed him."

Now his befuddlement had turned to outright disbelief.

"Why would she do something like that? Why would she kill Ron?"

"I had been suspicious of her ever since my sister was killed, so I confronted her about my mom."

"And?"

"And she seemed upset at first, but then she snapped right back to normal in a matter of minutes. I didn't find it strange because I just figured it was her trying to comfort me by dismissing it."

"So what happened at the park?"

"Well, I was supposed to meet Ron there to get an update about what was going on with his investigation. And I don't know how, but somehow, she found out. He was telling me what he had found out when…"

"When what? What did he say?"

"He told me that Kate hadn't done anything suspicious and that he didn't have any news. When I reached out to shake his hand, she shot him. And I was standing there with this guy's brains all over me! She just shot him, Seth! She just shot him!"

"Where did she come from?"

"I don't know. All I know is that he fell, and there she was behind him with a pistol in her hand."

"What happened after that?"

"I took her home."

Again, there was that look of befuddlement.

"You took her home? What in the hell did you do that for? Where's the gun?"

"She never gave it to me. When I woke up this morning she was gone."

"Why didn't you call the police? Wait, what do you mean *when you woke up*? Where was she when you were asleep?"

I was embarrassed to tell him what happened, but I had to because I needed his advice. And he was my lawyer for Christ's sake.

"So why didn't you call the police Peter?" he asked again.

"I did. I got scared Seth. I just couldn't go through with it. What if they thought I was in on it with her? After all, I did bring her home and didn't say anything after she left."

He sat there, deep in thought, rubbing his chin.

"Yeah, I could see that. You have anything to drink?"

"Yeah, some whiskey."

"Get it. We're going to need it." he said, rubbing his temples.

I ran to the kitchen and got the whiskey with two glasses.

*****

Kate ~ I woke up to a knock at the door and grabbed my pistol from beneath the pillow.

"Who is it?"

"It's June."

I got up and put the gun back before going to open the door.

"What do you want?"

"I hadn't seen you, and I noticed your car hadn't moved. I just wanted to see if you were okay."

The car, I hadn't even thought about that. What was I going to do with it? If June noticed it, who else would? I had been following the news day and night both on television and online. I crushed my phone and threw it out the window so that it couldn't be tracked. So I used the computer in the lobby to see if anybody out there *was* looking for me. I knew that I needed to get rid of the car and do it soon because that also could be tracked or recognized.

"I'm okay thanks," I said.

"Good. I was just checking."

I closed the door without saying another word so that I could prepare for the next step of my plan: getting rid of the car.

*****

Peter ~ Seth and I had been up all night trying to figure out what Kate might be up to and how I might be able to beat a harboring charge. But it didn't take a rocket scientist to know that she wanted revenge. She loved me, and somewhere in that love, she lost sight of what was right. To her, everything she had done to this point had been justified by how she felt. And I guess the real reason I didn't turn her in was because I loved her too and wanted to save her. I know that sounds crazy, but that was how I felt. I just wanted her to be okay.

"We'll go to the police," snapped Seth.

"What? Are you crazy? I'm not going to the police!"

"To report Kate missing. No one knows she committed the murders except us. Maybe we can put a fire up under her. When she finds out the police are looking for her, it might just flush her out."

That was why Seth was a lawyer. Granted, he didn't have the stress of his wife trying to kill him. But whether he did or did not, I still thought it was a great idea. If Kate thought the cops were looking for her, she might not take the chance of coming after me. And she just might tip us off to where she was.

"I'll go to the police and let you know if I find out anything else."

"Thanks Seth, and be careful."

"I will. Just stay here. Maybe call off work a couple of days until we can get this thing sorted out."

I agreed.

*****

Kate ~ I waited until after midnight to come out. I tried to close the door as quietly as I could before I walked downstairs into the shadows. I pressed the alarm button, hoping that the two faint beeps would not draw any attention. And I waited to make sure they didn't.

The coast seemed to be clear, so I ran to the car and was about to get in when...

"Going somewhere?" asked June.

I turned around, surprised to see June standing there holding a dog's leash.

"What's it to you?"

"It doesn't matter. I was just out walking Roger. I usually don't see anybody out this late, at least not around here."

I just hopped in the car, started the engine, and sped off without saying another word.

Nosey bitch. I thought.

"Gotta dump the car. Gotta dump the car," I repeated out loud.

I sped down the dark highway contemplating ways of getting rid of it when suddenly I knew. I pressed down on the accelerator and barreled the car over the embankment. The car went airborne before it slammed into a tree and flipped over twice, coming to rest right side up.

I had a horrible headache when I got out, the result of the airbag not deploying, and fell down.

"Get up Kate," I told myself groggily, feeling the pain in my shoulders now.

And when I did get up, I knew I had to get to work hiding the vehicle. I walked back to the car and pulled the keys from the ignition before I stumbled back around it to open the trunk. I stuck the key in but couldn't turn the lock.

"Shit! Shit! Shit!"

I tried again, and this time, I broke the key inside before I threw the rest of them into the darkness.

"What do I do now?" I said, sobbing.

I got up and walked up the embankment, ready to make my way back to the motel when the trunk popped open.

"YES!" I yelled, sliding back down the grassy hill.

I lifted the trunk lid and pulled out the shovel to begin rooting some nearby shrubs so that I could camouflage the car, hoping that it would not be seen from the highway. And after two hours, I had accomplished that goal and was ready to walk back.

It took me another hour to get back after I found the keys. And I tried as best I could to be inconspicuous.

"What happened to you?" June asked, running over to me.

"Where in the fuck do you come from? Every fucking time I turn around, you jump out!"

She stopped just short of me and said, "I live in number seven. I looked out and saw you walking, that's all. The owners gave me a job with room and board. So I kinda look out for the place, you know? I just happened to see you, that's all."

"Where's your family?"

"I don't have any. My mom and dad are dead, and I haven't heard from my brother in years. So it's just me."

"So you mean to tell me nobody knows you're here?"

"Nobody except God and the people that live here."

This was all too perfect I thought. She had no family, so no one would miss her if she went missing. Perfect.

CHAPTER 8

Peter ~ Kate had been gone two weeks, and I was paranoid. All I wondered was what in the fuck she was out there planning to do to me. I found myself staring at any woman who even slightly resembled her and some who didn't. Every scenario of how she would kill me ran through my mind. And it was taking its toll. And so I had the locks changed on all the windows and doors, aided by a new state-of-the-art home security system. And yet I still didn't feel completely safe. So I slept with my gun.

I guess it was the look on her face when she killed Ron that did it for me. She didn't even look like the woman I had known the last three years. Maybe she wasn't. Maybe she was *never* the woman I thought she was. In any case, I was worried, and I carried my gun everywhere.

I couldn't stand feeling like a sitting duck, just sitting at home waiting for something to happen. So I decided to go back to work. I opened the garage door from inside the house. Then I opened the kitchen door, gun in hand. I walked out to the car and looked in the front and back seats, then down at the tires. They weren't slashed, so that was a good sign. I got in, started the engine, and eased out, deciding to park on the street after today. At least I wouldn't be inside the garage trapped like a rat. Maybe I would even get off a couple of shots first, who knows. The odds just felt better that way.

When I got to work, I realized that it felt good to get out. But something was still missing. I didn't know what it was, but it just felt like I needed a change.

"Well, look who decided to save our asses with his presence."

"What's up Jose?"

"Man don't what's up me. What's up with you?"

I looked around and said, "Let's talk in my office."

Jose followed me in and closed the door.

"What's going on bro?"

"Okay, you remember Gail don't you?"

"What? Of course I remember Gail, and her money." he said, chuckling.

"No seriously, I think Kate killed her."

"Wait a minute... Your wife killed Gail? Yeah right!" He laughed.

"Dude, I saw her shoot Ron in the head!"

"Who's Ron?"

"A private investigator I hired to follow her."

"For what?"

"Because I think she killed my mom and Lilly too. So I hired him to follow her."

"What in the fuck are you saying to me man? Are you trying to tell me that Kate is some sort of serial killer?"

"I don't think she is a serial killer. I just think she feels threatened by people I am close to."

"What in the hell did you do to her dude? And what in the hell does that even mean?"

"Me? Nothing asshole. One day she was Kate, and the next day she was shooting people in the head in broad daylight."

I lifted my jacket and showed Jose my gun.

"No wonder you haven't been coming to work. My ass would've been in Mexico!"

We laughed, and it felt good, because just for that brief moment, my worries were all gone.

I could always depend on Jose for that.

"I've been thinking." I said.

"Okay, that's always a bad thing." Jose quipped.

"I've been thinking about making a change Jose. Seriously. I talked to Seth, and he thinks it's a good idea too."

"A change? What kind of change?"

"Like a change of scenery, you know. Get away from all this."

"All what? What about the business?"

"Nothing will change. While I'm gone, you'll be in control, and I'll contact you here and there. Just until we find out where she is."

"Where who is? Tell me you know where Kate is Peter. How do you lose your wife? What if she comes after *me*?"

Jose joked so damned much I didn't know if he was serious or not.

"Why would she? You're no threat." I chuckled.

"Man, that hurts. But okay, we'll do it your way."

"Thanks *hermano*. I appreciate you."

I really did think of Jose as the brother I never had. I met him while during construction on a movie theater when we were younger. And ever since the first day I saw him, he had always been a character. But besides that, in his own sort of way, he was one of the realest cats I had ever known, and I appreciated him for that.

Now here we were eight years later, the best of friends and business partners. And if there was anybody in the world I could trust to be there for me, it was him, and vice versa.

"So how are you planning to make this big change without anybody knowing?" he asked.

"I applied for a job in Connecticut."

"Connecticut? What's in Connecticut?"

"Nothing. That's why it's the perfect place."

"Sooo, you have your own company, making hundreds of thousands of dollars, and you're going to work for someone else?"

"That's the plan. Kate would never expect me to do that."

"So how long will you be gone again?"

"Just until this thing blows over, or they find out where she is. Don't worry. Once I get settled, I'll contact you. Okay?"

He nodded and gave me a hug.

"Whatever you need man. I'm here for you. Understand?" he assured me.

"I appreciate you bro. Thanks."

I grabbed a couple of things from my desk and walked into Jose's office after him.

"Here is the Anderson file. We're just waiting for the soil samples to clear, and we should be right on schedule to pour the foundation next week." I said.

"Did you hear from the electrician?"

"Yeah, he needs to order another four hundred feet of corrugated casing so that he can start wiring the first and second floors."

"Well, it looks like we're right on schedule. I'm going to miss you bro. I don't know what Lupe and Marisol are going to do without their Uncle Peter."

"Just tell them I'll be back soon and that I love them."

"Oh no, you're not sticking me with that. *You* tell them!"

We laughed again, and I walked out.

When I got to the parking garage, I looked around like always. But today I was a little more diligent in my observation.

I looked across the lot, and my heart stopped. Was that Kate sitting there watching me? I didn't recognize the car she was in, but I was sure it was her.

"Kate?" I said, walking toward the car.

I began to run, and when I got closer, she started the engine and sped away, almost running me down.

"Kate!" I yelled again.

The car stopped. I ran toward it, calling out, unsure of what might happen when I got there.

When I did get there, she was just sitting there crying. I reached for the door handle and pulled.

"Kate, open the door baby?"

She sat there trying not to look at me. I pounded on the window and said, "Open the door baby."

She rolled the window a quarter of the way down.

"What did you tell them Peter?"

"Tell who?"

"The police!"

"I didn't tell them anything, I swear baby!"

She looked like she didn't believe me. So I tried to convince her again.

"Baby, I didn't tell anybody anything! You need to come home so we can sort this out."

"It's too late Peter! Why are the police looking for me?"

"It's never too late baby. They are looking for you because I put out a missing person's report. When you left, I didn't know what to think. I needed their help baby."

"For us, it is too late Peter. And I'm not going to jail because of you. Do you understand that?"

She looked at me. And the look in her eyes told me she was serious. Maybe she was too far gone to save. It was ironic that here I was carrying a gun to protect myself from her while trying to convince her to come home with me. What in the hell was I thinking? But like I said before, I loved her, and I wanted to save her. And suddenly I wasn't afraid anymore.

She rolled up the window and sped off.

"Kate!"

I ran to my car so that I could follow her. But by the time I got to the gate, she was gone.

"Where in the hell did she go that quick?"

I turned right out of the parking structure and circled the block to see if she had doubled back to follow me. There was no sign of her.

The rest of the day I was on pins and needles looking around to see if she had been following me. Because, in my mind, I already knew that it was too late to save her. But in my heart, I just couldn't accept it. And now I *was* afraid again. For her safety *and* mine.

CHAPTER 9

Peter ~ I hadn't seen Kate since that day in the parking garage. And I didn't know how to feel about it. On one hand, I was glad because I saw her, and she didn't hurt me. On the other hand, if I *did* see her again, she *would* probably kill me. I had packed up the house and gave the final instructions to the movers. I would send my stuff to Pittsburgh and, from there, change moving companies to forward it to Connecticut.

I had planned it all out meticulously because Kate was still out there. And if she was following me, then she knew I was leaving. And if she wasn't, I knew she would find out soon.

That two weeks gave me enough time to relocate. I kept trying to convince myself that if I left and flushed her out, they would catch her and give her the help she needed. Was I crazy? I know. She killed my mom and Lilly, but maybe she was sick. I *was* crazy.

The day for me to leave finally came, and my covert execution of Operation Flush Out Kate was in effect.

At 4:00 a.m., I got out of bed. I say got out of bed because that night, I couldn't sleep. I was just too anxious and didn't spend a lot of time actually sleeping.

I sat at the edge and looked around. This would be the last time I would wake up in this room. Then I looked over to Kate's side of the bed and longed for the days when we were in love.

Pretty much everything I had was already on its way to Pittsburgh. So that meant I would be able to travel light with just a carry-on. I took a shower and got dressed. I only had a couple of hours until my flight, and I needed to get going. When I was ready to leave, I walked out the back door and put the keys beneath the mat for the realtor.

I rented a car the day before just in case Kate *had* been following me. And I parked it around the corner, hoping that she would not see it.

Fifty minutes later, I was walking through the terminal, still paranoid, looking to see if I was being followed. When I passed security, I went straight to the bathroom—not to use it but to peek through the door and see if she was somewhere out there. But after a few minutes and a couple of dirty looks, I was determined that the coast was clear.

Once I got on the plane, I felt tired all over again. So I decided to get some sleep. And before I closed my eyes, I decided to take one more look around. I looked through the seats and thought I saw her. My heart stopped just before it started to beat a thousand times a minute. I turned around, hoping that she wouldn't notice me as I poured through my mind, wondering how she found out where I was. And how did she know what flight I was going to be on? I had purchased my ticket with cash at the airport. Jose rented the car for me, and if Kate *did* see the moving trucks or spoke to one of the movers, all they knew was that they were going to Pittsburgh. I looked through the seats again.

"That jacket looks familiar." I told myself.

Damn, what was I going to do now?

I got up and walked down the aisle and saw her bend down, as if she didn't want to be seen. Every step I took, the more nervous I became.

"Sir, you're gonna have to take your seat."

"I'm just going to the restroom. I won't be long."

"Okay, but make it quick." said the already agitated flight attendant.

Just as I got to the end of the aisle, she showed her face, and… it wasn't Kate.

I exhaled visibly and walked into the small restroom, relieved. I was so relieved that I forgot to pee. I walked out and looked at the woman again just to make sure it *wasn't* Kate. It wasn't. So I was relieved all over again.

I went back to my seat, realizing that I still had to pee. I got up and saw the same flight attendant who told me to sit down. So that was what I did. Peeing would just have to wait for now.

The plane landed in Pittsburgh with me laughing at myself for being so paranoid. But could you blame me? I had a good reason to be.

I needed to be in Pittsburgh for at least a day just to make sure the transfer of moving companies went smooth so that I could be on my way to Connecticut. And the sooner the better.

*****

Kate ~ Over time, June proved herself useful, and we soon became good friends.

"Can I use your car?"

"Yeah, but be back by three. I have to go to the store." said June.

I swiped the keys from the desk and went down to the car. I was on my way to see Peter and try to explain why I left. I guess me seeing him must have spooked me, and that was why I sped off. But for the last couple of weeks, I hadn't even thought about coming near him. That was, until today. I thought that I could make it work by explaining how I felt, so I went to talk to him.

Three hours later, I was pulling up in front of the house. I got out, walked up to the door, and pulled out my set of keys. And just before I was about to stick them in, the door opened.

"May I help you?" said the young blond man.

"Who are you?"

"I'm Craig."

"And who are you, Craig?" I asked impatiently.

"I'm sorry. Do you have an appointment?"

"I don't need an appointment to come into my own home!"

"Your home?" Craig giggled.

"What's so funny?"

"Lady, I don't know who you are or where you think you are, but this house just sold."

"Sold? To who?"

"I'm afraid I can't tell you that."

The news was too much to bear, and I didn't know what to think or how to feel.

"Ma'am?"

I just stood there, consumed in thought, wondering where Peter had gone and when he had the time to put the house up for sale.

"Stupid, stupid, stupid!" I said, mad at myself.

"Ma'am!" the man said, touching my arm.

"Take your hands off me!"

He backed away and watched me run back to the car, still talking to myself.

I slammed the door and took a deep breath before I pounded the wheel violently.

"How could I let him get away? I should've been here!"

I beat my hands on the steering wheel again until they began to bruise and hurt.

The man walked off the porch toward the car.

"Are you okay?" he asked from outside.

I started the car and looked at him through tear-soaked eyes before I sped off. And what had taken me three hours to get to took just over two hours to get from.

I was distraught, feeling lost and betrayed at the same time.

"How could he just leave without telling me?"

Not taking into account that I left him first. But even with that fact, I still wanted to know where he was and why he left.

I sped into the parking lot and slammed the car into park. It had been a long drive, and the more time I had to think, the more upset I became.

When I got into the room, I threw the keys at June.

"What's wrong with you?"

"Nothing!" I said, flopping on the bed to pout like a second grader.

For the first time in a long time, I felt lost and alone because I was not in control. This threw my whole plan outta whack. Now I had to replan. And that started with finding out where Peter was.

I must have put his name into every search engine there was. In the state of California alone, there were 562 Peter Galvans.

I needed to stay close to June. We had spent a lot of time together searching names and finding photos for the Peters we had discovered. There was no doubt in my mind that I was going to find him. The only question was when.

He had his damned nerves leaving me like that. Not even giving me a chance to make amends. And when I *did* find him, I would show him why he shouldn't have left. And make sure he would never do it again.

CHAPTER 10

Peter ~ It had been eight months since I left California. And although things were not normal, they were as close to it as life had been in a while. I found a job working in a small realty office near Wallingford, trying to blend in while keeping my sanity.

Thanksgiving was about two weeks away, and I had just planned to get a twelve-pack and some food and sit back and watch some football until this happened.

"Hey, Pete. Do you have the Clausen file?"

I shuffled through the papers on my desk and gave the file to my coworker.

"You know Joe is having Thanksgiving at his place, and I was thinking about stopping by."

I kept typing, thinking that she was just trying to make small talk.

"Were you gonna stop by too?" she asked.

I turned and looked at Laura, who was beautiful and about four years younger than me. I guess I really never noticed how cute she was before because my mind was still in Los Angeles with Kate. I checked in every week like clockwork with Jose, first talking business and then eventually about Kate. He told me that she had come to the office twice, asking him where I was. But she had not been back recently. I often wondered what she was doing. If she was out there looking for me or killing someone else. I also wondered, was it time for me to move on with my life and leave this all behind? I was caught in a quagmire. And right now, I was just glad Jose was safe.

"So what do you think?" she asked.

"I think I'll be there. Do you need a ride?" I offered.

"I'm riding with Janet, but I could use a ride home. That is, if you wanna go out for drinks after."

Hell yeah I did! Now I know what you're thinking. I was still married, and I didn't even know where my wife *was*. I should be taking care of that before I go getting involved with someone else. And you would be right if my wife were not a killer. And besides, we were just two friends going out for drinks. It was nothing serious.

Over the last couple of weeks, I had been talking to Seth about how to divorce Kate without putting him or myself in any danger. We decided to have the sheriffs serve her. But we didn't know where she was. So until she surfaced, our plan would be delayed.

"Of course. I would like that." I said.

I was bubbling inside. It had been a while since I had been in the social company of a woman, and I was excited. It felt like Thanksgiving and Christmas all rolled up in one.

Over the course of the next week, Laura and I had developed a nice friendship. And although we had not spent much time outside of work together, our work relationship definitely blossomed. We would take lunch together, and our visits to each other's desks had become more frequent.

Finally, Thanksgiving was here, and I woke up very thankful for the peace of mind I was feeling.

I turned on the TV to watch the Thanksgiving parade and catch the beginning of the early game when I got a text.

"Can't wait to see you."

Now I was really excited. You see, over the course of that week, I had discovered Laura's true beauty. And I actually felt blessed to know it.

It was finally time to go, and I picked up my jacket to look for my keys. I scooped them off the dresser and walked out.

*****

Kate ~ I was reeling, frustrated, and tired of running into dead ends. I had been searching for Peter for months with no success.

Plus, after I talked to Jose, I felt something was fishy about the whole thing. So I would occasionally sit in the park across the street from Peter's office, trying to catch him sneaking in. He did have to work after all, right?

In a way, I did admire their friendship. Jose would always be in his corner, and I *always* longed for that same loyalty from Peter.

I had no option but to enlist June's help at this point. I finally realized that this job was bigger than me. So I had June searching all the social networking sites to see if he had put himself back into the dating game. She scoured thousands of profiles trying to find him, while I tracked down what she thought were potential leads.

*****

Peter ~ *"So bro, when do you think you will be coming back?"*

"I don't know man. I'm starting to like it out here."

"Are you kidding me? You're telling me you're giving up LA for podunk Connecticut?"

"I'm actually starting to get used to the seasons. Besides, the people are great out here. And I'm really starting to like Laura too."

"You barely even been through two of them. What do you know about seasons anyway? Or people for that matter?"

"I know I like them, and I know I like it out here."

"Oh yeah? So what about Kate?"

"I don't know. They still don't know where she is, and I'm getting pretty anxious."

"I think I may have just solved your problem."

"What are you talking about Jose?"

"Kate's back."

"What do you mean Kate's back?"

"I mean she's sitting across the street at the park."

"Are you sure it's her?"

"She's not trying to hide bro. I'm gonna go and talk to her."

"Don't do it Jose! Stay away from her!"

"You're slowing me down man. I'll call you back."

He hung up the phone, and my mind instantly wondered if I would ever see him again. I just had to wait…for now.

"Come on. Come on!" Jose said, repeatedly pushing the call button before he ran into the stairwell and rushed down the two flights to burst through the metal door onto the sidewalk, ignoring all my attempts to call him back.

*****

Kate ~ Strangely, I was starting to feel at home in my new persona, and now I was about to show Jose just who I had become.

So I baited him, and he fell right into my trap. I got up and walked away, knowing that he would follow me.

I could see him running through traffic, trying to keep up. He followed me over a bridge to a more secluded part of the park and stopped on the other side to catch his breath.

"Come on Kate, I know you're here. Come on out! We need to talk!"

I backed into the bushes.

"Kate, what the fuck man? What are you doing?!"

He walked toward the bushes and peeked in before he heard me come up behind him.

"Kate, what in the—" he asked, turning around.

I lifted the bat and hit him across the head.

"Kate?" he said, falling to the ground as I lifted it again.

He lost consciousness, and I continued to beat him without mercy, hearing his bones crunch as I crushed his skull.

"Can't let anyone find you out here." I said, panting heavily.

I leaned over and lifted his ankles to drag him farther into the brush to finish the job. I peered back through the foliage to see if anyone had seen me doing this dubious deed. No one did. And all I had to do now was finish and clean up. After today, Jose would never stand between me and my husband again.

Jose rolled over, and I picked up the bat and ran toward him.

"Oh no you don't."

I hit him in the arm and he screamed, which caused me to panic a little bit. So I hit him again.

I lifted the bat, bringing it to rest once more on his skull for good measure. And as I continued to beat him, I could hear him choking on the blood filling his mouth. When I saw his face begin to cave in and swell, I became even more excited, almost to the point of ecstasy. And strangely, there was no panic now.

It was no secret I hated Jose. I always felt that he was taking up too much of my time with Peter. And that feeling bred a deep-seeded resentment for him. So as I crushed his face and head beyond recognition, I began to feel a weird sort of sensation. An almost feeling of eroticism continued to grow inside me. And as the warm blood washed across my face, the more erotic I felt, until I finally climaxed, holding the neck of the bat tighter as I came on myself.

"That felt *so* damned good." I said, wiping the blood from my face.

I went over to the duffel bag I had hidden behind a tree and unzipped it to pull out the extra clothes inside. I looked around again before stripping naked to wipe Jose's blood from my body.

After I was clean and dressed, I put the bat and bloody clothes in the bag and peeked back through the bushes to see if the coast was clear.

It was midmorning, and usually there were people everywhere, running, walking, or just enjoying the day. Today, it was different though. There was no one by the lake, which even I thought was odd. It was just too perfect.

I grabbed the bag and walked out to the jogging path, trying to look as normal as possible on my way back to the car.

*****

Peter ~ Later that day, I tried to call my friend again. Ever since we hung up, I had been worried to death. I called him about twenty times, begging him to call me back in every one of the messages I left.

"Hey you."

I looked up to see that beautiful smile Laura was flashing at me.

"Hey." I returned.

"What's wrong?"

"Have you ever felt that something was wrong, and you just couldn't put your finger on it?"

"Not lately. What's going on?" she asked, concerned.

"I'm trying to reach my friend Jose, and he's not answering. That's not like him."

"Maybe he's just busy."

"Yeah, maybe." I said, trying to convince myself and hide what I feared may have already happened.

Laura didn't know much about my previous life. And I surely didn't tell her anything about my crazy-ass wife killing people. So I decided to put it to rest and wait until the next morning to try to call Jose again.

All that day, my mind had begun to get away from me. I had taken too much loss in my life over the last ten months or so. And it was all caused by the same woman. Now I didn't feel so sorry for her. In fact, I had begun to despise her, and I even contemplated flying back to Los Angeles to face her one last time. The only thing holding me back was Laura. Because if anything happened to me, what would happen to us? The answer was too frightening to think about.

I called the office the next morning.

"Mr. Marquez's office. How may I help you?"

"Janice, is Jose there?"

"Mr. Galvan, is that you?"

"It's me Janice. Is Jose there?"

"No Mr. Galvan. He hasn't been in today."

"Janice, listen. If Jose comes in, have him call me immediately. Do you understand? Immediately!"

"I understand Mr. Galvan. I'll have him call you right away."

"Thank you Janice."

I hung up the phone.

"Still no luck?" asked Laura.

"No, Janice said he hasn't been to the office yet. It's only eight a.m. in LA. I'll try and call him later."

I knew that if Jose was missing, chances are Kate killed him yesterday. I couldn't just stand by and let my friend, my brother, die in vain. So I decided to call the police…again.

I went into my phone settings and blocked my number before I called.

"LAPD, how may I direct your call?"

"Homicide please."

And after a short wait.

"This is Detective Garrett. How may I help you?"

"I'd like to report a missing person."

"And who would that be sir?"

"My friend Jose Marquez."

"When was the last time you saw Mr. Marquez sir?"

"About two months ago, but I talked to him yesterday."

"And what makes you think he's missing sir?"

"Because we talk every day, and I have reason to believe that my wife killed him."

"Who's your wife sir?"

"Her name is Kate Galvan."

There was silence on the other end. The detective could not believe what he was hearing. Kate had been the person of interest in my mother's and sister's murders. And now she was nowhere to be found. This call was the first time in months that he had even heard her name outside of his investigation.

"Who is this? Is this Peter?" he asked more intently.

"Yes, this is."

"Where are you Peter?"

"I'm in Connecticut."

"And how do you know your wife had something to do with Mr. Marquez's disappearance, if in fact he is missing?"

"When I was talking to him yesterday, he said he saw her. And I told him not to follow her, but he hung up, and I haven't heard from him since."

"Do you know where he followed her to?"

"Yeah, Hancock Park. Look Detective, I know this all sounds crazy, but I'm here to tell you that my wife is a dangerous woman.

The sooner you get her off the streets, the sooner the body count decreases."

"I'll check it out. Is there a number you can be reached at?"

I reluctantly gave him my cell number and hung up.

The next morning was Saturday, and Laura and I were having coffee when my phone rang.

"Hello?"

"May I speak to Peter Galvan, please?"

"This is he."

"Mr. Galvan, this is Detective Garrett. I'm afraid I have some bad news."

"What is it Detective?"

"We found Mr. Marquez."

"And…?"

My hands were shaking and starting to sweat.

"And I'm afraid he's dead."

My heart sank into my stomach, then rose back into my throat. I was speechless because my greatest fear had come true. And now I was truly alone. Jose was my last strand of hope and support, besides Laura. Now he was gone.

"Did you find Kate Detective?"

"I'm afraid not sir. But I will need you to stay available in case I have any questions."

"Thank you officer. I will."

I hung up the phone and began to cry as Laura scooted over to try to console me. It was a good thing too because if I had been alone, who knew what I would have done. So I told her everything.

"Babe, I have to tell you something."

I sat up so that I could look her in the eye.

"Well, you know I'm from California, right?"

She looked puzzled. Where was all this going?

"Yes, of course I know that baby."

I exhaled because the next part would be hard to say.

"Well, the reason I came to Connecticut was because I was try-ing to get away."

"Get away from what Peter?"

"It's more like who?"

"Okay, well who then Peter?"

"My wife."

I could see her heart breaking right in front of me.

"You're married?" she exclaimed, standing up.

"Yes, I am but…"

"But what Peter? You're married and didn't tell me? I thought you were being honest with me? Boy, can I pick 'em!"

"Baby, I was totally honest with you!"

"Except for the fact of you not telling me the truth!"

"Babe, I didn't tell you for your own protection."

"What do you mean for my protection?"

"My wife, Kate, killed my mother and sister. And the police think that she's killed more people, including Jose yesterday."

Laura was speechless, so I kept talking.

"I saw her kill a guy with my own eyes, and what scared me the most was when I looked at her, there was no remorse or guilt in her face. It was almost like she got off on it."

Laura still had no words.

"And so I came out here to get away from it all because it was just too much. And I thought that if she thought I was missing, that would draw her out of hiding."

"Why didn't you go to the police?"

"I was going to, but the night she killed Ron…"

"Who is Ron?"

"He was a private investigator I had following her after I became suspicious."

"Did you know she was killing people?"

"Not until she shot Ron in broad daylight. Right in front of me!"

"Oh my God! And you still didn't go to the police?"

I nodded.

"And now I think she killed Jose."

For the first time, I saw Laura scared, and I didn't like it because I didn't know if I could protect her. Hell, I didn't even know if I could protect myself.

"I was thinking about going back to California just so we could flush her out."

"You mean so you can become bait? And who is we Peter?"

"Well, what I meant is so the police could flush her out. The quicker they get her off the street, the quicker she stops killing."

"Okay, but what if you become her next victim?"

"Then nobody else will die, and that will be the end of that."

Laura sat quietly thinking. And *that* scared me even more than seeing Kate again. I wanted to be with Laura, and the thought of living without her was absolutely terrifying to me now.

"You're not going back to California. You're going to stay here with me and let the police sort it out."

I leaned over to kiss her. She moved away.

"I'm still mad at you. So this will be the last night we sleep in the same bed until you're divorced or we're married."

I could accept that. To tell you the truth, I was happy with it. At least she still thought of us as a couple.

I had come clean with Laura, and it felt good. But there was still something else I needed to tell her.

"Babe, you were asking me why I didn't go to the police?"

"Yes, I did."

"I know I should have turned her in. And if I were on the outside looking in, I would have asked why also. But the reason I didn't was because I still loved her. And for some strange reason, I thought that I could save her. And possibly get her some help."

"Save her? What made you *think* you could save her? And why would you still care about someone that killed your *mother*?"

"You know, I thought maybe I could get her some help or something, I don't know."

"And how do you feel now? You still think you can save her? Do you still love her?'"

"I just feel that she needs to be off the streets, and to be honest, I hate her now. I just can't do it anymore. I'm done, I promise."

You know, I often wondered why she did what she did. With everything that had happened, I never thought of asking. I just chalked it up to her ass being crazy, which seemed like a pretty good reason to me.

She took away the people I loved in the name of love. And *I* had moved all the way across the country and lied for love. It's true. Love *is* a fickle mistress. And over the course of this last year, it had taken me to my deepest depths and my highest highs, leaving me to grasp what was left with Laura. And there was no way I was going to let that go. *Over my dead body!* Should I have even said that?

CHAPTER 11

Kate ~ Two months had passed, and I still hadn't found Peter. And with each passing day, I became more irritated with that fact.

"Have you found anything yet?"

"No, not yet, but this guy is cute." June said.

She slid the laptop around to show me who she was talking about. When I looked at the screen, I could tell that June saw something in my face that she had never seen before: optimism.

"June, you are wonderful!" I said, kissing her on the forehead.

"What did I do?"

"You found him!"

Yep, there he was in full color on some bitch's Facebook page, looking right at me.

"Whatever happened to you guys?"

"He was an abusive asshole and a loser. And now that I've found him, I can finally get some closure."

I lied. He had never once raised a hand in anger toward me. He would never do that. He loved me too much, and I knew that.

"You see? That's why he left me, because he wanted a life with this slut! I wonder if he's beating her ass too."

I started to cry as part of the charade. But what June thought were tears of sadness were actually tears of joy. I had found Peter, and now I needed to be with him. After all, it had been just under a year, and all my hard work had finally paid off. And now I was ready to go forward with the plans I so painstakingly developed to get him back.

The first thing I had to do was fake my death so that I could travel without suspicion, or attention. I was so anxious to start that I almost killed June right then and there. But that would have to wait because I still needed her. And now was not the right time because I hadn't tied things up on this end yet. But it would be soon, and I would be ready.

Ever since June had found Peter, I kept her close. And in some sort of weird way, she had actually become my friend. And I found myself actually caring for her.

I always had my own money. But I would have never *ever* thought I would be using it to finance a revenge plot. But here we were.

I bought a ticket to Connecticut, and only a week after I found him, I was landing in Hartford. He lived only a couple of hours away, and within three hours of touching down, I was sitting in front of his house.

*****

Peter ~ "Baby, did you get the wine for tonight?" Laura asked.

I was on the couch half-asleep, watching basketball. I had totally forgotten about it.

I sat up and asked, "Huh?"

"You didn't get the wine, did you?"

"I'll go and get it right now." I said, hopping up.

"You don't need to."

"Babe, I'll go."

And five minutes later...

"No, I'll go and get it after I go to the post office." she said.

Now come on. Was she messing with me? By the time she had told me that, I was ready to walk out the door.

"Hold on." she said, rushing after me.

Uh-oh, here comes the mini lecture.

"I need you to pick these up too."

She handed me the list and gave me a kiss. Was she still messing with me? She had already known that I was going to the store, didn't she? That was why she already had the list made out. I don't know, maybe I was overthinking things again.

I grabbed my keys and said, "I'll be back."

I walked out, looking over the list, deciding it was better to walk than take the car. She only needed a few more things anyway, and the crisp air felt good.

I walked down the stairs onto the sidewalk and casually glanced across the street, instantly feeling terrified. Did I just see Kate? I didn't want to look back, but I knew I had to. When I did, my worst nightmare had come true. There she was sitting calmly in the car, looking at me. How in the hell did she find me?

I started to walk over to the car so that I could face my demon. But before I got off the curb, she had started it and drove calmly away.

I was scared all over again. I ran back into the house, sweating and panting heavily.

"You can't be back already?" Laura joked.

"Laura..."

All I could do was look at her. Which I knew freaked her out.

"What is it baby?" she asked, walking over to comfort me.

"I just..."

She stood in front of me, patiently waiting for me to finish.

"You just what baby?"

"I...just saw Kate."

She backed away from me in disbelief. I had just told her what happened in California, and now here I was telling her that Kate was in Connecticut. It was like a surreal dream that I couldn't wake up from.

"You saw Kate where?"

"Outside, right out front!" I pointed.

We both walked into the living room and peeked through the blinds.

"Do you see her?"

"No." I said nervously.

"Was she in a car?"

"Yeah, a blue Chevy."

"What happened?"

"I walked outside, looked across the street, and there she was, just sitting there, looking at me."

"We need to call the police."

"And tell them what Laura? That my wife is in town, and she scared the shit out of us when we saw her sitting in front of our house?"

"Yes! And don't be a smart-ass Peter!" she said, peeking out the window again.

"How in the hell did she find me?" I wondered aloud.

I pulled my phone out and pressed Detective Garrett's name.

"Shit!" I said, taking the phone from my ear.

It went straight to voice mail, so I decided to leave a message.

"Detective, this is Peter Galvan, and I just saw my wife…"

I looked over at Laura.

"My ex-wife sitting out in front of my house. Please call me back when you get this."

Laura was still looking out the window as if she half expected Kate to walk up to the front door. And to tell you the truth, so was I. But that never happened. Thank God.

"Maybe I should call the local police too." I said, pacing.

Now instead of worrying about Kate, Laura was worried about me.

"I'm sure she will turn up again. And that's when the police will get her."

"You're probably right baby." I said, already knowing that that was not going to happen.

I don't have to tell you how I felt: worried, confused, and mad all at the same time. And although I loathed Kate for what she had become, I still loved her for the time I knew her as a kind, gentle, and beautiful soul. So if I saw her again, I would try to reason with her. But if she tried to hurt me or Laura, who knew what I might do? I didn't even want to find out.

What I didn't know at the time was that Kate went straight back to California. And now that she knew where I was, I think she thought it better to start whatever she was planning as soon as possible.

The only thing I was worried about now was keeping Laura safe. At first I decided to pack up and run. But that wouldn't be fair to ask Laura to do that. Just leave the life she had built and go on the run from my wife? I didn't think so. So I decided to stay, fight, and protect Laura any way I could. And that started with helping the police find Kate.

*****

Kate ~ I pulled into the parking lot of the triple B and got out.
"How was your mom?" June asked.
"She's doing much better, thanks." I said, exhausted.
"That's good. I was hoping she would be okay."
I pulled the small travel bag from the front seat and walked to my room with June not far behind.
"June, can you stay with me tonight? I'm still worried about my mom, and I can really use the company."
Step 1: The Bait.
I had never been afraid of anything or anyone. And now my excitement was peaking, especially now that I could put my plan in motion. But as the black widow, I still needed to spin my web. And so I put mine under construction, all in an effort to catch my husband.
"Sure. Just let me go get my overnight bag, and I'll be right up."
June started to walk away before she stopped to turn around and say, "You know, at first you tried to be a hard-ass, but I knew you were a softie. I'm glad we became friends."
I smiled back and said, "Me too."
As soon as the door closed, I got to work, loading the small travel bag with rope, duct tape, and a crowbar. I really liked the feeling I got when I killed Jose. So much so that I almost had an orgasm just thinking about it. And so I decided that beating or stabbing would definitely become part of my modus operandi. And I was truly fine with that, unless another method presented itself of course.
"Let's see now. Do I have everything?"

I snapped my fingers and walked over to the drawer to pull out the small bottle of chloroform I had.

"Knock knock."

I dropped the bottle in the bag and zipped it up before I kicked it under the bed.

"Why do people say "Knock knock" when they don't actually knock?" I asked.

"Well… I guess the "Knock knock" takes the place of the *actual* knock."

I smirked. I was going to miss June.

"June, I need you to help me with something."

"Of course, anything."

Despite June's beauty and gorgeous golden-brown skin, she was lonely. She never really had many friends. And the ones she did have had either moved away or just lost contact altogether. Her mom and dad were not dead like she told me. They were alive and well and living in Vegas.

The truth behind June becoming anonymous was that her dear father would sexually abuse her every chance he could. He even went as far as to call her his *real* wife. Sick bastard. She was tired of sleeping with him. And the two abortions he had put her through took an irreparable toll on her, both emotionally and physically. So she left. At seventeen, she was homeless and sleeping with truckers for rides, wandering aimlessly until she came to the Bakersfield Bed and Breakfast—the triple B to the locals—where she found a home. It was true nobody knew where she was, but that was by choice, not by circumstance. She had felt betrayed by her mother, who had sided with the monster, so she decided to start a life elsewhere. And for now, the Bakersfield Bed and Breakfast would provide her the opportunity to do just that.

"I need you to help me get rid of my car."

"What happened to it?"

"I crashed it a couple miles down the five, and I need you to help me get rid of it so that my husband won't find it. Or me."

Step 2: The Set up.

"How would he do that?" asked June.

91

"Because the car is registered to him, and if the cops find it, they will notify him. And he *will* come and find me. I don't want that June. So will you help me?"

June sympathized with me, feeling the bond of abuse between the two of us. If there *were* such a thing.

*****

Peter ~ Meanwhile, back in Connecticut, Laura and I were still spooked by Kate's untimely visit.

"So what are we going to do now?" asked Laura.

"Nothing," I said.

"What do you mean nothing."

"I mean nothing! I'm not going to run from her again. And if I see her, I'll just call the LAPD. They'll come and arrest her ass, and this will all be behind us." I said as manly as I possibly could.

"I'm scared Peter. Who knows what she's capable of?"

I did. I walked over and put my arms around her.

"Don't worry baby. I won't let her hurt you."

This coming from the guy who ran across the entire country to hide from her.

*****

Kate ~ It was just after eight, and the sun had gone down hours ago. And this particular December night, it was cold in the California desert.

"Where's the flashlight?"

June reached into the bag and passed it to me.

"I know it's around here somewhere." I said, pointing the beam of light into the darkness.

The wind from the passing traffic was bone-chilling as we walked along the shoulder looking for the discarded vehicle when...

"Can I help you ladies with something?" asked the CHP officer pulling off the road, lights flashing.

How did I not see the cop pull up? *That was foolish*, I thought.

"No sir, we're fine." I blurted out.

"What are you doing out here ladies?"

There was silence.

"I asked you a question." he said.

The cop put his cruiser in park and got out.

"What are you looking for out here ladies?"

He pulled out his flashlight and pointed it down the embankment.

"I was walking home from the store, and I dropped my keys. They've gotta be here somewhere." June said, looking around.

"Yeah, this is not the first time this has happened." I said, playing along.

"I'll help you look then."

I couldn't think of a reason fast enough not to have him help us. So I continued to pretend. June eased her keys from her pocket and leaned over.

"Oh, here they are!" she said, jingling them above her head.

The officer and I walked over.

"Are you okay ma'am?" He asked looking at me.

"Yes officer. I'm just cold."

And nervous.

"Well, I can drop you guys off if you like. Where are you going?"

"Oh, we're just down at the triple B."

"Okay, well hop in, and I'll give you ladies a lift."

"That's okay. It's just down the road. We can walk back."

"Well, I can't leave you out here on the shoulder. It's too dangerous. So I'm afraid I must insist."

We walked to the car. When we got there, the officer opened the back door and gestured, "Ladies."

We got in the cruiser, and I wondered if this was how I would end up one day.

Fuck that. I'll be dead first! I thought.

Ten minutes later, we were pulling into the parking lot with me anxious to get out.

"Thank you officer," I said, walking past the cruiser.

"My pleasure ma'am."

I hurried up the stairs and into my room.

"Shit, shit, shit!" I said, falling back on the bed.

June came in just after me.

"What are you carrying on about?"

I sat up and said, "I have to get rid of that car! Peter can *never* find me! Do you hear me? Never!"

June sat down and said, "Don't worry. We still have time."

I looked at her, waiting to hear why she was so optimistic.

"I know the chippies around here, and that was the last pass for a couple hours."

It was 9:30 p.m., and with that news, my optimism had returned. I was determined to keep as close to schedule as I could. And with no CHP in the area, I just might be able to pull it off.

"So you're saying we can go back tonight?"

"Yeah, but we should leave a little after ten or so just to make sure he didn't stop at the Sunshine for a cup of coffee."

"Okay, that sounds good. Thank you." I said, walking over to hug June.

Boy, was I gonna miss June.

It was a short wait, and now it was time to leave.

"Do you remember where the car is?" June asked.

I thought for a second. "I know it's near a billboard with some old guy smiling."

"I know where that is. That's down by Route 34."

"Okay then, let's go." I said, grabbing my murder bag.

June turned out the lights as we hurried out of the room.

"How are we gonna get down there without being seen?" I asked.

"I know a small trail across the highway where I used to take my johns."

What June didn't know was that she was in fact helping me to kill her. She had just shown me the perfect place to carry out the devilish deed without her even knowing it.

About forty minutes later, we came up on the car.

"THERE IT IS!" I yelled.

I ran to it and started to remove the branches.

94

"How are we gonna get it back?"

"Back where?"

"To the triple B."

"And June, why would I take it back to the triple B?"

June thought for a second and said, "I don't know."

I chuckled. I was *really* gonna miss June.

"Come over here and help me! I was thinking we could get rid of the car down the road. It looks pretty deserted."

"It's not deserted. That's the end of old man Randall's farm. He breeds horses, and that used to be his grazing pasture. But ever since he bought another twenty acres of additional land up by Mill Creek, he grazes his herd about five miles north of here."

Perfect.

Step 3: The Murder Scene.

I walked around the car, opened the bag, and walked up behind June, who was still clearing the branches.

"What are you gonna do with that?" she said, looking back.

"It has to be a reason why I crashed the car, right? I'm gonna take out the lug nuts from the wheel."

I walked past June and went to work on the passenger-side tire. Shortly after she finished removing the branches, I stood up and called her over.

"Hey, come do me a favor. Get rid of these lug nuts while I get the gas can out of the trunk."

"What do I do with them?"

"Throw them in the desert, but not in the same direction. It has to look like they came off and scattered everywhere."

June threw the lug nuts as far as she could, continuing to be the good friend who would pay for her loyalty with her life. And just after she threw the last one, I hit her with the tire iron.

She fell to the dirt dazed and confused, staggering to her hands and knees, waiting for me to hit her again. She fell hard to the dirt and started to bleed profusely from her head.

She was barely conscious when she had become the unwilling and helpless victim of a psychopath like me.

I wiped the small spatter of blood from my lips and looked around before I knelt down to roll her over on to her back.

When I looked down at her, I felt the loss of my friend for only a moment before I kissed her and placed her head gently back on the ground.

I steadied myself and lifted the tire iron again, bringing it to rest across June's face, just under her nose. I wiped her face again before I put my hand on the ground to prop myself up. I started to bludgeon my friend again, this time much faster and much harder.

I took a deep breath and put my hand into June's mouth to remove her teeth like seeds from a pumpkin gourd. Then I lifted the tire iron again to continue my assault. And after hitting her several more times, I reached back into her mouth to remove some more of her teeth as I watched her convulse and cough up blood.

I hit her several more times before I reached into her bag to take out the small flashlight and a pair of pliers.

I clicked on the light and placed it in my mouth before I looked around again. I put my watch under the light and told myself, "Okay, I've got time."

I put the light back in my mouth and opened June's, positioning it so that I could see the few remaining teeth to pull. I put the pliers in her mouth, clinched a tooth, and began to wiggle it to remove it and the rest of her already loose teeth.

Ten minutes later, I was finished and a little winded, but I was still not done. I looked down and saw that I was sitting in a pool of June's blood, and that excited me tremendously. I reached for the tire iron and lifted it to bash the rest of June's head in, discovering that I had become increasingly hornier than I had ever felt in my life.

I sat up on my knees and started to gyrate my hips while simultaneously clubbing June. This made me more orgasmic by the second until…it happened—orgasm. Oh, shit!

I didn't know what was coming over me. Suddenly the power of taking a life became more exhilarating, which apparently led to orgasm. Either way, I had no complaints. It seemed as though it had become the reward for killing. And I had to admit that I liked it.

Now here I was immersed in my friend's warm blood, beginning to salivate. And after a very satisfying conquest, I dug into my pants and rubbed my silky ejaculation across my face as the tremors in my legs violently subsided. Now I was starting to get tired, but I still had work to do, so I got right to it.

I picked up June's teeth and put them in a sandwich bag to place in my pocket.

I stood up feeling the cold air, aided by the draft from passing cars on the highway, chill my very soul. I went to the trunk and lifted the spare. Beneath it were a change of clothes and a bottle of tequila. I only grabbed the bottle.

I looked around again and twisted the cap off to take a healthy drink.

I swallowed half the pint before I walked back over to sit in June's blood again. I picked up the pliers, and this time, I put them into *my* mouth.

I bared down on one of my front teeth and began to pull. It hurt like hell. So much so that I had to take another drink from the bottle. I reached in again and attempted to extract the tooth, feeling the momentous pain before I drank almost all of what was left of the tequila.

Again I reached in and began to pull, as I felt and heard the roots being ripped from my gums. Success! The first one was out!

I picked the bottle up and looked at it. And now I was beginning to feel its effects. I placed the pliers back into my mouth and started on the next one, enduring the pain as I yanked the bone from flesh. My mouth had begun to fill with blood. So much so that I couldn't spit it out fast enough.

I was beyond drunk now, and the only thing keeping me awake was the pain I was in. But eight teeth later and after a little nausea and a lot of crying, I was finished. Not because it was a part of the plan but because my mouth hurt like a son of a bitch.

I took the teeth I was holding and threw them in the front seat and on the floorboard before I wobbled back over to June. I tried to focus on the bottle of alcohol so that I could pour the last of it into my mouth. And if I thought it hurt before, that was nothing compared to how it hurt now. I should have gotten another bottle.

"GODDAMMIT! SHIT!" I yelled, jumping around.

The tequila felt like fire in my open wounds. I spit the remainder of it, mixed with blood and pieces of my gums out, while I tried as best I could to get back to the car. Once there, I opened the door and threw up.

I was in bad shape. And when I leaned over to throw up again, I wondered if this had been a good idea. But whether it was or not, it had to be completed now because I was in too deep. So I pushed on.

I stumbled over to June and leaned over, feeling the dry heaves mount in my stomach. The eruption of vomit shot out and spewed all over June's body.

I wiped my mouth and leaned over to lift her so that I could pull her to the car. Finally, when I got there, I put her in the driver's seat and carefully placed her smashed-in face on the steering wheel.

"Comfortable?" I joked, patting her on the back.

I stumbled back to the trunk, using the car as a crutch to get a bottle of water to pour over my hands and face. I took out the shovel to cover the spot June had bled out in, feeling sick and tired but not in the usual sense. I really was *sick* and *tired*.

I wobbled back over to the puddle of blood and began to turn the hard ground over to cover it, hoping it would seep out of sight over time. When I was done, I picked up the flashlight to see if any evidence was left. And as I wobbled in place, I decided there was none.

I stumbled over to the pile of branches and placed them over the spot I had just dug up.

"Phew, almost done." I said, chuckling through my toothless grin.

I walked back to the car, dragging the shovel behind me before I reached back into the trunk to grab the change of clothes and the can of gas.

I walked a short distance from the car, fighting the urges to throw up from the fumes. I doused the car and threw the empty can back into the trunk before I lit the match and began to cry. I *did* miss

June and wished in some macabre way that she could be here with me. But she wasn't. So I threw the match to cleanse the crime scene and hopefully my emotional state.

The car caught fire and instantly washed the dark desert with light. I knew I had to get out of there quick because undoubtedly the fire would bring attention. So I hurried over and grabbed a dry branch to light the small pile of branches, covering the spot where I had killed my friend. I grabbed my clothes and ran back toward the deserted horse pasture.

It was 1:15 a.m., and the fire did catch the attention of a passing CHP cruiser, who immediately called for a fire unit with paramedics.

I was relieved and kinda surprised to be out of sight. I looked back through the trees to watch the car explode in a fiery silhouette before I took a deep breath and began to walk and cry. And yep, you guessed it, I *missed* June. Unfortunately, I couldn't accomplish my plan without sacrificing my friend in the process. Plus, I had no way of knowing if June would have bought into my murderous plot. Anyway, I definitely couldn't afford to find out. What if I told her and she threatened to call the cops? I would've had to kill her anyway. So this had to be the way.

I walked over to an old watering trough and reached in, surprised to feel the cold water on my fingertips. I cupped it and began washing my friend's blood and my guilt away.

CHAPTER 12

Peter ~ I hadn't seen Kate since she came to Connecticut, but we were still vigilant. We looked for her everywhere. And this particular evening, something just seemed different. Something I thought I would never live to hear.

"BABY, CAN YOU GET THE PHONE?" Laura yelled from the other room.

I ran over to the phone, still trying to catch a little more of the Lakers game I had DVR'd.

"Hello?"

"May I speak with Peter Galvan?"

"This is he. Who am I talking to?"

"This is Sergeant Krist of the California Highway Patrol Bakersfield office. I'm sorry to bother you. I'm calling to inform you that your wife is deceased."

I couldn't believe it. Kate was dead? How? I just stood there dumbfounded and said, "How?"

"We found her car burned on the side of the highway. It looks like she hit a tree, and her car caught fire."

"How could that have happened officer?"

"Well, far as we can tell, she sped off the road, down the embankment, and hit the tree. We're still investigating the scene. When we have more information, I'll let you know."

"When did this happen?"

"Late last night or early this morning. Witnesses report seeing the car on fire shortly before two a.m."

I had nothing to say. I couldn't believe it. I mean, I did feel sorry Kate was dead, but come on. It also meant that I was free. That *we* were free. I just stood there swaying between the two emotions.

"Mr. Galvan?"

"Yes, I'm here officer."

"So can you come out and identify the body? I mean, there's not much of her left. Or you can always wait until we get the DNA sample back from the lab. You were the only one listed as her next of kin."

I decided to do the latter. I certainly wasn't going back to California. I just wanted to leave that nightmare behind. And if Kate truly was dead, that meant that I should do just that.

"I'll wait officer."

"Okay, then I'll call you at this number when we find out."

"Thank you."

I hung up the phone, moving like a zombie.

"Baby, who was that?"

"The police."

"The police? What did they want?"

"They wanted to tell me that Kate was dead."

"Kate's dead? How?"

"Car crashed near Bakersfield."

And now there were two zombies.

We both couldn't believe it, and when I looked at Laura, I saw her starting to bounce through her own gauntlet of emotions.

*****

Kate ~ Two days later, I jumped awake from the nightmare I was having. It was 2:00 p.m., and my mouth tasted like stale cigarettes and rotten meat. It smelled like it too. I rolled over and focused on the digital clock before sitting up.

"I gotta get going." I said, pushing my fingers through my hair before I picked up the last half of a joint to light. It felt funny smoking weed with missing teeth and swollen gums, but I made it work. And after I got high, I was ready to shower. Something I had not done in at least two days.

The warm water felt good running across my face, and it gave me the soothing relaxation that only warm water could. I wiped the water from my eyes and called out, "June, can you get the towel I left on the chair?"

Expecting a response and getting none caused me to peek through the curtain.

"Goddammit June, did you hear me?"

I was ready to step out the shower and really tear into her when I remembered.

"What in the fuck am I doing?" I just laughed.

What a question.

I stepped out of the shower and got the towel, with a little saner brain.

By 5:00 p.m., I was dressed and almost ready to go. I just had one more thing to do first. Find a plastic surgeon. You heard me, a plastic surgeon. I put down the beer I was drinking and walked out. I had also decided that finding a dentist would be a good idea too.

The sun was bright and high. And even though there wasn't a cloud in the sky, it was chilly. I closed my wrap around me and walked to the office.

The computer I had used to find Peter belonged to June, and well, June was dead, and the computer was locked in her room. So I was forced to use the one in the office.

"Wow, it's kinda cold out today." I said, hurrying in to close the door behind me.

"Rob, can I use the computer?"

"Of course. What happened to you? It looks like you got in a fight with a wildcat."

"Yeah, something like that."

"You want me to call a doctor?"

I stopped and stared at him.

After seeing the look on my face, he walked to the end of the counter and pulled back the latch on the small door.

"Come on in."

I walked behind the counter and followed him into the office.

"She's all yours."

"Thanks Rob."

I waited for him to walk out before I sat down.

Once I logged in, I started my search, typing in "best plastic surgeons," with twenty or so names popping up on page 1.

I scrolled halfway down the list and stopped at Patrick Krane, who was a very prominent doctor from Philadelphia. When I clicked on his bio, I read every word of it.

He was thirty-eight and single with a daughter, Eliza, who was battling a rare form of leukemia. He attended Northwestern's prestigious Feinberg School of Medicine and had been in practice for a little over seven years.

I clicked on "Krane and Associates" and scoured every link and page on the site before turning my efforts to his social media.

"Google is a great fucking thing." I told myself smiling.

There was a light knock at the door before it opened.

"Kate, there's somebody out here who needs the computer."

"Okay Rob, I just need to print some things first."

"Okay, you got five minutes."

"More than I need Rob."

I printed what I needed before punching Dr. Krane's office address into June's phone. Then I quickly looked for a dentist before deleting the browser history.

It would take six days to get to Philly if I took my time. And that was exactly what I had planned to do. First I needed to go to the dentist and stay low-key to support the story of me being dead. They would be investigating the area around the triple B, and it was no longer the place for me to be. So I hopped in June's car and started the drive cross-country immediately, assured that no one would be looking for *her*.

*****

Peter ~ Three days had passed since I got the news, and I was feeling anxious. After all, what if it wasn't Kate. But...what if it was? What would I do? Go on living a fairy-tale life with Laura?

Whatever I was going to do, I needed to do it fast and live with it. But if she *was* dead, that would make the decision a lot easier.

I was sitting downstairs reading the paper when my cell phone rang.

"Hello."

"Mr. Galvan."

"Yes Detective, what did you find out?"

My hands were sweating, and I was nervous.

"Well, we found some teeth and ran them against some of your wife's previous dental records, and..."

"And what?"

"They came back a match."

I didn't know what to say, so I just said, "Thank you." and hung up the phone.

I walked into the kitchen and kissed Laura, almost feeling guilty for how happy I was. Now I know what you're saying. I'm a cold, hard-hearted dog and an asshole. But what I would like to say in defense of that is...she killed my mother and sister, case closed. And as far as I was concerned, so was that chapter of my life.

So now I was happy. And the feeling of guilt seemed to melt away when I told Laura. We both seemed to be relieved. And honestly, we were ecstatic because we could start our lives now. Our life *together*. Keep your opinions to yourself please.

*****

Kate ~ It was 7:00 a.m., and I was sitting in Denny's, enjoying a short stack and eggs, thankful for my new teeth, when I looked up and couldn't believe my eyes. There he was standing right in front of me—Dr. Krane.

What was he doing here? I thought.

I had been driving all night after leaving the dentist in Indy when I decided to stop before going to get some sleep. And in my haste to do that, I hadn't noticed that I was just down the street from the good doctor's office.

I was so excited that I stuffed half a pancake in my mouth along with some eggs and coffee before I dropped a twenty on the table and waited for him to walk out.

Dr. Krane paid for his coffee and walked out, with me not far behind.

I followed him halfway up the block to a small medical plaza, electing not to follow him in.

What was I going to do now? I inhaled the crisp winter air to calm myself down. I knew where he was now. So I decided to go get some rest before coming back to convince him to see things my way. Plus, my mouth still hurt like hell.

I was so tired that I slept all of that day and half the next. I woke up just before three, feeling well rested and ready to go.

I had decided to get dressed and go back to case the doctor's office. It was just a short walk, and in no time, I was there. I saw him walking out with his daughter. And I also saw the way he looked at her, the way he embraced her when they hugged. I knew then I had to take her and that she would be the perfect pawn.

So now I just had to figure out how to get her and where I would keep her. I really had to think about that because at that moment, she became the most important piece of the puzzle.

A short time later, I was back in the hotel room looking through the paper for a suitable place to keep the girl. Somewhere nobody would notice.

"Let's see, it's got to be somewhere that's secluded but comfortable."

I came across an ad for a small house rental about an hour outside of town.

"Perfect."

Three days later, I was ready. I put on my jacket and slid the small bottle of chloroform I had into my pocket, along with a white face towel, grabbing my keys on the way out.

Over the course of the three previous days, I had been busy. First I had to find out where the good doctor lived. But before I broke into his house, I had to find out his family's schedule. This would prove useful when deciding the best time to grab the girl. I looked at the notes I had taken at the triple B and entered the good doctor's address into my GPS.

Step 4: Get the Bait. I walked up to the house, which seemed homier than I had expected a successful doctor's home to be. I took the pick from my pocket and looked around before going to work on the lock. And a couple of minutes later, I was ducking into the house. The three-bedroom Virginian was stocked with memories. There were pictures of the family in every room, even the bathroom.

"When me and Peter have our kids, we won't have any pictures of them in the bathroom." I said as I wiped myself and flushed.

I walked through the entire house, and now there was only one more room to search. I found it at the front, just left of the door. I walked in and looked around at all the books, thinking to myself that I would *never* want to read this many books on purpose.

I walked around the desk and sat down before reaching for and opening his appointment book.

"Let's see…"

Thumbing my fingers through the pages, I searched for the opening I would need to steal my bargaining chip, when…viola! There it was, the annual children's walk for cancer.

"I could snatch her there. Yes, that would be perfect. With all those people there, I could put her to sleep and use the crowd as cover."

I closed the book, put it in my pocket, and walked out of the house.

CHAPTER 13

Kate ~ The four days I had to wait seemed like an eternity. But Saturday was finally here, and in just a couple of hours, I would have what I needed to acquire the services of one Dr. Patrick Krane.

I made arrangements to meet with the owner of the house I hoped to rent that morning. And an hour and a half later, I was getting out of the car to meet its owner.

"Mrs. Marshall?"

"June?"

"Yes ma'am, that's me."

"You're early."

"Yes ma'am. I just got a job working for a medical practice in Philly, and I volunteered to help out at their annual health fair. I thought that I would come out and meet you before I go."

"Volunteering? That's nice. I wish more people did that these days, including me."

"I'm just doing it to look good for my boss." I chuckled.

Mrs. Marshall looked down her nose as if she had just lost the respect I had just earned.

"Well, I'm sure you'll come to realize that charity is selfless."

"Yes ma'am."

"You seem nice enough though," she said.

If she only knew.

"I suppose you want to see the house. It's this way. Follow me."

I followed her down a small path past a field of corn to a small house on the edge of a lake. It was absolutely beautiful.

"Well, here it is. It has all the comforts of home."

Outside didn't look like much, but inside...inside was spectacular.

The small one bedroom had beautiful oak flooring with central heating and a small air conditioner in the bedroom. The kitchen wasn't as big as I would have liked, but it did lead out to a rear patio that was perched just above the lakeshore.

"Perfect."

The small older woman turned around and said, "Well now then, it's just the small matter of the payment."

"Oh of course."

I dug into my jeans and pulled out a wad of cash.

"That's a lot of money for someone who just got a job."

"It's my savings ma'am, from the job I had back home."

"Back home?"

"Omaha."

"Nebraska huh? You're kind of far away from home, don't you think?"

"Not far enough."

Mrs. Marshall looked at me again with that same distasteful chagrin. Who did this bitch think she was? I just wanted to punch her in the throat and dismember her mean ass. But for now, I just paid her. I had enough on my plate, but you could be sure that if she got in my way, I would kill her quick. Just as sure as water is wet.

"Well, what about you?" I asked.

"Well what about me?"

"What's your story?"

"My story is that I'm your landlord, and I expect my rent every first of the month. I don't want any loud music blaring at all times of the night, and *no* wild parties. Do you understand?"

"Yes ma'am."

"Here are the keys. Where's your stuff?"

"It's at the motel. I'll bring them when I come back this evening."

She turned and walked back up the path, leaving me standing there.

The small house was furnished, so all I really needed was a place to keep the girl. I walked into the bedroom. It was small with barely enough room for the bed and dresser.

"This won't do."

I walked out into the kitchen and opened the patio doors. The air felt good, cupping my face as it whisked by. I looked to the left and saw a small gate that led off the patio.

"What's this now?"

I walked over to it and saw a small footpath on the other side.

"We might be on to something here."

I opened the gate and walked down the small path that led to the back of the house. Just beneath the patio were two cellar doors. My eyes opened wide. This would be the perfect place to hide the girl. And at night, there would be no light back here. So if I could keep Mrs. Marshall away, I wouldn't have any problems. Or at least *she* wouldn't.

I opened the door and pulled the string that turned on the dusty light bulb at the center of the room.

"A little dusty, but this will do just fine."

I ran back upstairs and looked under the kitchen sink to find all the cleaning supplies I would need.

"This is just too perfect." I gloated.

And an hour later, I was finished cleaning, standing in the middle of the room admiring my work, before looking down at my watch.

"Oh shit, I gotta get outta here!"

*****

Peter ~ It really hadn't begun to sink in that Kate was dead. And even though the police said that it was definitely her they found, I still had a strange feeling that we hadn't seen the last of her just yet.

Laura and I had started to plan our wedding, and we had even set the date. The formal wedding with guests at a church would be later. But for now, Atlantic City would have to do. We had decided to go that coming weekend.

"Baby, do you have everything?"

"Yep." I said, looking around.

I grabbed both our bags and walked out of the house.

"Baby, don't forget to lock the door."

I took the keys from my pocket and locked the door before I threw the bags in the back seat to hop in the car.

"Do you have the directions to Linda's?" Laura asked.

"Yeah, right here in my pocket."

Linda was Laura's sister who lived just outside of Philly across the river in Camden.

The idea was to pick her and her husband Carl up and head on to Atlantic City.

Laura hadn't seen her sister in a while and wanted to make this a holiday of sorts.

She had planned to ask her to be her maid of honor both here and at the wedding for family and friends.

For most of the trip, we had been talking and laughing. So much so that we hadn't noticed that we were almost there. The trip was just under six hours, and we had decided to stop and get something to eat before heading on to Linda's.

"Hey, pull off. I know this great cheese steak place not far from here. My father used to take me when I traveled with him."

I pulled off the expressway right into traffic.

"What the hell is going on here?" I said, frustrated. I had been driving all day. And besides the cramping in my butt, I was hungry. And all these people in my way made me hungrier and grumpier.

"It looks like some kind of fun run or something." Laura said.

We stopped at a light, and Laura rolled down the window.

"Excuse me. Excuse me!"

A woman and her daughter walked up to the car.

"Excuse me ma'am. What's going on here?"

"They're having the annual walk for cancer for the children's hospital of Philly."

"Oh great." I said.

It wasn't that I didn't think that childhood cancer was not a worthy cause because it is. It was just that I was tired, I had to pee, and I was hungry.

"Calm down. I know a shortcut right past the park."

And little did I know, Kate was at that same park in the middle of her diabolical scheme.

*****

Kate ~ I sped into the parking structure across the street from the medical plaza, screeching to a halt in the nearest space.

"It's going to take me all day to find her. I should have left earlier." I told myself.

I leaned over and opened the glove compartment to take out the chloroform and face towel. I slammed it shut and hurried into the park.

*****

Peter ~ "Take a left up here." Laura pointed.

I turned left, not looking before I came to a hard stop just in front of two men and their kids.

"Sorry." I gestured.

"Baby, you have to be careful. There's a lot of people in the park today."

"Thanks for the news flash baby," I said, irritated.

"Somebody's testy today."

"Somebody's hungry today baby, and plus, I have to pee."

"Well, just be careful then. The restaurant's just across the park, and we can get you some cheese with that whine."

I laughed and agreed.

"It's not far now, just down the road a bit on the right."

Besides hearing Laura say she loves me, those were the sweetest words I had heard from her lips…ever.

We just had a couple of blocks to go, and most of the commotion from the cancer walk was behind us. With every rotation of the wheel, I felt hungrier as my bladder swelled. And all I could think about was the relief I would feel not soon enough.

I pulled into the crosswalk.

"Back up baby. These people want to cross."

I put the car in reverse when the woman standing behind us pounded on the trunk.

*****

Kate ~ "HEY, WHAT THE HELL ARE YOU DOING?" I yelled at the asshole backing into me.

*****

Peter ~ I looked in the rearview mirror but couldn't' see the woman's face. So I rolled down the window and said, "Stop hitting my car lady!"

*****

Kate ~ I couldn't believe it. This fucker almost ran me over, and now he was yelling at me, just as I had found the doctor and his daughter. I was following them from a distance when I walked into the street and saw this asshole backing into me.

"Watch where you're going muthafucka!" I said, pounding the trunk.

*****

Peter ~ I pulled the door handle and was about to get out when Laura grabbed me and said, "What are you gonna do when you get out baby? Beat her up?"

She was right. She knew as well as I did that I wouldn't do anything. Plus, I was still hungry, and I still had to pee. So I closed the door and sped off.

*****

Kate ~ I was ready, and I had my small pocketknife with me, because if this asshole was going to get out, I was going to make sure that he wished he hadn't.

Then all of a sudden, he closed the door and sped away.

"THAT'S RIGHT ASSHOLE. YOU HAD BETTER LEAVE!" I shouted defiantly.

*****

Peter ~ I looked back in my side-view mirror to see the woman screaming in the street behind me.

Laura looked over at me and asked, "Honey, what's wrong?"

I must have been as white as a ghost because I had just seen one.

"It couldn't be. Could it?" I asked myself.

"Couldn't be what?"

I didn't even know Laura had asked a question. I just kept driving in a daze.

"Babe, you're scaring me. What happened?"

I snapped out of it and said, "I'm sorry baby. It's just that I thought…"

"You thought what?"

"I thought that I saw Kate just now."

Laura looked at me like I had just lost all of the few marbles I had left.

"What do you mean? You saw Kate? Where?"

"That lady who was yelling. I could have sworn it was Kate."

"Oh be serious Peter!"

She just didn't know how serious I was.

*****

Kate ~ I watched the man drive down the street and pull over. If I had more time, I would have followed them and shown them I was the wrong one to mess with. But I had no time for fun. I had to keep an eye on the doctor and his daughter.

*****

Peter ~ I got out and looked back down the road, trying to sift through all the people in the park. I was searching for the salmon-colored coat the woman was wearing to see if once again my worst nightmare would come true.

"There she is!"

Laura looked in the direction I was pointing and asked, "Are you sure?"

I wasn't.

"That couldn't be her." She squinted and said, "And besides, I thought you had to pee?"

She was right. I did have to go, because as soon as she said that, I felt my bladder swell again. Just the thought of seeing Kate made me forget that I even had to use the bathroom. Crazy huh?

*****

Kate ~ I rushed across the street so that I could keep up with the doctor and his daughter. I had to wait for the right time to pounce and claim my prize. Because right now, there were just too many witnesses.

I followed them for hours, and no time seemed to be the right time, especially with all these people around. There really were no opportunities. I had begun to sulk in my failure when I saw them getting into a private car.

"Shit, why did I walk?"

I made my way quickly through the thin crowd toward the car, putting urgency in every step as I began to trot and then jog.

I was only twenty feet or so away when the door closed, and the car drove off.

"Fuck!" I said under my breath.

I turned and started to walk back to the hotel, furious that I had let this chance slip away. But I was sure that it would *never* happen again.

Back at the hotel, I plopped on the bed, still upset. I was hungry. I walked into the small kitchen area and pulled a sandwich from the fridge. When I took my jacket off to throw on the chair, it made a strange *thud* when it hit the wall.

"What was that?"

I walked over and picked it up and discovered the schedule ledger I had taken from the doctor's house. And damn, I was so happy that I started to dance.

"You tight, Kate. You tight!" I sang.

And now that my focus was back on track, I wasn't hungry anymore.

I opened the book and said aloud, "Let's see here. Looks like little miss Eliza has a recital at her school near the park later this week. That's when I'll get her."

The next four days, I moved what little I had out to the house. Only a little at a time though. In part to waste time and because I still needed the room. It was closer to the school, and I needed it to watch the doctor and to make Mrs. Marshall think that I was working. I had to keep her suspicions and her personal angst at bay, because if I didn't, I would have to kill her, and I just had no time for fun. But if it came to that, I would definitely enjoy it, for sure.

I hadn't been out of the room all day, and it was finally time for me to go. I drew the blinds and walked out. From across the park, I could see the people beginning to file into the auditorium to get the perfect vantage point to record their kids.

I snuck up behind a family, and before I was able to walk in, a staff member stopped me.

"Good evening ma'am. Who are you here to see tonight?"

"Eliza Krane."

"May I see your invitation?"

Invitation? This was definitely not in the plan. I opened my purse and looked in, pretending to search for it.

"I know I have it." I said, still looking.

"Ma'am, I'm afraid—"

"Look… I'm from out of town. My name is June. I can show you my license. Hell, you can keep it. Just let me in to see my friend's kid sing. Please?"

The woman looked embarrassed and said, "That's okay. Let me show you to the auditorium."

"Thank you very much." I said, pretending to be relieved.

When I sat down, I noticed that I was only three rows behind the doctor. But that was neither here nor there. What I really had to do was figure out how to get Eliza.

Twenty minutes later, the house lights went down, and the curtain went up. And there she was, Eliza, the little princess, center stage, looking like an angel.

I was surprised that she *could* sing. So much so that I almost forgot why I was there. I got up and walked up the aisle toward the usher.

"Ma'am, I'm going to have to ask you to take your seat during the performance."

I looked the woman in the eye and said, "Look lady, if you don't let me go to the restroom, I'm going to throw up all over your pretty little carpet and put on a performance of my own."

We both stood staring at each other, that is, until I began to dry-heave.

The usher waited a couple of seconds to see if I was bluffing. I showed no sign that I was, so she opened the door and escorted me to the restroom.

"Ma'am, are you going to be okay?" she asked.

"I think so." I said, rushing into the nearest stall.

"I'll go and get you something to drink to settle your stomach."

I walked out and went to the door to peek out. I saw the woman round the corner and walk toward the concession stand. As soon as she was out of sight, I eased out of the restroom toward the backstage entrance.

I went over and stood behind one of the large columns that adorned the lobby and saw another staff member standing sentry at the door.

"Shit, this place has more security than Fort Knox! What do they think is going to happen?"

I thought for a second and laughed at myself.

"Oh, right."

I walked over to the man sitting in the folding chair and looked at his nameplate.

"Mr. Griffin?"

"Yes?"

"There's a woman in the restroom that could really use your help?"

"And who would that be?"

"I don't know her name, but she has red hair, about 5'7" or so?"

"Are you talking about Mrs. Neal?"

I shrugged my shoulders and said, "I didn't get her name. All I know is that it's some woman in there that's sick, and she asked me to go and get another staff member. And here you are."

The man sat there, obviously distrusting my story, until the other woman came out the restroom calling for me. Luckily, I was standing behind the column, just out of her line of sight.

The man got up and walked toward the woman, which allowed me to slip through the stage door.

"Mr. Griffin, did you see a lady in a black jacket walk past here?"

"Yeah, she's right over—"

He paused because I was not where he had left me.

"She's right over where Mr. Griffin?"

They walked fast toward the stage door.

"Go that way. We'll cut her off if she's back here. The only way she could escape is to walk out onstage."

The pair split up and searched through the darkness for me.

I could hear them closing in, and I felt trapped with every step they took. So I opened the door I was standing in front of and walked out onstage to hide behind the paper-mache Mount Rushmore.

"Did you see her?"

The woman shook her head no as they started to walk back toward the door.

I could still see backstage from where I was standing. I could also see the man and woman walk back out the door into the lobby. They never thought to look onstage for me for whatever reason, and I was thankful for that.

I went back over and opened the door just before the next scene change and ducked into a dark corner to wait for the perfect time to pounce.

A minute later, another teacher was leading the children's chorus through the dim pathway behind the curtain.

"Okay children, we've got to be quiet back here."

She put her finger to her lips to quiet the children while I peeked from behind the spare curtain to locate Eliza.

I looked as closely as I could at each child's face. Then I saw her, standing near the back of the line, keeping to herself.

"Baby, you have to go on last because you'll be doing the first solo. Remember?" the teacher told her.

I reached into my pocket and pulled out a pair of rubber gloves to snap on quietly before I pulled out the small bottle of chloroform to douse the rag with.

A few moments later, the curtain was down, and the stage crew had started their behind-the-scenes chaos to get it ready for the next performance.

The teacher led the children onstage, and walked right past me standing in the shadows. Then Eliza walked past as I frantically tried to open the bottle, almost dropping it in my haste.

"Shit." I whispered, frustrated.

"No baby, you stay here until I call you, okay?" the teacher told Eliza.

I calmed myself down when the new opportunity presented itself.

Carefully, I opened the towel and doused the clear liquid into it. I closed the bottle and slipped it back into my pocket.

Then I eased slowly from behind the curtain and walked as quietly as I could toward them.

"She couldn't have gone far." I heard the woman say, still searching for me.

I stopped. What was I going to do now? I was almost there, so I kept going.

Finally, I was only a few feet away and had already made up my mind to hurt anybody standing in my way. If *anybody* tried to stop me, I was prepared to stab my way to freedom.

"Let's check backstage again." the man said.

"Okay."

I put the rag over the teacher's mouth and nose and held on tight before I felt her go limp. I quietly laid her on the floor when Eliza turned around.

"Baby, can you come here? I'm going to need your help." I said, kneeling down.

She nodded yes and skipped toward me.

"Teacher is sick, and we have to get her some help. Could you stay here while I go and get some?"

She trustingly nodded yes.

I got up and pretended to walk away. And seeing Eliza's attention focused back onstage, I quickly walked behind her and held the rag firmly across her face, until she succumbed to the poison.

She collapsed into my arms as I drug her into the darkness, just in time to see the two staff members discover their fallen colleague.

"Oh my god! Go and get help!" ordered Mr. Griffin.

The woman immediately ran toward the stage door and pulled out her phone to dial 911.

Eliza was small and heavy, and I was beginning to struggle with her limp body. I even had to catch her a couple of times to keep us hidden behind the curtain.

A couple of minutes later, four more staff members rushed to aid the teacher, all frantically calling out their own set of orders.

"Is her husband here?" one asked.

"Has anyone called 911?" asked another.

"Please, everyone stand back!" ordered Mr. Griffin. "Please, everyone, keep calm. Help is on the way!"

"Does anyone know CPR?" asked yet another teacher.

"Mrs. Craig does."

"Where is she?" asked Mr. Griffin.

"In the ticket booth I believe."

"Good, go get her!"

The lady sprinted toward the stage door out into the lobby.

It was hot, and I was starting to sweat. From behind the curtain, I could hear the ambulance race into the parking lot as one of the teachers ran to open a side door to signal the EMS.

"Over here!"

I peeked from behind the curtain and saw two women and a man rush through the door with a gurney.

"Okay, I'm going to need everyone to step back and let us do our jobs!" one of the women ordered, rushing to aid the teacher.

The small crowd opened up to allow the emergency personnel to begin their work.

I peeked out the other side and saw that no one was watching the door.

I turned Eliza around to face me before I bent over to lift her. I put the child on my hip and rested her head on my shoulder before I made my escape.

"Okay, let's go baby." I whispered.

It looked like I was only twenty feet or so from the door. And in just a few steps, I could be free.

"MOVE OUT OF THE WAY PEOPLE. WE'RE ABOUT TO TRANSPORT THE PATIENT!" yelled the same woman as before.

I was halfway out the door before Mr. Griffin yelled out. "HEY!"

I squeezed Eliza close and ran down the ramp and around the building.

And just as I ducked around the corner, Mr. Griffin was at the door.

"Where did she go?" he asked aloud.

"SIR, CAN YOU PLEASE MOVE OUT OF THE WAY?"

He jumped when he heard the small woman yell.

He moved from the doorway but stayed close, hoping to get a glimpse of the strange woman he was chasing.

He walked out right behind the paramedics, searching the parking lot for me. I saw him turning in circles to see if I might reveal myself during my getaway.

I ducked and ran along the narrow passageway that led behind the school into the teacher's parking lot. Eliza seemed to weigh a ton now, and I was getting tired of carrying the dead weight. I stopped for a second to catch my breath until I heard, "Check behind the school! She can't be far!"

I inhaled and ran into the parking lot. There was no way for me to get to the car without being seen. So I decided to travel light.

As I ran to the other side, I heard the teachers approaching fast. I ran behind a large blue van that had "McElroy Marching Monarchs" painted in large gold letters on the side and knelt down to lay Eliza on her back.

"Everybody, spread out. She's got to be here somewhere!"

From under the van, I could see the flashlights getting closer. I scooted beneath it and reached out to pull Eliza toward me. I was tired but determined, and so I took this opportunity to adjust my plan.

"Okay." I panted. "Gotta get to the car and come back to get the girl."

I looked over to see if Eliza was still unconscious. She was. I scooted beneath another car while keeping an eye out for the posse.

The route to the car was slow and tedious. And now I was close enough to it to be able to duck so that no one could see me.

When I got to the car, I reached in my pocket and pulled out the keys. I looked in both directions and stuck them in the lock. I pulled the door open and quietly tried to crawl inside.

And when I got inside, I sat and watched the police search the parking lot and everyone in it. The good thing was that I was at the far end of the lot, not far from the teacher's entrance. So getting out would not be that difficult, I hoped.

If I can just get out of the parking lot, I could park the car and get the kid, I thought.

Another cruiser came speeding through the park with its lights flashing and sirens blaring. I started the car and turned off the lights, hoping that their noise would mask mine.

I put the car in drive and steered slowly toward the exit, turning right on to a small service street made specifically for daily drops-offs and pickups. I parked at the end, beneath two large oak trees, which provided the perfect cover of shade at night.

I turned the car off and looked in the rearview mirror to see if I had attracted any attention.

No one was there, so I reached over and opened the door slowly, reaching up to turn off the interior light before I got out.

"Fuck! I gotta be careful." I exhaled.

I looked around and slid out of the car to run to the gate.

When I got there, I knelt to monitor the activity in the parking lot before I made my way back to the kid.

"MR. GRIFFIN!" shouted one of the teachers.

"Just a second!"

I saw him get closer to the van, and that made me mad. This asshole was not going to stop me. And if he tried, I would kill him. I ran my thumb along the cold steel of the knife blade in my pocket, planning to do what was necessary to get the kid. Even if it meant killing this asshole.

"I'm trying not to kill nobody tonight. Please don't make me kill you man," I whispered.

"MR. GRIFFIN!" the woman yelled again.

He turned and looked toward the van.

"Mr. Griffin!"

He shined the light on the van, then he turned to see who needed his attention so urgently.

"Yes Tammy, what is it?"

"Mrs. Craig needs you to give a description of the lady to the police. They're waiting on you now."

He turned and looked back at the van, and just as he began to walk toward it, the other teacher said, "Mr. Griffin, she said to come now because Eliza Krane is missing too!"

122

He turned and looked at the woman with defiance before he looked back at the van. He followed her back across the parking lot, still searching it with his flashlight.

Seeing this energized me because this was my opening. I ducked over to the fence and slid the latch up. When I pulled the gate open and tried my best to stop its squeaking from giving me away. But to no avail. I opened it slowly before running to slide back under the van.

"Okay, let's get you out of here."

I slid the girl from beneath the van and felt her move.

I froze. Shit, was she waking up?

I rolled over and reached into my pocket to pull the rag out again. I pressed it back across her face, and she was out instantly.

"Fuck!" I exhaled again.

I got up and put the rag back in my pocket before lifting her up.

"Okay, come on." I groaned.

I was almost to the car when I heard it.

"Cordon off the park and stop anyone coming up or down Walnut!" one of the cops yelled.

Now I knew I had to get out of there. And I planned to do just that as expeditiously and as quietly as I could.

I got to the car, opened the door, and laid the kid across the back seat. Then I stood up to see if anyone had noticed me yet. No one had.

I ran to the front of the car and saw that the utility road ended near a small hill that led to a residential street on the other side of the park.

I got in, put the keys in the ignition, and shifted the car into neutral.

"Okay. You can do this Kate."

I got back out and started to push the car toward the hill, quietly grunting while using all the strength I could muster to finally push it up over the small curb.

And as it began its creaky roll, I ran and jumped in, trying to maneuver the car through the trees and picnic tables as it picked up speed, which made *that* even more difficult to do.

What seemed like seconds later I was at the bottom pulling the emergency brake.

I felt the car come to a screeching halt just inches away from a pickup truck parked across the street.

I turned and looked over my shoulder, half expecting the hill to be flooded with white lights and police dogs. But there was nothing but darkness.

"Okay let's go." I said, relieved.

I turned the key and put the car in reverse before speeding cautiously down the street. I had what I needed now, and I was elated.

CHAPTER 14

Kate ~ Six a.m. the next morning, I was up sitting in bed, watching the news, eating cereal from the box.

"Good morning. I'm Jan Anderson, and we begin this news hour with every parent's nightmare: a missing child. Well, that's what has happened to local Dr. Patrick Krane. While at the McElroy School's winter recital, she was taken by this woman..."

I stopped eating.

"That doesn't even look like me!" I scoffed.

"No one knows who the woman is, but she reportedly told one of the teachers that her name was June. We ask that if anyone out there knows anything, please contact your local law enforcement agency. And remember, you can do it anonymously. And...you can make a difference."

I hated the smug way the reporter read the story. As if *she* could do anything about it and if she were here with me, I would show her a thing or two.

I got up to begin the process of transferring the kid to the other house. And after an hour or so, I was ready to walk out the door. I opened it and put two bags outside. And soon after, I was back in the room, lifting the kid to be carried to the car. After securing her in the back seat, I walked into the office and rang the bell repeatedly until the manager came to the desk.

"Okay okay, I'm here!" he said, coming out of the back irritated.

"I'd like to check out please."

"I can see that," he said with an attitude.

He grabbed the keys from the counter and looked around me into the car.

"Picked up some extra baggage, did we?"

I followed his eyes and said, "*We* did not pick up anything. She's my niece, and I'm taking her home. Just mind your own business please."

He slid June's credit card through the machine and picked up a pen.

"Sign here please."

I snatched the receipt and the card, then walked out before speeding out of the parking lot.

*****

Peter ~ I woke up that day still feeling uneasy about seeing who I thought might be Kate.

I should've been happy, right? My life was finally becoming what I wanted it to be. But I wasn't. There was something eating me up inside. It just felt like I was in danger. And that scared me because if Kate was out there, then I would have reason to be. I mean, I should have been over the moon, right? I was getting married today to the woman of my dreams, and I seemingly had no problems. But something was still telling me that everything was not all right.

"Baby, I was thinking we could go and get something to eat before we go down to the chapel." Laura said.

I hadn't heard a word she said because I was trapped in my own thoughts, still wondering why this feeling had swept over me all of a sudden.

"Honey?"

I snapped out of it and said, "Huh?"

"Did you hear anything I said?"

"I'm sorry baby. My mind was somewhere else."

Laura walked over, kissed me on the cheek, and asked, "So you weren't thinking about me?"

I turned to her and said, "I always think about you baby."

"Good. Well, think about getting up. We have to meet Linda and Carl downstairs in thirty minutes."

I got up, still wondering if Kate was out there somewhere stalking me. I didn't know. And I hoped not. That woman yesterday, although from a distance, looked exactly like her. That was crazy, right?

*****

Kate ~ I drove down the short dirt road that led to the back-house as slow as I could. I looked over to see if Eliza was still sleep and hoped that Mrs. Marshall was too. But there was no such luck. As soon as I stopped the car, I saw her walking across the meadow toward us.

"June?"

I jumped out quickly and ran around the car so that she couldn't see who was inside.

"Hey Mrs. Marshall, is there something I can do for you?"

"I didn't see you this morning. Did you stay out last night?"

"Yes I did. I stayed with a friend in the city."

She craned her neck and asked, "What's in the car?"

"Just a few of my things."

"Okay." she said skeptically.

I walked backwards to make sure that she had no more inquiries. And to stop her just in case she got nosey. After she was gone, I ran back to the car and pulled the kid out just in case she decided to come back.

Her body was limp, and I lifted her with a groan. Then I walked around the house to the cellar door and propped her against the wall.

"I just have to get you settled in, then I can go and see your dad. Let's hope for your sake that he loves you enough to do what I ask."

I walked inside with the child and sat her on a small futon before I pulled the handcuffs out to lock her small wrists together.

"That should hold you." I said, tugging at the cuffs.

I thought it might be better to gag her, and so I did before locking the door.

"And now it's time to go and see the good doctor."

Of course I knew where he lived. But I decided to go to his office to persuade him to follow my plan. And an hour later, I was standing in front, waiting to see if he would come in today, when suddenly, "Doctor? Doctor, may I have a word with you?"

I ran over to him, surprised that he was alone.

"You're not a damn reporter are you?"

"No, sir, I'd like to employ your services."

He looked at me irritated.

"You could have just made an appointment with my staff you know?"

"I needed to talk to *you*, Doctor."

"Listen, miss…"

"Call me June, please."

"Okay, listen June. I'm going through a personal tragedy. And even if I decided to see you, I wouldn't be able to get to you until after it's resolved."

I got serious.

"So, Doctor, let me ask you something," I said as he walked away.

"And what would that be?" he asked without turning around.

"Do you ever want to see your daughter again?"

He stopped in his tracks and turned around.

"Did you have anything to do with my daughter's disappearance?"

I looked around calmly and said, "Let's go inside Doctor."

"Look here bitch, if you have anything to do with my daughter's disappearance, I'll—"

"You'll what? Never see her a-fucking-gain? I'll make sure of that. So what you're going to do is shut the fuck up and walk into your office so that we can talk."

"Look, if it's money you—"

I stopped him and spun him around.

"I don't want your fucking money, you cockless dweeb. I have better things to attend to other than blackmailing you. Now walk!"

The doctor turned around befuddled. If I didn't want money, what did I want? That thought had to be racing through his mind.

We walked into the office.

"Oh, hey Doc, I thought you weren't coming in today." said the receptionist.

"I need to talk to this patient. So hold all my calls, okay Brenda?"

The receptionist nodded, and I followed him through the door.

"Wow, what a nice place you—"

"Look, you psycho bitch, what do you want?"

I stopped looking around and focused solely on his face.

"That's mighty tough talk for someone who says they want their daughter back. The way you're talking to me now suggests that I should just call my boyfriend and tell him to strangle the little bitch after he's had his way with her."

I pulled out my phone.

"Wait! Wait! I'm sorry. What do you want from me?"

I walked over, sat down in front of him, pulled out Laura's picture, and slid it across his desk.

"Who is this?"

"Never mind who that is. Can you make me look like her?"

"Look, I don't know what you want, but—"

"I already told you what I wanted! Are you stupid? Can you make me look exactly like her or what?"

I waved the picture in his face.

"Yes! I think I can. Yes, just don't hurt my baby!"

"Well, now that depends on you Doctor. Doesn't it? If you do what I ask, I can promise that your daughter will be returned unharmed. But if you call the police or if I wake up and I don't look like this, your daughter dies. Instantly. Understand?"

He nodded yes.

"Now…when do we get started?"

"Tomorrow, meet me at St. Dominick's at nine a.m. Someone canceled."

I stood up, pulled down on my jacket and said, "Okay Doctor, remember, no tricks, or you'll get your daughter back in a box. And *no* police. You understand?"

"I understand." he said, sniveling.

I walked out knowing that I couldn't keep the kid quiet for long. And I didn't want to be worried about what Mrs. Marshall might find while I was under the knife either. I knew she needed something stronger to keep her quiet…but what?

I walked down the hallway and caught the elevator to the lobby.

The doors opened, and what I hadn't noticed on my way up was the most pleasant surprise now. The pharmacy would surely have what I needed to keep my pawn under control. But how would I get it? I walked over, sat on a bench, and pulled out my phone to search for a sedative. I found one: Seconal sodium, a barbiturate that was used for light surgery and by some psychiatrist to keep their subjects calm. That was exactly what I needed to keep the kid under wraps. And with her cancer in remission, this would hopefully make it easier.

I got up and walked in, pretending to shop when I heard, "Can you take those boxes around back while I help these customers?"

"Sure." said the small woman in the lab coat.

I hurried out and ran around the building to wait for her.

It was a blustery day, and the wind seemed to pierce through my hoodie. I pulled the hood around my face and waited for the woman to come out.

She opened the door just as I reached into my pocket to open my knife. I walked hurriedly toward the woman and stuck the blade deep into her abdomen just as she turned around. She grabbed my wrist to try and stop me from pushing the blade in further, but that didn't do any good. I head-butted her and watched her fall back over the bags.

"Please don't kill me." she said, scooting away.

"Oh, I'm not going to kill you. Time will."

I lifted the knife and violently stabbed her ass twelve more times before I stood up to watch her bleed out.

I knew I had to move fast. So I walked around, put my hands under her arms, and drug her behind the dumpster.

I took her badge and hurried back inside to see the pharmacist helping the last customer.

"Ruth?"

I stood motionless, listening as the woman called out futilely.

"Ruth, where are you?"

I ran and stood next to the door just in time to watch her walk through it.

"Hey!"

The woman turned around, startled to see me standing there frowning and covered in blood. I stabbed her in the neck, unleashing her own geyser.

She fell holding her neck, while I stepped over her to pull the door closed. I stabbed her again just as she took her last breath. I saw her blood beginning to pool, and I tried my best not to track in it. I looked at her, disgusted, before walking over to the door to swipe the key card.

I opened the door to the vault and pulled out my phone.

"Seconal sodium, Seconal sodium."

I followed the different names alphabetically until I came to the Ss.

"Here it is."

Man, this was just too easy, I thought.

I slipped two of the small white boxes into my pocket before going over to the drawer marked syringes.

"Shit, do they lock up every damned thing here?"

I walked back into the storeroom and searched the woman for her keys. There were none.

Shit! Now I had to go back outside and search the other one.

I ran through the back behind the dumpster and searched the first woman's pockets.

"Bingo!"

I looked at her and said, "Don't look at me like that. If I would have asked you for the keys, you would have said no. And I would have had to kill you anyway."

I stuck out my tongue and walked back into the building. After pulling three or four of the needles from the drawer, I said, "Fuck it." and pulled out the entire box.

I looked myself over and saw that there was blood on the sleeves of my jacket as well as on my pants and face. I took the jacket off, walked over to the coatrack by the microwave, and took the blue wool one from it.

"This will do just fine. Besides, they don't need it anymore."

I buttoned it up and walked over to the sink to clean my face. Then I cautiously walked out the door and hurried back to the car so that I could head back to the farm.

It was late afternoon when I returned, and Mrs. Marshall was waiting outside.

"What the fuck does she want now?" I asked myself.

"Hey Mrs. Marshall how are you?"

She walked down the steps toward me.

"I thought we said no pets?"

"Did we?"

"Yes, we did."

The truth was I knew that she had said nothing about pets, but I decided to play along.

"What's going on, Mrs. Marshall?"

"Why don't you tell me young lady."

I really didn't know what she was talking about until I remembered.

"Eliza!"

"Who?"

"My niece."

"You left her here alone?"

"No, she's with my sister. I just remembered. I have to pick her up tomorrow."

"Did you buy her a puppy or something?"

"No, why?"

"Because it's something in the cellar of the guesthouse. I heard it when I went to the lake this morning."

"Don't worry yourself Mrs. Marshall. I'll take care of it. It's probably a possum or something."

Mrs. Marshall looked smugly at me and said, "Okay, but if you need some help, let me know. I know a guy over in Junctionville that helped me in the past."

"Okay I will."

I hurried into the house, thinking that I might have to kill Mrs. Marshall soon.

But that was something that I would ponder later.

Now I had to get to and quiet the kid.

When I walked in, I could hear her groggy and whining through the floorboards.

When I rushed out the back, I half expected Mrs. Marshall to be there looking at me. Thank God she wasn't. For her sake.

I opened the door and saw Eliza awake but still kinda out of it. And for some strange reason, she didn't appear to be scared. And for that same strange reason, I respected her.

She tried to talk through the gag.

"What are you saying?" I asked, pulling it from her mouth.

"Where am I? Who are you?"

"My place. And I'm a friend of your father's."

"Where is your place? And where is my father?"

"Look, I ask the questions here, not you. Do you understand?"

"Do you want me to answer that?" she quipped.

I was losing my patience with her, but I knew I couldn't hurt her. Besides, it seemed like she knew that too.

"Are you hungry?"

"Yes."

"Okay, I'll bring you something to eat."

"What do you have?"

"Does it fucking matter?"

"Yes."

"And why is that if you're hungry?"

"Because I don't like certain things."

"Well, here you have *no* choice in the matter."

I had had enough, so I walked back over and put the gag back in her mouth.

Ten minutes later, I was walking back downstairs with a plate of chicken nuggets and a bottle of water.

"Here you go."

I put the plate down and went over to pull out the gag.

"Do you like chicken nuggets?"

"Yes."

"Good, because I thought for a minute I was going to have to force-feed you."

I went over and locked the door before reaching into my pocket for the keys to the cuffs.

"I was wondering when you were going to loosen these."

I stood over her. Who did she think she was? She didn't act like any child I had ever seen before, with or without cancer. She seemed more in tune instead of detached.

"Don't get too comfortable because they are going back on as soon as you've finished eating."

"Awwww." she whined.

I was tired. It had been a long day, and all I wanted to do was get into the bath and then into bed. After all, I had a big day tomorrow, a day that would change my life for the better...or worse, depending on Peter.

I decided that it would be easier to keep an eye on the kid if she were upstairs with me because I didn't want to drug her if I didn't need to.

Besides, she was just a kid after all.

"Come on. You're coming with me."

"Aren't I already with you?" she said, stuffing a nugget in her mouth.

"Just come on smart-ass."

She got up and followed me upstairs into the house.

"Go and turn on the television, and don't bother me. I'm going to take a bath."

I went into the bathroom and started the water before coming back out to handcuff her to the bed.

"I thought you said we wouldn't need these."

"Oh yeah, well I guess I lied. Calm down. If you're good, I'll take them back off."

"Are you lying?"

"Maybe." I said before I went to check my bathwater.

I was really excited about my appointment with the doctor. So much so that I couldn't sleep. Today was the day. It was 4:00 a.m., and I was wide awake. So I decided to get up and get ready.

First I took out my phone to video the kid sleeping comfortably.
"That should be proof enough for now." I whispered.

I went to my purse and pulled out one of the needles along with the sedative. I stuck the needle in the bottle and pulled the plunger back. Then I reached under the bed and slid out the small overnight bag to douse a rag with chloroform.

Beneath the rag, I could feel her laboring to breathe before it evened out to a slower but steady pace.

"Good, good." I said.

I picked up the shoestring I had taken from her shoe and wrapped it around her arm, tapping it to produce a vein.

"There you are."

I pushed the plunger to release the excess air from the cylinder before I put the needle down.

Fuck, I didn't want to kill her, and I had no time to research. I didn't want to be late to my new life, and nothing was going to deter that.

I was no doctor. I hoped that what I was doing wouldn't kill the girl, who seemed to be resting comfortably now in her sedated state. It had already been proven that chloroform was not enough, right? So I had to try something different.

"That should hold you for awhile," I said, settling on the small amount I had given her.

"I gotta get going!"

I gagged her, got dressed, and ran out the door.

CHAPTER 15

Kate ~ 8:30 a.m. and I was already walking through the lobby of St. Dominick's.

"Good morning ma'am. How may I help you?" asked the security guard.

"I'm here to see Dr. Krane. I have a nine o'clock."

"What's your name, ma'am?"

"June, June Galvan."

You know that I could never use my real name. And now that the cops might possibly be looking for June, I decided to combine the two.

"Okay, I see you here. Go through these double doors, make a left, and take the elevator up to five. When you get off, take another left and go into L-10. That's Dr. Krane's office."

"Thank you." I said, walking off.

As soon as I walked through the door, Dr. Krane came out all nervous and jittery and shit.

"Come right in." he said.

"I'll need you to go into that room and take off your clothes please. But first, I need to see if my daughter is okay." he said, grabbing my arm.

"I figured you would say that. But don't get cocky. I'm the one running *this* show." I said, snatching it away.

I pulled my phone from my jacket and showed the doctor his peacefully sleeping daughter.

"Oh thank God." he said.

"Remember our deal?"

"Yes, of course. I didn't tell anyone. I promise."

"Good, because if I don't come back, your daughter doesn't come back."

He sat down in front of me and began to explain the procedure while chalking off my face.

"Look who's anxious to get started." I joked.

"We'll have to do the procedure in pieces, meaning that we work on one part of the face, let that heal a bit, and begin the next phase."

"Don't stall for time because we can keep the girl as long as it takes."

"I'm not stalling. It's just that this procedure can be very painful if not done correctly."

"How painful?"

"Very, if rushed. Depending on your threshold for pain."

I looked him in the eye and said, "Do the job as fast and as well as you can. The quicker I am satisfied, the sooner I am gone. And the sooner you'll be back with your daughter. Got it?"

"Got it."

"So the shortest time frame would be?"

"If we do each piece a couple of days apart, it might take two to three months…maybe more."

I sat back and said, "Okay, let's get to work. And don't worry about my threshold for pain. Leave that to me."

He got up and opened the door.

"Nurse, can you take her down to be prepped for surgery?"

"Sure Doctor."

He was scared, and I knew it.

He was scared that he wouldn't get his daughter back.

And what if he messed up and the surgery didn't turn out as planned? Would I still kill the kid? He didn't know, and that was the one thing he didn't want to find out. Trust me. He knew I was dangerous because just after I had left yesterday, security, conveniently for me, had discovered Dr. Nyugen and Dr. Jansen dead in the pharmacy. Did I do it? He didn't know, but the coincidence was just too close for comfort.

An hour and a half later, I was prepped for surgery and dozing fast.

"Today we are going to shape the eyes and nose. Then Friday we should be able to contour the jawline before finishing with the chin and ears."

I was so groggy that I couldn't even respond. And to tell you the truth, I really didn't give a shit about what he was saying, just as long as he did a good job. And five hours later, there I was slowly easing back into consciousness.

"How are you feeling?"

I felt the bandages wrapped tightly on my face and said, "Horrible."

"Yeah, well, it's going to hurt for a bit. Get some rest, and I'll be back to see how you're doing later."

My face felt like it was on fire, and I could barely see through the bandages. I had no time to hurt though. I had to get up and go check on the kid because she was my key to success in all this, and I couldn't take the chance of losing my only bargaining chip.

A nurse came in to check on me a few minutes later.

"Hun, are you all right?"

I pretended to be asleep so that she would check my chart and leave.

I opened my eyes as soon as I heard the door close and began to rip the tape from the tube that held the IV in.

"Ouch!" I said, watching the small stream of blood run down my wrist.

I took the tape and reapplied it along with a pad of gauze before I walked over and started to put on my clothes. The first thing I picked up was my jacket to search the pocket where I kept my knife. It was still there.

"Good."

I loosened the thin gown from behind and let it fall to the floor.

"Wait, wait what are you doing?" asked the doctor, walking in.

"Going home."

"You can't go home!"

I stood there trying my best to mask the tremendous pain I was in.

"Look, Doc, if I don't show up at home, there's going to be problems. And neither one of us wants that, right?"

"Okay, stay right here. I'll bring you something that will help with the pain."

I grabbed his coat and said, "No tricks."

"No tricks." he agreed.

Minutes later, he was back with a syringe.

"And what do you plan on doing with that?"

"This is going to make the pain a little more bearable, but not by much."

He took the syringe, thumped it, and pushed the plunger.

He moved one of the bandages to the side and injected the medicine directly into my face.

"Fuck, that hurts worse than if I had no medication at all!"

"Calm down. You'll feel better in a minute." he said as I walked out.

I was exhausted when I got back. And when I pulled down the small dirt road, I wondered where Mrs. Marshall might be hiding.

And what if she were to pop up? How would I explain the bandages?

"If she gets too nosey, I'll just kill her." I reasoned.

I drove around back, turned off the car, and got out.

It seemed like every step I took brought pain to my face, and all I wanted to do was go to sleep. But as soon as I opened the door, I knew that would have to wait.

"Hello lady, is that you?" said the small voice in the darkness.

"My name is not lady."

"You never told me your name."

"It's June." I said, turning on the light.

"Okay then June, I'm hungry."

"Fuck you! You little rug rat! Didn't I just feed you? And did you shit on yourself?"

"Yes, you did, last night. And yes, I did. Just before you came in."

I exhaled and walked toward her to loosen the cuffs.

"Wait. How did you remove the gag?"

"It wasn't hard. You didn't put it on all that tight."

I was tired and in pain, so I just shrugged my shoulders and said, "Chicken nuggets it is. But first, we need to get you in the shower."

"I had chicken last night."

"And you're having it tonight. Now get ready to get in the shower."

"Awww."

"Cut it out, or you'll go back in the cuffs. Do you need a washcloth?"

"Yes."

I walked to the freezer, pulled out the nuggets, and poured them on to the tray to put them in the microwave. Then I walked over to get her a towel from the linen closet.

"Well, go ahead then. I'll be in in a minute."

She got up and ran into the bathroom, slamming the door behind her.

I walked in after her and turned on the water.

"Hurry up. I'm very tired, and I need to rest. And don't forget to wash yourself good! Because you smell horrible." I said, walking out.

Twenty minutes later, I was pushing the plate of nuggets in front of her.

"Eat your food and don't give me any problems. Okay? I picked up some more clothes for you. So after you've finished with your dinner, go and get dressed for bed."

She nodded while I shoved two Motrin into my mouth.

"I'm going to go and run some bathwater. I'll be right back. Do you want me to turn on the television?"

She nodded yes and asked, "What happened to your face?"

"Nothing that should concern you. Eat your food and get dressed. After I'm done, we'll watch a movie or something."

I walked into the bathroom, sat on the edge of the tub, and turned the knob to adjust the water temperature. I stood up and took off my jacket and shirt before walking back out to check on the kid one last time.

"What the fuck?"

I ran around the small cabin, frantic.

"Where did she go? Kid!" I called out.

I ran out the door and down the steps that led to the cellar.

"Kid!" I called out again.

I ran back upstairs on to the path that led to the lake.

"Kid!"

And when I came into the clearing, I saw her sitting on the dock, eating her chicken nuggets.

"Jesus kid, what are you doing? You can't be out here at night with just a towel on. You'll catch your death of cold. Now come on. Let's go back inside."

"I like the water."

"I don't want you out here unless I know about it, okay?!"

"Where's my father?"

"Your father is busy, and he left me in charge. So you'd better do as I say, or I'll have to lock you up again. I can't have you getting lost. After all, what would your father say?"

I had planned to lock her up anyway. And now that this little incident happened, I decided to do it sooner than later.

"Sit at the table and finish your food." I ordered.

I walked into the bathroom and saw the tub overflowing.

"Shit!" I screamed, turning off the knobs.

All this was just too much for me to handle. I needed order again, and I needed it now. So I decided to tame the wild card. I turned off the water and reached into my jacket pocket, which was drenched now from the bathwater, and pulled out the rag, which was drenched too.

I looked around the room and pulled the extra face towel off the rack. I twisted the cork from the chloroform with my teeth so that I could douse the rag and put her to sleep.

I was wet, cold, tired, and my face hurt like hell. Plus, I needed to get some sleep. This was day 1, and I would not go through the rest in misery.

I walked lively into the other room and put the rag across her face. And after a short struggle, there was peace again. And I was in control.

I laid her across the bed before going to close the door and pulling the shutters. I peeked out to make sure Mrs. Marshall wasn't lurking about. I just stood there staring, wondering why I hadn't seen her today. Where was she? I was tired and in pain, so Mrs. Marshall would just have to be a worry for another day.

After a long hot bath, I was ready to hibernate for the next couple of days until my next appointment, planning to wake up periodically only to feed the kid.

At 4:00 a.m. the next morning, I awoke to a light moan. I opened my eyes to try to focus through the darkness. Then I heard the disturbing noise again.

I rolled over and felt the bandages on my face before I sat up and heard the moaning again.

"Kid?"

There was no answer.

"Kid?"

There was still no answer.

I got up and walked over to the small cot Eliza was sleeping on and woke her up with a gentle nudge.

"What's wrong kid?"

"I had a nightmare."

"Oh yeah, about what?"

"I dreamed that I was trapped in a castle, and there were monsters all around."

She looked up at my bandaged face and asked, "Are you a monster?"

What a question.

"Why do you ask that?"

"Because sometimes you act like one. And those bandages make you look like one too." She chuckled.

Kids. Was I *sure* I wanted them?

"I'm not a monster." I said in my most reassuring tone.

I got up from the cot and turned around. "Do you wanna come sleep with me?"

"Yes."

I grabbed the keys from the table and unlocked the cuffs.

She immediately threw the covers to the floor and ran to jump in bed with me, nestling comfortably under my armpit.

Kids. Okay, maybe I did want them now. Maybe.

The next couple of days were pretty uneventful, with me and the kid just hanging out inside the cabin or walking down to sit by the lake. Surprisingly with no sign of Mrs. Marshall. And before I knew it, I was waking up to prepare for the forty-minute drive to the city for my second procedure.

"Wake up kid. I have to feed you before I go."

Eliza got up and rubbed her eyes before walking into the bathroom.

When she came out, I had already placed the microwave nuggets on the table.

"Is this all we have to eat?"

"Beggars can't be choosers."

"I'm begging for another meal." she said, disgusted at the sight.

I looked at the girl, who reminded me so much of myself. Not in any physical way but attitude-wise.

"I'll get you something else if I'm not feeling too bad when I come from the doctor."

She nodded and picked at her food before she started to eat.

"Hurry up because I have to leave in a little while."

I took out the bottle of chloroform and put it on the table.

"You don't have to do that." she said.

"Do what?"

"Make me go to sleep. I'm tired of sleeping."

"Well, then I'll have to lock you up."

"Why? I thought you were not a monster."

I wanted to slug her right in the mouth but resisted, only because I had to go.

"Look, I can't have you running around here while I'm gone. And I definitely can't have you escape. I mean getting lost."

"I won't, I promise!"

Twenty minutes later, I was in the car, pounding on the steering wheel.

"I can't believe I did that! What if she escapes? What if that nosey -ass Mrs. Marshall starts snooping around? I'd be fucked, that's what!"

What could I do? I was halfway to the city and needed to make my appointment if I were to stay on course with the plan. So *that* was exactly what I did. For now, I would have to trust the kid. And after driving another half hour or so, I was pulling into the parking structure at St. Dominick's.

"Hey Doc."

"How is my daughter doing?"

"Take a look for yourself."

I pulled out my phone and switched on the video of me and Eliza singing by the lake.

His eyes began to well with tears when I snatched the phone back and said, "The sooner we finish here, the sooner *she* will be here."

The doctor motioned me to lean back so that he could take the bandages off.

He picked up the scissors thinking, *I could stab her right here and get my baby back*, which was impossible considering he didn't know where she was. So he did what he was supposed to do to ensure her safety.

"Everything is looking good." he said, unwrapping the rest of my face.

"I think we can move on to the next procedure. Have you eaten anything this morning?"

"No, not since last night."

"Okay good. I'm going to call the nurse."

I remembered the routine from just a couple of days ago, so I got up to walk toward the prep area to take my clothes off.

But before I went under, I followed my own protocol and threatened the doctor with his daughter's safety again.

Six hours later, I woke up in recovery, even more sore than the first time.

"Well, look who's awake." the doctor joked.

I could feel the bandages squeezing my face as if they were almost suffocating me. I could also feel the cheekbone implants that were pushing my eyes closed.

"I think we might be able to finish the process with the next procedure. We did a lot today, and just a couple of tweaks will do it I think."

"I need to get out of here."

"I'm not releasing you yet."

While I was sleeping, the doctor had the bright idea of trying to hold me hostage. What was I going to do? Go to the police? I guess he felt that if he could keep an eye on me, he might be able to ensure his daughter's safe return.

I slumped back into bed and said, "Okay Doc, you know best, but if you try any funny stuff, I'll make the call."

I searched the bed for my phone.

"WHERE IS IT?" I yelled.

"What?"

"My phone asshole!"

"Now what would I be doing with your phone?"

"Don't play with me motherfucker!

If I don't check in, your precious Eliza *will* be dead!"

"I don't believe you."

It hurt to yell, so I began to speak in a more docile tone.

"I'm only going to tell you one more time to go and get my fucking clothes. And my fucking phone! Or I'll have my boyfriend mail your whore of a daughter's head back to you in a box. Do you understand?"

He stood there, trying to call my bluff.

I smiled and said, "Look, even if you turn me in and I spend the rest of my life in prison, your daughter will still be dead. So tell me, is this little stunt you're pulling worth your daughter's life?"

He looked down at me and said, "I'll be right back. Don't leave."

A few minutes later, he came into the room with a plastic bag filled with my belongings.

"Here you go."

I snatched the bag from him and sat up to rifle through it. After making sure everything was there, I grabbed my phone.

"Wait! Wait please!" pleaded the physician.

"What can you say to me that will save your daughter's life after pulling this shit?"

He began to cry as he reached out to vie for my sympathy.

"Please don't hurt my baby! I'm sorry. I'll never do anything like this again, I promise! Please!"

I was upset now. Who did this fucker think he was, trying to pull my card? I should really fuck him up. If I didn't need him, I would have killed him a long time ago. But it was never too late. Never.

I put the phone down and said, "Come here."

He was confused. Why did I want him to come closer? We were the only two people in the room. But through all the pain I was in, I needed to be clear.

"Come here."

He stepped closer and leaned in.

"You don't have any more fuckups Doc. Do you understand? Remember, the quicker you get this done, the quicker your daughter comes back. So stop fucking with me before I stop your heart by cutting hers out."

Over the course of the next three months, I had finally been transformed and ready to proceed with the next part of the plan.

"Wow, you really look different. Is it because the police are looking for you?" Eliza asked.

I stopped and looked at her.

"Why? Don't you like it?"

"I didn't say that. Did you do something bad? I mean, besides steal me from my daddy?"

"I didn't steal you! I kinda used you as collateral."

"Collateral?"

"Yeah, it's kind of like insurance."

She still didn't understand what I meant. All she knew was that she missed her father. And all she wanted to do was see him again. And the only person keeping her from him was me.

"Well, it won't be long now. I'm going to take you to him in a couple of days."

Her face lit up with hope.

"You mean I get to see my daddy?"

"In the flesh. And you two can live the rest of your lives in peace."

Two days later, I woke up, intending to keep my promise. And this morning found me in a particularly good mood. I was in the kitchen putting the finishing touches on breakfast, singing, eager to put the next phase of my plan in motion.

"Kid!"

I sat two plates on the table along with two glasses and a bottle of orange juice.

"Kid!"

Eliza walked out of the bedroom, rubbing her eyes.

"Voila!"

She rubbed her eyes again.

"Wow, you've changed. You don't look like June anymore?"

"June doesn't live *here*…anymore." I said with a smile.

She walked cautiously toward the table.

I looked at her, trying to read her reaction to the transformation.

"Kid! It's still me."

"I know."

"Well…?"

"You don't look like June, that's all. You look different."

"Well, I mean, that *was* the whole point. Where were you during all of this?"

"Sleeping." she said, staring at me. I think that she was looking for any proof that I *was* who I said I was. I knew it might have been too much for the kid, but such is life.

"You need to eat up because I'm taking you to your daddy today."

Her eyes lit up with joy as she picked up a piece of bacon and began to sing, *"I'm going home to Daddy, Daddy, to Daddy. I'm going home to Daddy. Yes, I am."*

"You just hurry up. I have some things I need to get to today. And I don't want you slowing me down."

A little over two hours later, we were pulling into the parking structure of the medical plaza.

"Are you ready kiddo?"

Eliza sat quiet.

"Hey, do you hear me?" I said, waving my hands in front of her face.

"I'm going to be sad."

"Why baby?"

"Because I'm going to miss you."

"Awwww."

I was actually touched by her candor.

"I'm going to miss you too baby. But I won't be far away, ever. And if you ever need me, you can *always* ask your dad to call me, okay? He knows how to contact me." I assured her, lying.

She reached over and gave me a hug, holding my neck long and hard.

"Come on kid. Your dad is waiting for us."

She got out of the car, followed closely by me. I grabbed her hand when I joined her on the other side because if this asshole was gonna try anything, I could snatch the kid and go.

I was beside myself. I knew that this could be last time I would see the kid. And that bothered me for a second.

I didn't tell the doctor when I was going to bring the kid, just in case he got any bright ideas about turning me in.

Just as we walked into the lobby, the doctor, who was walking toward us, could not believe his eyes. Why was his daughter holding this psycho's hand?

"Eliza, come here baby. Come to Daddy, please."

She ran to her father and gave him the same love she showed me moments earlier.

"I missed you Daddy! Where were you?"

"I missed you too baby! Daddy had a lot of work to finish, but I'm here now. And I'll never let you outta my sight again." he said with tears in his eyes.

He pushed her back so that he could take a good look at her.

"Are you hurt baby?"

"No Daddy, I'm okay."

He stood up, still holding his daughter close, and said, "Thank you for returning my daughter safely."

"You kept your word, and so I kept mine."

I pulled him close.

"But if you ever say anything to anybody, I'll rip out your intestines while you watch and take the kid with me. And *nobody* will ever see her again. Do you understand?"

The doctor, still holding his daughter, reluctantly agreed before he turned to leave.

I hurried to the car, paranoid, looking around to see if the good doctor had betrayed me yet.

I pulled my keys from my pocket and turned them in the ignition. If they were going to try to catch me now, I was going to give them one hell of a ride.

I pulled off slowly, checking the mirrors to see if anyone was following me. No one was.

"I can't believe it! This fucker actually kept his end of the bargain."

And just after I said that, I saw five police cars speeding my way.

"No, no, no, no!"

Three cars sped down the road while the other two slowed to look inside of the ones they were passing.

"Okay Kate, stay calm. You can do this."

I unwrapped the bun in my hair and combed it over my face with my fingers.

I needed to cover up, so I put on my sunglasses, hoping that if the cops pulled up, they wouldn't be able to recognize me.

"I'm going to kill that fucker! I promise!"

But first things first, I had to get back to the farm and settle things with Mrs. Marshall.

It was a little after three o'clock when I drove down the small road that led to the cabin. And who did I happen to see? Mrs. Marshall sitting on the porch, waiting for me.

"Hey Mrs. Marshall."

"What are you doing in my home?"

I looked toward the front house and said, "I thought *that* was your home?"

"If you don't tell me what the fuck is going on, I'm calling the cops! And what did you do to your face?" she asked, still trying to get a good look at me.

Between here and the city, I had added a few more accessories, namely, a hat and a scarf.

I closed the door and started to walk toward her.

"You don't want to do that. And I'd really advise you to mind your own business right about now."

Her face was suddenly flooded with confusion.

"Wait...who are you? How do you know my name? And where's June?"

"You know who I am." I said, taking off the hat and glasses.

She pulled out her phone to call the police.

"Wait, Mrs. Marshall, it's me, June!"

"Stand over there! Don't come any closer!"

"Mrs. Marshall, will you let me explain? Please?"

"What did you do to your face?"

I looked ashamed to make the performance more believable.

"I'm hiding from my husband. So I came out here to get plastic surgery so that he wouldn't find me."

"And what about the girl?"

"She's my daughter."

"If she's your daughter, then why do you need these?"

She pulled out the small bottle of chloroform and the handcuffs.

"Well, that's for...you know...kids." I said, stumbling to find an answer.

"What kind of sick bitch are you? Drugging your kids while you're out getting all gussied up with your fancy face-lifts."

That was it. It was time to kill this bitch, and fast. She was simply becoming a nuisance.

"Please, Mrs. Marshall, let me explain."

"Explain what, you psycho? Explain it to the police."

"Please, Mrs. Marshall!"

I gestured toward the house.

"I'm not going anywhere with you."

"Okay, so…can we at least sit on the porch?"

"Go ahead. You've got two minutes, then I'm calling the police."

I went and sat on the porch. She followed and sat across from me.

"You see, we got married really young. My husband had a trucking business that kept him away most of the time. Nothing cross-country, but he was always up North. Well, one day, I answered the phone, and it was this…this woman who said that she was his *real* wife. And that he had a whole other family up in Mission, kids, the whole bit. All those holidays I thought he was working, he was upstate with another woman playing daddy."

I started to cry. Damn, I was good.

"So what happened?" she asked.

"Well, I confronted him about it when he got home one day, and we began to fight. By the time he got there, I was already pretty drunk. So I went in the kitchen and grabbed a knife. I didn't know what I was going to do with it. As matter of fact, I really don't know why I went and got it in the first place."

Mrs. Marshall passed me the handkerchief she had in her pocket.

"I guess when he saw me with the knife, he freaked out and hit me. Beat me up pretty good too. He put me in the hospital for a week. But I stayed with him. And the longer I stayed, the easier it became to hit me. It felt like he was punishing me for pulling a knife on him that night. And he didn't want me to ever forget it. In his own special way, of course."

I saw a gardening spade not too far away in an old flowerpot.

I continued, "One day, I just got tired of it all and decided to leave. That's when I came out here from California."

"Pennsylvania's a long way from California."

151

"The longer the better." I chuckled through tears.

Mrs. Marshall was so moved by the account of my made-up marriage that she began to tear up. She turned away to try to hide the emotion she was feeling. This gave me the perfect opportunity to grab the spade.

"So where's the girl now?"

"With family."

We sat in silence and looked out across the meadow.

"Mrs. Marshall, I can—"

"No need to explain. Just pack your things and leave. I think it's time for you to go anyway."

She bobbed her head and wiped her nose and eyes.

I picked up the gardening tool and said, "I'm really sorry for any trouble I've caused you."

Without looking up, Mrs. Marshall said, "Just...please...leave."

"Okay, if you say so, I'll leave."

"Good." she said, right before I jammed the spade into the top of her skull.

She started to convulse, squirting blood everywhere. I had never seen this before. And I definitely was not ready for it. But I had to say that I did enjoy it though.

She reached around and tried to remove it from her head while I watched, almost dumbfounded by the fact that she wasn't dead yet.

I ran over and pulled her hands down when she started to scream.

"Be quiet."

I leaned over and picked up one of the cobblestones that lined the planter to hit the old bag in the head with, sending her crashing heavily to the dirt.

"I told you to be quiet! You...don't...listen, do you?" I said as I pounded her face with the stone.

I kept lifting it over my head, pounding until I crushed her face, trying to avoid her flailing arms in the process.

"Would you just die already, you old bitch!"

I hit her again, hearing the bones break in her face as her skin split open to release the river of blood from her head.

I leaned over her, breathing heavy. I was tired and wanted to rest. But first I had to bury my nuisance.

I stammered to my feet and walked around the cabin to get a shovel from the cellar.

I didn't mind killing Mrs. Marshall. But this was just bad timing. Or was it? I reasoned. Finally, I came to the conclusion that I wasn't going anywhere soon, so I took my time. I walked around and dragged the dead woman to the back of the house near the lake so that I could bury her in the soft dirt that surrounded it.

I pulled her by her feet through the reeds, talking to her faceless corpse.

"You just couldn't leave well enough alone, could you? You should have just stayed out of it, you mean old bitch! I really didn't want to kill you..."

I thought for a second.

"Okay, yes I did. But only after you started talking shit!"

I dragged her through the willows that bordered the lake's edge and began to dig.

I stuck the spade in the dirt and looked at the corpse again.

"You know, a demon like you deserves to burn in hell. And I hope that's where you're going. Maybe I'll see you there one day."

I climbed out of the shallow hole and went to the cellar to get a gas can and some matches.

"You should be excited. I'm going to send you home now." I said when I returned.

Fifteen minutes later, I was kicking Mrs. Marshall into her final resting place, dumping almost the entire can of gas on her.

I lit the match and threw it in the hole.

I watched as the fire consumed her body before I covered it with dirt.

"To hell with you demon! To hell with you!"

I tidied up the grave and put the tools back in the cellar before I went into Mrs. Marshall's house.

I was tired, and all I wanted to do now was take some Vicodin while sitting in the tub with a glass of wine.

I walked in and looked around. She had a lot of pictures of family too, just like the doctor.

I knew one day that Peter and I would know that happiness. So it didn't hurt to see the smiles on their faces, at least not as much as it used to.

"Okay, first of all, I need a drink."

I walked into the kitchen where I saw a nice Merlot already opened and got a glass.

"Letting it breathe, huh? Well, you could have been breathing with it if you weren't such a bitch." I told the picture on the fridge.

I grabbed the glass and the bottle and walked into the bathroom.

I sat on the edge of the tub and ran the water before going to sit at the vanity.

I opened the Vicodin and popped two of the tablets in my mouth, followed by a generous portion of wine.

I looked in the mirror to admire the fine work of the doctor. And for the first time in my life, I hated myself.

What the fuck was I doing? Did this man even want me? Well, if he didn't, I would kill him and start over. Either way, I didn't put myself through this shit for nothing.

My hair was blond and flowing instead of the usual dead black. My eyes were blue instead of brown. And I looked entirely like another woman—a stranger who had my husband's heart.

Fuck her! She wasn't going to win! And truthfully, I think that was the real motivation behind what I was doing. I simply couldn't let her win. I needed to rejuvenate. I turned the water off and eased my sore bloodstained body into the soothing warm water.

I said, "Fuck it." and took a sip from the bottle.

I just wanted to get fucked up and sleep my soreness away. So what better time than now? And what better place than here?

"Ahh, now this is the life." I said, sinking into the bubbles.

CHAPTER 16

Kate ~ Three days later, I woke up refreshed and ready to make the drive up to Connecticut. The soreness in my face had subsided a little, and the anxiety of getting to Wallingford seemingly overwhelmed me. And although I was anxious to get there, I took my time to get ready for the trip.

First I cooked breakfast for myself before taking a relaxing thirty-minute bath. I even napped a little before packing the car to leave.

*****

Peter ~ "What do you have to do today baby?" I asked.

"I have a late meeting, then I have to stop by the store." Laura said, packing her bag.

"I asked because I'll be a little late myself tonight." I said.

"Why?"

"I have a late showing over on Crispin Lane. The buyer is flying in from Boston and won't be here until early evening."

"Well, that's a bummer. What time do you expect to be home?"

I got up and walked over to my wife, cradled her face, and said, "I know this is no honeymoon" She laughed. "But I will be back as soon as I can tonight, okay?"

"Okay," she said softly.

She kissed me and walked out.

The next couple of days, Laura and I were really busy. I was trying to sell houses, and she was fundraising for her nonprofit. This particular day, she was working from home.

"Yes Emily, I need those numbers right away because I'm meeting with our primary investor today at two."

"Are you going to be home later today?"

"Yeah, I'll be here. I have some other things to look over, and there are just too many distractions at the office."

"Okay boss, there's just one more thing..."

"Hold on, hold on, there's someone at the door."

Laura walked to the door and looked out the window. And what she saw was a woman standing there with her back to her.

She opened it and asked, "Can I help you?"

When the woman turned around, Laura almost passed out. She just couldn't believe what she was seeing.

*****

Kate ~ "Who are you?" Laura asked, frightened and confused.

"No, the question should be, Who am I about to become?" I said smugly.

I walked toward the woman who stole my husband and pushed her into the house.

"What's going on? Why do you look like me? Who are you?"

I looked down and saw the phone in her hand.

"Get rid of them." I whispered.

Laura looked at the phone and hesitated as she tried to sort this all out. I knew what she was thinking. Why was this woman here? And who could I possibly be?

And probably, why did I look exactly like her? And possibly, what would her fate be now. So many questions.

I grabbed her wrist and whispered again, "Get rid of them."

She lifted the phone to her ear and said, "Em, I'm going to have to call you back."

"Is everything okay Laura?"

I snatched the phone and put it to my ear.

"Hello, Laura, hello..."

I hung up the phone and put it in my pocket before motioning Laura toward the kitchen.

"I don't understand what's going on here. Who are you?"

"Sit down, and I'll explain it to you. Do you have any coffee?"

Laura sat stunned beyond belief. How was this happening?

"Coffee...?"

"Um, yes, in the cabinet over there." She pointed.

I took my jacket off and walked to get the coffee.

"I know you might be confused by all of this."

To say the least.

"But by the end of this cup of coffee, you'll understand."

I looked around for the coffee maker before turning to ask her where the filters were.

"You see, you have something of mine, and of course, I'm here to get it back." I said while loading the machine.

She had no idea what I was talking about though. She just sat there trying to figure it all out.

"I don't even know you! So how could I have anything of yours? I don't understand why you're doing this."

I put the coffee down and walked over to her.

"Didn't I tell you by the end of this cup of coffee you would understand?"

"Yes."

"Well, shut the hell up and listen then!"

I walked back over to the coffee maker and continued, "Now... where was I? Oh, okay, I remember now. *You* have something that belongs to me, and I'm here to get it back."

"Wha—"

"Uh-uh-uh, let me finish." I said, wagging my finger.

This was something that just never happens. Well, not to her anyway. Or anybody she knew, for that matter.

"I really shouldn't say something as opposed to someone..." I continued.

She looked deep into my eyes, trying to catch on to the game of cat and mouse.

"Kate?" she blurted.

"So you do know who I am? Has Peter mentioned me? Did he tell you I was his one true love?"

"He told me that you were as crazy as bat shit!"

She put her hand under the table.

"YOU DON'T THINK I SAW YOUR LITTLE RING!" I yelled.

"What are you going to do to me?"

"I mean, you don't think you can get away with whatever it is you're planning to do, do you?"

"Well, that depends on Peter now, doesn't it? If he comes back with me and you promise not to interfere, then I'll leave you alive and alone. But…if it goes the other way, well…"

"Well what?"

"Well… I won't really need you then, will I?"

"And what does that mean?" she asked with tears in her eyes.

I poured her a cup of coffee and sat it on the table.

"That means that this could be your last cup of coffee honey."

I walked back over to the counter and poured myself a cup.

"Now I know this may seem to be so absurd that it could *never* be true. But let me assure you. *This is reality.* Go ahead. Drink your coffee before it gets cold."

*****

Peter ⁓ I had been feeling bad the last couple of days. Here I was with a new wife, and already she was feeling neglected. I wanted her to know that although I wasn't there, she was still on my mind. So I called her.

*****

Kate ⁓ Her phone rang. I took it out of my pocket, looked at it, and smiled.

"It's Peter." I said, sliding it across the table.

Then I pulled the large knife from my coat and sat it next to her.

She picked up the phone.

"Put him on speaker." I ordered.

"Hello?"

158

"Hey honey, I've been thinking…"

I knew he could feel the awkward silence on the other end. He always had a knack for knowing when something was wrong. I just wondered if she would give away our little secret.

"Baby, what's wrong?"

I picked up the knife just to show her I meant business.

"Nothing baby. I'm just really busy, that's all. How's your day going?"

Laura figured the longer she kept him on the phone, the more time he would have to figure out something wasn't right. But she was wrong because if she did try anything, I would simply just have to kill her quicker.

"I called you because I have something to tell you. Do you have a minute?"

"Sure." she said after I prodded her to the right response.

"Well, I just wanted you to know that I love you. And I know it hasn't been easy as of late. And when we do go on our honeymoon, I'm going to show you just how much."

"Baby, how much *do* you love me?"

I could see that although Laura was in a compromising position, she still had her pride. And that very pride would cost her her life.

"I love you to the edge of the universe and back, baby, you know that?"

"Do you love me more than Kate?"

My eyes got big, and I scooted closer to listen.

"Yes baby, of course! That crazy bitch could never hold a candle to you."

I stood there furiously tightening my grip on the knife handle because in just a little while, all those compliments would be mine alone.

"Baby, you are the only *woman who ever meant the world to me."*

And now the look on my face must have went from interest to absolute disgust.

"That really means a lot to me baby." She said, sobbing.

"Baby, don't cry. I'm gonna make everything okay. Do you want me to come home?"

"No! No baby, I'll be okay. Go and do what you need to do so that you *can* come home."

"Okay." he told her, completely clueless, hanging up the phone.

She looked me square in the eye, knowing that I was hurt. I had never expected Peter to *ever* say that about me. And even though he felt it was true, it still hurt.

"Get up!"

"What?"

"I said get the fuck up! Now!"

I grabbed her by the arm and shoved her into the dining room. "Sit down!"

"I will not be ordered around in my own house!"

I showed her the knife and walked around the table.

"Well, we don't have to fight now, do we? We could end this all right now?" I said, poking her with the knife just hard enough for her to feel it.

She sat down, and I immediately went to work, pulling the cuffs from my pocket to lock her arms behind her.

"I know what you did!"

"I didn't do anything." she defended.

"Do you think that if he knew I was here, he would've said all those horrible things about me?"

"Yes." Laura said as calmly as she could, knowing she had me at an emotional disadvantage.

"Well, you're wrong! If he knew I was standing here, he wouldn't even remember your name!"

"And why wouldn't he remember his wife's—"

"*I'm his wife!* I…am…his…wife! You got that!"

We faced off, trading our evilest scowls.

"Well, we are going to have to see about that now, won't we?" she said.

"He's my husband! Don't you think he's going to know that you are not me? You could never be me no matter how much surgery you've had!"

I took the rag out of my pocket, ready to douse it with chloroform, then I put it back.

I walked over to her and placed my hands on both sides of her head and said, "All you are is a substitute bitch. You could never take my place. But now I'm going to show you just how easy it is to take yours."

"Look who's talking. You come to my house looking like me, and I'm the substitute?"

I held her head up and spit in her face. Then I walked behind her and snapped her neck.

"That's why when Peter gets home, you…will be gone." I said disdainfully, spitting on her again.

I unlocked the cuffs and watched her fall to the floor.

"What's this?"

I knelt down and pushed her hair aside just above the left ear.

"What is this now?"

There behind her ear was a birthmark shaped just like the state of California. Now how did I miss this?

Was fate playing a trick on the cruel? I pulled my phone out and snapped a picture before I removed her wedding ring.

I waited the forty minutes or so for it to get dark before going out to the car to get the shovel I brought with me.

And after I changed, I got into Laura's car and drove across the river to bury her.

*****

Peter ~ I was able to wrap up the business I had early and was on my way home when I pulled my phone out and tried to call my wife. There was no answer on her cell, so I decided to call the house-phone when the machine picked up.

"Hey honey, I was able to get done early and just thought I would come home and spend some time with you. If you get this message, call

me back. I'm going to stop by the store to get something to drink before I come home."

*****

Kate ~ I opened the trunk, pulled her out by the ankles, and dropped her in the cold wet mud.

It had started to rain again, and I could feel the vibration of her phone in my pocket. I pulled it out and listened to the message.

"Shit, I have to get back before he gets home."

I dragged Laura through the mud behind an old barn.

"I have to get rid of you first though." I said wet and out of breath.

I ran back to the car and got the shovel so that I could do just that. I went into the farthest stall in the rear of the barn and removed the hay so that I could get to the dirt.

"I told you, you were just a substitute, didn't I? And now it's time for *me* to go home and be with my husband. I told you, didn't I?"

*****

Peter ~ I decided to go and get the wine she liked, which cost me another forty minutes in traffic. But I decided it was worth it.

When I got home, I walked in and saw my wife walking toward me.

"Hey honey!" she said, running over to kiss me.

Where did this come from? I had seen Laura excited before, but it was never like this.

She spun me around, squeezing me hard. It was as if she hadn't seen me in years. I didn't mind it though. It felt good. But I still didn't know how to take it.

*****

Kate ~ When I spun him around, I noticed that I had left my murder bag on the table.

"Baby, let me take that from you. Go and have a seat, and I'll pour us some drinks."

He went into the living room, plopped down on the couch and asked, "How was your day baby? Were you able to finish what you needed to?"

I ducked into the dining room to put the bag away.

"Baby?"

I dropped the bag.

"Yes dear?" I asked, kicking it behind the hutch.

A few minutes later, I was bringing him his drink.

"Thank you." he said, gulping it hastily.

"Where's yours?"

"In the kitchen."

"Well, don't you want it?"

I jumped up and walked back to pour my own.

*****

Peter ~ I knew we hadn't been spending a lot of time with each other, but...*was* she changing? She rarely drank with me at home. And I didn't know, but either way, I liked it. It just made me feel closer to her.

"BABY, I'M GOING TO TAKE THE TRASH OUT. I'LL BE RIGHT IN." she yelled from the kitchen.

I reached over and picked up the remote, wondering again, *Who is this lady?*

As long as I had known Laura, she had *never* taken the trash out. Hell, even when I met her, the can in her kitchen was overflowing. I asked myself again, Was she changing?

And if she was, it was most definitely welcomed.

I took another drink and heard thumping coming from the back.

"Baby, do you need any help?"

"No, I GOT IT!" she yelled back.

I sat back down and got comfortable until she returned.

"Okay, okay, I'm back." she said, rushing in.

"Baby, what was all that thumping I heard out there?"

"It was nothing. Just something I finally got rid of."

"Well, it must have been huge."

"Larger than it should have been baby."

We sat and watched a movie that night. And although we hadn't spoken much, there was something strangely familiar about her, something I hadn't felt since I was with Kate.

And there was something else I didn't know at the time. And that was, she was really smart. And boy, was I stupid not to see it. She stepped right in and took over Laura's nonprofit without missing a beat. She even landed the sponsor Laura had been trying to lock down for months with ease. It just seemed at that moment that we had the perfect life, that is until...

"Baby, are you happy with me?" she asked.

I finished what was left of my drink and said, "Of course I am sweetie. Why? What's on your mind?"

I reached across and grabbed her hands, which tonight seemed coarse and hard.

"Baby, what's up with your hands? It feels like you've been doing construction or something."

She snatched them away and asked, "What are you trying to say Peter?"

"Nothing baby. It's just that I've never felt your hands like this. They have always been so soft."

And a little smaller.

She snatched them away again and rubbed them together before she got up to go to the bathroom.

"Baby, I didn't mean anything by what I said. I'm sorry."

"Forget about it. Let's just have a good time and enjoy this time we have together. We haven't had a chance to enjoy each other in a while. Let's go out. I'll be ready in a minute."

I agreed, and a while later, we were pulling up to the valet at Tambourines.

"Hey guys, welcome to Tambourines." said the bartender.

"Hey." I said. "Can I get a Jameson and ginger ale and a Tom Collins for the lady?"

She cleared her throat and said, "I'll have a Long Island iced tea please."

I furrowed my brow and thought, *This looks like my wife, but this is not the wife I know.* I mean, Laura always had a Tom Collins when we came here. Now here she was sitting across from me looking around as if she had never been here before in her life.

"Baby, is everything okay?" I asked.

"Yes, why?"

"I don't know. It just seems like something is different."

Suddenly, all her attention was focused on me.

"Different how?" she asked defensively.

"I mean, you're sitting here looking around like you've never seen this place before when you're the one that bought me here in the first place."

"What are you saying Peter?"

The server sat the drinks on the table and asked, "Shall I run a tab for you?"

I whipped out my credit card, fearing I might need some help to make it through the night. That which only liquor could provide.

I took a sip from my drink, hoping that the silence would make her forget. It did not.

"So what do you think is different about me? Is it my hands again? Are they still too rough for you?" she asked.

I took another drink.

"I didn't mean anything by it. It's just that you were acting a little strange."

Suddenly, I saw a familiar scowl, but a scowl I had *never* seen on Laura's face.

I took a bigger drink, almost finishing the glass.

"So are you saying you don't know who I am all of a sudden?"

"No, I'm not saying that at all. That's crazy."

"Well, what are you saying? Are you calling me crazy?"

I gulped down the rest of my drink and called for the server again.

"Can I get another one please?"

"So what now? Do you plan to get drunk and have me carry your sorry ass home?"

Who was this woman?

The server *had* to know what I was going through because it seemed like only a minute had passed before she was sitting my drink on the table.

"Thank you." I said, grateful for her expedience.

"Oh, so now your flirting in front of me?"

I had *never* seen Laura like this. Quite frankly, she was starting to act like Kate. No, that couldn't be right. Could it? Maybe I was just paranoid, knowing that Kate may be still out there somewhere. Or possibly buzzed. Whatever it was, I didn't like it.

"Peter, are you going to sit there and ignore me?"

I took another drink.

"Okay, go ahead and drink yourself into a stupor. I'm not going to carry you home!"

I put my drink down and said, "Honey, whatever I said to make you upset, I'm sorry."

She got up and stormed away without saying a word. I was going to go after her. But then I looked down at my drink and thought it better to order another one.

We had been together for a little over a year now, and I *know* it takes time to get to know a person. But I thought we had passed that point a long time ago. All of a sudden, Laura was doing all kinds of crazy shit. Shit Kate used to do.

My head was spinning by the time the server sat my next drink down. And with the next drink I took, I had decided to put my concerns aside and make peace.

*****

Kate ~ I marched into the bathroom.

"GET OUT OF MY WAY, YOU TROLL!" I yelled at the woman walking out.

166

I went to the mirror and looked in my purse for my lipstick. And just as I was about to apply it, I looked at myself. I mean really looked at who I was and who was staring back at me. I started to laugh out loud while the women who shared the mirror looked as if I had gone crazy. I had.

I realized that I had forgotten who I had become. You see, while I looked like Laura, inside, I was still me. And in my mind, I was supposed to know that. But now that I had realized my error, I adjusted my attitude and went back to the table. I didn't want to fuck this up.

*****

Peter ~ I stood up. "Baby, are you okay?"

She took my hand and sat down. And yes, they were still rough even after the lotion.

"I know I must have acted atrociously tonight, and I apologize. Let's go home, and I'll show you how sorry I am. It's just been a long day, and I thought that coming here would give us a chance to enjoy each other. And now all I want to do is go home."

I took another drink and called for the server.

"Can I have the check please?"

She sat across the table, seducing me with her eyes. And I was starting to feel the whiskey take effect. And at that moment, I didn't care who she was. I just wanted to go home with her.

A short time later, we were pulling into the driveway, and I was fully aroused. I ran around the car to open her door. And when I did, I saw the strangest look on her face. It was like she hated and loved me at the same time.

I reached out and grabbed her hand to follow me into the house. And before we even got inside, we were in full throw. I reached around and gripped her ass, which at the time felt as it always had, just a little smaller. Her lips felt different too. I mean, they were cold and hard, not warm and soft like they had been previously.

She reached up and pulled my head close to hers, something Kate always did. That could have been a coincidence, right?

The sex was *amazing*! I had never felt this way with Kate, Laura, or any other woman for that matter. And what came next was something that I had never expected.

I had never heard Laura snore in almost eighteen months, probably because I did. And while I was looking down at her I swore, in her face I saw Kate. I sat up, rubbed my eyes, and looked at her again.

"You're seeing things because you're still drunk." I told myself, lying back down.

The next couple of days, we really didn't see each other. We pretty much just fell back into our own separate careers and routines. And one day while sitting behind my desk, I received a phone call.

"This is Peter."

"Mr. Galvan, I'm Dean Croft, your late business partner Jose's attorney."

"What can I do for you Mr. Croft?"

"Well, I'm going to need you to come back to Los Angeles."

"For what?"

"To decide what to do with the company."

"What do you mean?"

"I mean, would you like to sell your shares or just liquidate the entire asset? Or would you still like to run the day-to-day operations? Whatever you decide, we need to move forward on this?"

"I'm not selling my company or its shares Mr. Croft."

"Well, then I need you to come out here and square things away."

"Okay, I'll be there as soon as I can."

"Sir, you need to be here sooner."

"Okay, I'll be there tomorrow."

"I'll see you then. I'll send a car for you."

I had anxiety about telling Laura I had to travel, which really was just baggage left over from Kate. But nevertheless, I was still nervous when I walked in the room to tell her.

"Who was that on the phone babe?"

"Jose's lawyer."

"What did he want?"

When Jose died, I told Laura everything. And when I told her about Kate, she suggested that the real reason Kate wanted me dead was to lay claim to our company. But when I told her Kate would never kill me, just anyone who interfered with her *being* with me, she changed her mind. But Kate already knew about Jose because she was the one who killed him. But what she didn't know was if I had told Laura…or so I thought.

"He wants me to go back out to California and decide what I'm going to do with the company."

"What *are* you going to do baby?" she asked.

"I'm going to keep my company. Besides, I owe it to Jose. Foundation was something we built together. It just wouldn't be right to sell it all off."

There was silence. I looked at her, waiting for a reaction, but she just sat there and stared at me.

"Honey?" I said, waving my hands to interrupt her daydream.

She looked at me and asked, "Does that mean we have to move back to California?"

"What do you mean back? I thought you had never been to the West Coast."

"Babe, you know what I mean. So are *we* moving to California or what?"

I had so many other things on my mind that I really didn't dwell on her slipup. I needed to pack for the flight home and figure out what I was going to do next.

"I have to go back and sign the papers that will make me the majority shareholder. And I'll have to stay there to run the company. So yeah, I guess we're moving to California."

I really didn't need to work in real estate. It was just something to do while I was on the lamb from Kate. Jose ran the company better than I ever could, and the money he was putting in my account allowed me to live more than comfortably.

I thought I was going crazy because at times, Laura seemed like she was mad that we were in fact comfortable, and that confused me. Oftentimes, a show of affection toward her would illicit a jealous rant toward me. But again, love had me blind, and maybe this was a chance at a better life. Out in the open. A chance to live our lives on our own terms without the threat of Kate hunting us down.

"Well, I guess I should start making plans to move our offices to the West Coast."

"Are you sure you wanna do this?" I chuckled nervously.

"Well, that's where you're from, so I think we should go back. Lay some roots."

"I love you so much baby. Thanks for understanding."

"Well then it's settled. We're moving to California." she insisted.

I looked at her and fell in love with her all over again. All I wanted to do was provide her with the best life. And share *that* life with her.

I knew things were a little crazy as of late, but moving back to LA would definitely be the fresh start we needed.

CHAPTER 17

The move home for me was easy because this was where I was from and where I wanted to be. And it seemed like Laura was adjusting well to the move too. We moved into a nice two-story two-bedroom house in Pasadena, and life was sweet. We had been having sex like teenagers, and both of our professional careers were skyrocketing. I mean, everything was going great!

One day, we decided to have lunch when my suspicions arose again.

"Do you want to drive?" I asked.

She smiled and grabbed the keys.

It was a beautiful day, and lunch at the beach would have just added to its splendor.

"I used to go to this place in Manhattan Beach when I lived out here. Do you want to go?"

"What's the name of the place?"

"O'Hurley's." I said.

We were pulling out the driveway when I asked her.

"So how are you liking Cali?"

"It's fine. I still have some things to get used too though."

"Like what?" I chuckled.

"Well, the weather for one thing. It just feels very dry to me."

Again I chuckled.

"What else?"

"Well, let's see? The traffic, definitely the traffic."

"Yeah, I've lived here my whole life, and I don't think that I've ever gotten used to the traffic."

"Are those all the things you dislike about being out here?"

"I mean, everyone looks so perfect. Everybody in Connecticut looks frumpy?"

"No they don't!" I blurted out.

"Yes they do!"

"Janis didn't look frumpy."

She stopped laughing and asked, "Who?"

Did I make a mistake and say the wrong the thing?

"Janis who?" she asked again.

"Janis from work. You remember Janis, don't you?" I said.

She didn't respond. She just stared at the road as if she were in deep thought, like she was trying to figure out what to say next.

"Honey?"

She turned, looked at me, and said, "So what about her?"

"Nothing, I'm just saying she didn't look frumpy, that's all."

"And how would you know?"

"Because we work together."

"Not anymore." She snorted.

I was quiet because I had made what was not a problem a problem. So I really shouldn't have told her the news I had. But I decided to anyway.

"I asked Janis to come take a position at Foundation."

The look she gave me made me think that she was about to drive the car off the road and kill us both.

"You what?"

"Baby, watch the road!" I said, reaching for the wheel.

She slapped my hand and said, "I know how to drive!"

"Yeah, but do you know how to do it safely?" I blurted.

That slipup caused her to look at me again like she wanted to kill us both. Again.

The rest of the way was quiet as you could imagine, with me wondering how I would peacefully get through lunch. So I decided that I would do it drunk.

We pulled into the parking lot, and when I got out, there was only one question I needed her to answer.

"Have you been here before?"

"Ye...no," she corrected.

"Have you, or haven't you?"

Okay, it was more than one.

Look, we had only been in LA a couple of weeks, and I had never even mentioned this place. So how did she know how to get here without GPS? I didn't tell her how to get here, and yet *here* we were.

"You know I haven't been here before. Why would you even ask me that?"

"All I know is that you're the first person that I have ever seen find a place she had never been to before without directions."

I was positive that if she *were* driving now, I'd be dead or really, really hurt.

She stopped and asked, "So what are you saying Peter?"

I looked at her in disbelief because I thought I had already said it.

"I'm simply asking. How did you know how to get here?"

"When you suggested it, I looked it up."

Liar!

"I didn't tell you until we got into the car baby."

"What are you trying to say Peter?"

Again, you know the rest.

Laura seemed to be a whole different person these past few weeks. Short-tempered and all, which reminded me horribly of Kate.

"What are you trying to say to me Peter?" she pressed.

"Nothing." I said under my breath.

"Excuse me?"

"*Nothing.*" I said louder.

All through lunch, I just couldn't get it off my mind. How in the hell did she know how to get here? I didn't want to drag this out in public. Just to have her turn it around on me. So if I was going to be the bad guy, I was going to drink like one.

I was at the bottom of my fourth drink, still trying to figure things out when the day got worse. I looked up, and who was walking down the strand? It could have been anybody in the world, but it wasn't. It was Janis.

I gulped the drink and raised my hand for another one, hoping Janis wouldn't see us.

She did.

"Peter!"

Fuck.

"Hey Pete!" she said, walking toward us.

I raised my hand again, not to acknowledge Janis but to hurry the server.

She walked over to the table.

"Hey boss."

"Hey." I said nervously.

"What are you doing here?" she asked.

"Having lunch with Laura."

I motioned toward my wife.

Laura looked at her as if she had never seen her before but wanted to kill her anyway.

"It's nice to see you again Laura."

"Well, it's good to see you too." she said smugly.

Wait a damn minute. Didn't she almost rip my head off in the car over this very same woman? And now she didn't know who she was? Maybe I was paranoid. Or maybe I was drunk. Either way, I still thought it was crazy.

Laura and Janis had seen each other at least a dozen times before. They never talked much, but this encounter just seemed extra cold and strange.

Janis turned to me, looking confused.

"Soooo I guess I'll see you at work then. Enjoy your lunch."

"Okay then, I'll see you at the office." I said, gulping my drink.

"Who was that?"

"That was Janis."

"So that's Ms. Not-So-Frumpy, huh? What are you going to have her doing?"

"Sales."

"She *is* cute."

What the… I didn't even respond to that. I just excused myself, telling her that I had to go to the restroom, planning to detour at the bar on the way back.

At this point, I thought Laura was losing her mind. I was seriously contemplating getting her help, or even better, getting some for me.

I went into the restroom, not to use it but to look into the mirror and try to grasp what was left of my sanity. Luckily no one was in there with me, so talking to myself didn't seem so crazy.

"What the fuck is wrong with her? Or is it me? This shit is crazy!"

I turned the water on and washed my hands, not because I needed to. I just had to do something with them.

I finished up and walked out to the bar.

"Sir, did you need anything?" said my server, who was getting drinks for another table.

"Another Jameson and ginger ale please."

"Okay, I'll bring it right over."

"Thank you."

I was kinda hoping to spend some time at the bar to try to sort things out. But now I had to walk back because Laura was looking right at me.

Fuck.

"Is everything okay baby?" she asked, sipping her drink.

"Yeah, I just had to pee really bad."

"I bet you did, with the way you've been drinking. I'm worried about you baby."

"I'm okay." I insisted.

"Yeah, but will I be?" she joked.

She had her damned nerves.

The server sat my drink on the table, and immediately I was swallowing the top half.

What was going on? Would every woman I meet be their own special kind of crazy? I suppose that we all are. But this was just too damn strange. I was quickly becoming more distrustful of Laura because of the way she was acting. But I guess I just needed more time to sort things out my own way, whatever that was.

"So when do you think you'll be starting work?" she asked.

"I'm going in tomorrow."

"I have an early meeting with a potential funder about an outreach program, but after that, I'm free. Do you wanna have lunch?" she asked.

"I don't know. I might be kind of busy all day baby."

"Well, we don't have to go out. I'll just bring something by."

She looked at me and said, "You do want to have lunch with your wife, don't you?"

Now what was I supposed to say? So I said what I should have. "Of course baby."

"Good," she said, grabbing my hands.

"Because we need to spend more time together. Don't you want that?"

"Yes baby, I do," I agreed, still buzzing from the drinks.

"Well then it's settled. Don't worry about this. It's my treat. Can you go pull the car around while I pay the bill and stop by the little girl's room?"

I finished my drink and stumbled out to the parking lot.

Being half-drunk was a brilliant excuse to be quiet on the ride home. And I didn't think she minded the silence either. And to avoid any conflict, *I* drove home.

When we got there, we said little or nothing to each other before going to bed. And no matter how it sounded, I was okay with that. I just needed the peace.

The next day at Foundation was just as busy as I had imagined it would be. Jose's attorney came in with Seth to go over the paperwork for the transfer. Plus, I still had a couple of contracts to finalize before construction could begin on our next project. And then I had to look over the layouts for Cherry Blossom—a new living and retail space in Little Tokyo—all before Laura came for lunch.

I had just walked out of a meeting with one of the architects when she walked in.

"What are you doing here?" I asked.

176

"We had plans for lunch, remember?"

"What time is it?"

"One o'clock."

"Okay, let me give these to my assistant, and I'll be right out."

She walked over and, just my luck, sat on the couch in front of Janis's office before getting up to walk in.

"Knock knock," she said, remembering the joke she and June had shared.

"Oh hey Laura."

"Mrs. Galvan." Laura insisted.

"Okay, Mrs. Galvan, what can I do for you?" Janice asked, a little irritated.

"So you're Janis?"

Janis sat behind her desk, quiet and confused.

Kate sat down just as I walked back into the lobby. I stopped in my tracks because whatever I got away with yesterday at the beach I surely would not get away with today.

"Yes I am." Janice said, still wondering where all of this was going.

"You're the woman Peter talks about all the time, huh?"

Janis leaned back in her chair and asked, "Don't you know me? We must have had at least a dozen conversations in the past. I started working with Peter just after you left the firm. I'm sure you've seen me before."

She sat quietly, trying not to blow her cover.

"So how long have you been working with my husband?" she asked, deflecting the point.

Again the look of confusion washed across Janis's face.

"I think you know that already." Janis said.

"If I knew that, then I wouldn't be asking you, would I?" asked the impostor.

As soon as I heard her voice elevate, I stepped in.

"Come on baby. I'm ready to go."

Both women looked at me for an explanation, but I was determined to only give one. And that would be to my wife. The rest would have to be addressed later.

"Come on." I said again.

She walked over to me before turning to look back at Janis and say, "So this is the one you don't think is frumpy, huh?"

Janis looked at me, even more confused than when I had first walked in.

I turned to walk my wife out before I turned back to mouth *"I'll explain later"* to Janis. Luckily, she was okay with that.

"What's going on honey? What was that back there?" I asked.

"Why didn't you tell me that was Janis at the beach yesterday?"

"Baby, what are you talking about? You've met Janis plenty of times. Don't you remember meeting her boyfriend Mark at the Christmas party? And I did tell you. I actually introduced you to her."

Again she was quiet. She looked back toward Janis's office and said, "Well, if I don't remember her, then evidently, she's not important."

And that was good enough for me right now.

Later that night, we were at home, and I was on the couch in the den, watching the Lakers.

"Honey, do you want something to drink?" she said, coming downstairs.

I didn't hear her until she was standing behind me.

"What did you say baby?"

"Do you want something to drink, I said."

"Yes baby. Thank you."

I didn't even look up at her because if I had, I would've noticed the evilness on her face and said no thank you to that drink.

She walked into the kitchen as I watched the Lakers go down by 3 to Detroit.

"Here you go baby, just like you like it."

I had been drinking way too much over the past couple of days, trying to figure out what was really going on. I didn't know whether to steal her DNA to prove that she wasn't Kate or what.

I just wanted to find out if she was truly my wife. But tonight, I didn't want to think about any of that. I just wanted to drink and watch the Lakers.

She walked back into the room about ten minutes later to find me passed out on the couch as she slipped the bottle of Seconal sodium into her pocket.

"Baby, I'll be back in a minute." she said, rushing out the door.

We only lived about a mile from my office, and Laura was there in less than ten minutes.

It was 6:23 p.m., and the sun had just set to provide her the perfect cover to wait and follow Janis home.

*****

Kate ~ I parked beneath a large maple tree and got out to walk the short distance to the building when I saw Janis coming out of the rear entrance.

"There she is." I told myself on the way back to the car.

I waited until she pulled off and was halfway down the block before I pulled off to follow her. And after following her to the grocery store, the cleaners, and the coffee shop, I watched her pull into her driveway.

I turned off the cabin light and opened the door when I saw her boyfriend come out.

"Do you need some help?" he offered.

"Yeah, can you get the bags from the back seat please?"

I closed the door, slouched into my seat, and said, "Did you know your girlfriend is a whore? Did you know that?"

He pulled his head out of the car and looked around.

I sank deeper into my seat, just enough to see over the dash.

"Are you looking for your slut's integrity?"

I was both mad and excited as I watched him pull the last bags from the car.

I pulled out my knife and got out. All I could think about was what I was going to do when I got inside, so much so that I didn't even close the car door.

I strode fast and with purpose across the street, bounding up to the door before knocking.

From inside, I heard him tell her that he would get the door. And when he did, I pushed it open and shoved the knife into his stomach.

"Shhhh, shhhh, shhh, we don't want to draw attention now, do we?"

He fell away from me gripping the handle as I turned to close the door. Quietly, of course.

"Babe, who was at the door?"

Janis came from the kitchen and saw him hunched over the stairs.

"Oh my god, Mark. What's wrong baby?"

He sat up and showed her his bloody shirt.

"Mark, what happened?"

He tried to point at me. And when she turned around, I hit her ass with one of the bookends from the shelf.

Mark was helpless because the pain he was in had paralyzed him. And all he could do was lie there and endure every painful breath, watching as I spewed my rage.

"Do you see her?" I said. "She's a whore! She's sleeping with my husband! And did you know that they have been fucking for over a year now?"

When Janis woke up, I knelt down, grabbed her by the hair, and said, "Tell him what you've been doing, you whore!"

"I… I don't know what you're talking about Laura." she said, still groggy.

"Don't you fucking call me that! My name is Mrs. Galvan! Do you hear me slut?"

I stood up and kicked her in the head, before I spit on her, and pulled her by the hair over to her lover.

"No, no, you're gonna look at me bitch." I said, turning her over.

"You tried to take something from me, but tonight, I'm going to show you just how that's done. And why *you* shouldn't have done what you did.

Did you really think that you could run back and forth from my husband to your boyfriend, and there would be no consequences?"

I flipped her boyfriend on his back and pushed the knife further in.

He groaned in pain as he tried his best to be brave.

"Oh no you don't." I said, grabbing Janis by the hair again to stop her from squirming away.

And I punched her in the back of the head, for good measure, just to make sure she didn't try it again.

"I see that I'm going to have to restrain you. Either way, you're going to watch, bitch."

I walked over to the couch and pulled out the tie straps I had in my jacket pocket.

"I think that these will do just fine."

After restraining her, I hit her in the face four more times. Then I gagged her.

She belted out a muffled plea, "Please, please don't kill us."

"I'm afraid I can't grant you *that* wish. You wanna know why?"

She nodded yes slowly as I placed my nose just inches away from her face.

"Because I'm not a genie, stupid ass!"

I got up and walked over to Mark, who was barely conscious now.

"You know, the human body is amazing. But what's even more amazing than that is human sexuality. Let me show you."

I took my finger and rubbed it around the knife's handle before running my hand down to Mark's crotch to unzip his pants.

Janis's eyes got big because she had no idea of what was about to happen.

"I know what you're thinking. Am I going to fuck your man before I kill him?"

I smiled, looked down, and said, "Yes, I am. You see, turnabout is fair play, and I plan to play, just not fairly. While, at the same time, proving a point!"

I reached into his open zipper, pulled out his penis, and began to stroke it ever so gently.

"Damn Janis, you're greedy. I mean you wrestle with this big ol' thing, and then you fuck my man too?"

Although Mark was in excruciating pain, he couldn't help becoming aroused.

I leaned over and put my mouth around his dick and began to suck until it stiffened even more. His eyes rolled up into his head before I lifted his bloody shirt to position myself on top of him.

I stood up and pulled my pants off, teasing him ever so slightly with the sight of me in my panties. I straddled him and pulled them to the side before I put him inside of me.

"I know you like that, don't you?" I said as I slowly gyrated my hips and my tight pussy on his penis.

He started to cry. Not because he was in pain but because he couldn't stop what was happening.

I got off and started to stroke his dick again. And despite his best efforts, he couldn't control his arousal.

"You like these?" I said, ripping open my blouse to rub my breasts in his face.

All he could do was hold the knife as still as he could to minimize the pain.

I started to suck his penis again, which sent him into a sort of painful ecstasy, before I mounted and put him inside me again, riding him while staring at Janis until we both climaxed.

"You see, the point I was trying to prove was that, even though your man was in excruciating pain, he experienced blissful pleasure at the same time.

So you see, human sexuality *is* a powerful thing. Even more powerful than love. It was human sexuality that made your man cum inside me. And it was human sexuality that aroused him in the first place."

I looked down on myself and said, "I am a baaaaad bitch. You see it, don't you?"

"So now you know that you're not the only one that can fuck someone's man. But…after tonight, you won't have to worry about that."

I saw Janis crying, and it felt good. I was on top of the world because tonight was the night Peter's affinity for her would die with her.

"Awww, hurts, doesn't it bitch? But not like this."

While he was still inside me, I pulled the knife out and plunged it into his chest. The sight of the spewing blood sent me into an almost euphoric state of being as I continued to roll my hips, feeling his hard dick inside me.

"I…killing…your…boyfriend…whore!"

I pulled the knife out and stuck it back into his chest two more times as he lay on the floor, wheezing from a punctured lung. He just laid there trying his best not to drown on the blood that was pooling in his throat.

"Okay I'm bored." I said before I cut his throat open to watch him gag violently and eventually succumb to his wounds.

"That was not pretty."

I chuckled and wiped off my face with the back of my hand.

Janis screamed. And although she was gagged, the shrill still pierced through.

I got up and walked over to her, adjusting my panties on the way.

"I thought you were going to cooperate, but now it seems that you've thrown that all out the window."

I kneed her in her big-ass head and knelt down beside her.

"Sit up for me."

Janis was shaking uncontrollably, scared and peeing on herself. Why was her boss's wife doing this? What had she done to deserve this?

I *knew* these questions had to be running through her mind. But I didn't care. I just wanted her to suffer, and that was part of it.

I wiped the excess blood from the knife's blade on to Janis's cheek before I pulled a chair in front of her from the dining room.

"Look at it this way honey. The last thing you're going to see is this pretty face staring back at you. And you'll die knowing your boyfriend had some good pussy before he died."

I raised the knife above my head and dropped it, stopping just inches from her chest.

"I bet you thought you were a goner, huh?"

She started to sniffle before she started to whimper. And I was tired of seeing her this way. So I lifted the knife again and pushed it into her face again and again and again and again.

"Shhhh, go away now. All of *my* troubles are over."

I lifted her head to kiss her face before I pulled the knife from it to leave. But before I did, I cut her throat too. Just to be sure.

"Oh my god! That was sooo exhilarating!" I said, walking out after I got dressed.

"I bet Peter won't think she's so pretty now." I laughed.

CHAPTER 18

Peter ~ I woke up after eleven to find Laura sleeping next to me. She looked so peaceful. And if *she* was at peace, then so was I.

I closed my eyes and was startled by the phone.

"Hello."

"Hey Peter."

"Maggie, good morning."

"Hey Peter, is Laura there?"

"Yes, she's right here, but she's asleep now. Do you want me to wake her up?"

"No, no, don't wake her up. I just wanted to tell her that I was thinking about coming out to see you guys."

"That's a great idea. You can stay with us."

I thought that if anybody else saw how she was acting, I wouldn't think that I was crazy. So I invited her mother.

"I don't want to be a bother."

"You won't be a bother at all. When were you thinking about coming?"

"I was thinking in the next couple of days, probably around the weekend."

"That's fine. Do you need me to pick you up?"

"No, I'll take a cab."

"Okay, then it's settled. We'll see you in a couple of days."

Saturday, 9:27 a.m. I was downstairs, putting on my shoes to go out and mow the lawn, when Laura walked downstairs.

"Good morning baby," she said.

"Good morning."

"What are you doing today?" she asked.

"I'm about to go and get some trimmer wire before I cut the grass. What about you?"

"I really didn't have anything planned. I feel lazy."

"Good, then you'll be here when your mother comes."

"My what?"

"Your mother."

"How do you know my mother is coming?"

"I talked to her Thursday."

"And you didn't tell me?"

I sat there with the most stupid look on my face because I really had no explanation of why I had not told her. Or should I have told her that I wanted her mother to verify that I wasn't crazy because of the way she was acting? Was that crazy?

"I'm sorry." was all I could say.

"You don't tell me my mom is coming, and all you can say is you're sorry? Oh my god. You are right about one thing, though. You *are* sorry…a sorry ass, giving me a sorry-ass apology. Who in the hell are you?"

Shouldn't *I* be asking that question?

"I said I was sorry. I must have gotten sidetracked," I said.

"Yeah, sidetracked." she said, walking back upstairs.

"Where are you going?"

"My mother is coming. You know that, right? I'm going to get dressed."

I knew she wasn't happy. But I had to get another witness here without her knowing what I was up to. And who better than her mother? My suspicions were growing because the woman I thought was my wife was acting like a familiar stranger. I just wanted to see how her mother would react when she had one of her episodes. That was why I didn't tell her. But I couldn't tell her that.

I was pulling up to the house when I saw Maggie's cab pull up.

"Okay. It's showtime." I told myself.

I hurried out of the car and walked into the house.

"Hey mom, how are you?" Laura said, greeting her mother with open arms.

"Great, I guess. I still haven't heard from your sister."

"I'm not supposed to tell you, but I spoke with Linda, and she wanted to surprise you. She's supposed to be coming out on Sunday."

Good, another witness.

"Hello ladies." I said with a Cheshire grin.

Maggie got up and gave me a hug. I looked deep into her face to see if she had noticed anything strange or different about her daughter yet. And from what I could tell, she hadn't.

"So how are you Peter?"

"I'm good. Your daughter has been keeping me busy though."

"Baby, do you want some coffee?" Laura offered.

"No baby, I have work to do, maybe later."

I walked out the door, hoping that I would hear Maggie ask, *Who are you?* and I would run in to finally expose whoever was pretending to be my wife. But it never came, and so I depended on patience.

That night at dinner, we were all sitting around the table when Maggie asked, "So, Laura, when are you and Peter going to start a family?"

We both looked at her.

"We plan to start one soon mom." said my wife.

Huh? The Laura I knew was not eager to have kids at all. She wanted to be established in her career, according to her. And now she was telling her mother that we were planning to be parents soon. Where was I when this happened?

"You mean, you guys are working on my grandchildren?"

I just smiled while Laura said, "Yes mom, we are. Aren't we baby?"

Oh my god, who was this woman?

I got up and walked into the kitchen to pour me a scotch, which over time turned into many scotches. And while I was standing there guzzling another one, I came up with an idea.

"Does anybody need anything before I start cleaning up?" Laura said, getting up to clear the table.

"Here, let me help you." said her mother.

I waited for her to leave the room so that I could talk to Maggie.

"Maggie, is there anything that distinguishes Laura from anybody else?"

"What do you mean?"

"I mean, is there something you look at that tells you that that's who she is? That beyond a shadow of a doubt, she's your daughter?"

"Yes Peter, there is. It's called her face."

"Come on, Maggie. I'm serious."

"Like what? What are you getting at Peter?"

"I don't know. Like a chipped tooth, a crooked nose, or a surgical scar. Something."

"Peter, she's your wife. You should already know what you're asking me."

"Please Maggie, can you think of anything?"

"Let's see."

I sat across the table, hanging on every facial expression she made until she said, "What about her birthmark?"

"Her birthmark? Where?"

"I don't see how you're gonna give me grandbabies when you're not even familiar with your own wife's body."

"Maggie, where is the birthmark?" I urged.

She looked at me and realized I was serious. But *she* was still confused.

"She has a birthmark behind her left ear shaped like the state of California. I can't believe you didn't know that."

"Maggie, since you've been here, have you noticed anything different about your daughter?"

"Different like what Peter? What are you getting at? What's going on?"

"Has she done or said anything around you that she just doesn't normally do?"

She sat and pondered my question.

"No, no, I can't say that she has Peter. Why would…?"

Laura walked backed in.

"Everything okay?" she asked.

I looked at her mother, praying that she wouldn't say anything.

"Let me help you finish clearing the table baby." Maggie said, getting up.

And that was my que to get up from the table and walk into the den.

"In other news, a Redondo Beach couple was found stabbed to death inside their home early this morning. Police say Janis Sorenson and Mark Wood were stabbed to death in what seemed to be some sort of personal vendetta. When asked how they came to this conclusion, the detective told me that nothing of value was missing in the house. The safe was open, and no money or jewelry were missing."

That was what I heard when I turned on the TV. I just sat there in disbelief. I couldn't believe Janis was dead! Who would murder her and why? I guess deep down inside, I knew who and why.

I turned and looked in the kitchen. But how could I prove that she did it though? If Kate wasn't dead, could she be smart enough to pull off becoming Laura?

I decided that I was too drunk for that to even be rational. But I didn't forget it. I just put it in the back of my mind.

I had been drinking, so naturally, I passed out on the couch. And when I woke up later that night, I found myself in bed with Laura tucked under my arm.

"How did I get here?" I asked, rubbing my eyes.

I eased my arm from beneath her head and got out of bed, still uneasy about who I had been sleeping with.

I walked into the bathroom and peed before I washed my hands to splash my face.

I just hoped that when I wiped it dry, Kate wouldn't be there with a knife, exacting her revenge.

I walked out and saw that Laura was still sleep. I was starting to feel like Gregory Peck in *The Omen*, when he found out who Damien really was. I left the bathroom light on so that I could see. And when I pulled her hair to the side, I saw...a birthmark.

Okay, she had the birthmark, and now I was really confused. What would make the sweet, lovable girl I had known for two years act like she did? Even worse, act like Kate. Did I really know who I was married to? Hell no was the answer to that.

The rest of the week, nothing else unusual happened. Laura's mother left convinced that I was losing my mind. And I was halfway convinced of it too. Now here we were at Janis's funeral with Laura by my side playing the dutiful wife.

"I don't see why we have to be here." She snorted.

"*We* don't have to be anywhere." I returned.

She stared at me with that I-can-kill-us-both look again before she got out of the car.

We were walking into the church when Lance and Toby walked over.

"Man, I can't believe this happened to Janis. Who would do something so horrible?"

I looked over at Laura to gauge her reaction. There was none.

"Yeah, what a shame." I said.

What could make Laura hate Janis so much? They rarely saw or talked to each other. And she never ever hinted a dislike toward Janis until that day at the beach. So why was she acting like this now?

I mean, their encounters had never been overfriendly. But I never thought Janis would be dead over that.

We got to our seats, and all through the ceremony, Laura seemed disinterested, to the point it was becoming offensive. So I got up and said, "Let's go."

I grabbed her arm and guided her to the lobby, stopping just outside the door to ask, "What is wrong with you? Did you really have to act that way?"

"What way?"

I stood there and stared at her because she knew what in the fuck I was talking about.

"OH, SO NOW I GET IT. YOU THINK MORE ABOUT HOW *THEY* FEEL ABOUT YOU THAN HOW YOU TREAT YOUR OWN WIFE. GOOD JOB, ASSHOLE!" she screamed.

"What are you talking about? I was here to show my condolences for a friend."

"A friend huh?"

"Yes, a friend!"

"Well, you and your friends can go to hell!"

She walked out and stood by the car. Where was my whiskey when I needed it?

I walked out behind her and opened her door before walking to the other side to face her hostility head-on. But oddly enough, there was none. I mean, she didn't say *anything* until we got home. And I hate to admit it, but I was thankful for that.

"Are you hungry?" she asked, walking in.

Hell no! I thought, but what I actually said was, "No, I'm okay."

I watched as she calmly walked into the kitchen. It was like she just changed instantly from hothead to her normal calm demeanor. And at that moment, I had no way to tell how she was feeling or what she was going to do. And that shit made me nervous.

She walked into the den, grabbed her laptop from the table, and walked into the bathroom, locking the door behind her.

I walked in and yelled out, "BABY, WHERE ARE YOU?"

I heard a muffled response. "In the bathroom."

This gave me the opportunity to get the drink I so desperately needed.

*****

Kate ~ I sat on the toilet scrolling through the pages of Peter's website, searching every face and person on it. His accounting manager, Aggie Simmons. The community liaison, August Harris, and even his vice president, Amy Howell. I was going to make sure that no one would ever take him from me again. And strangely enough, destroying his way of life was the way I would do just that. Just ask Janis.

*****

Peter ~ A couple of weeks had passed, and again everything seemed to be normal. But this time, I felt that it wouldn't be that way for long. So I decided that I would be the one to set it all off.

I sat down and wrote out all the things Kate didn't like, like different foods, places, and hobbies. Just things that I felt would piss her off if I pressed her on them. Then I wrote down some of the things I knew Laura liked and went to work cross-referencing the two.

I let a couple of days pass before I put my little experiment into motion. I knew it was a fucked-up thing to do—to test my wife because my suspicions made her a killer. But they were my suspicions, and I was determined to see them through.

I went downstairs and saw Laura sitting on the couch.

"What are you doing baby?" I asked.

She looked at me, and then the book, to bring my attention to it.

Vaughan? She never read Vaughan before. In fact, she told me that he was egotistical and chauvinistic and that his simplistic story lines made her nauseous. And yet here she was, seemingly intrigued with one of his most famous works. There was someone who did read Vaughan though, and that was Kate.

I ran upstairs and pulled a pad from the drawer to add "reading Vaughan" to the list.

"What was that for? All of that running upstairs and stuff."

"Oh, I just remembered something and had to write it down, that's all." I said, walking back down into the living room.

"Well, it must have been important."

"I think so. Hey, I was thinking of going down to Cap'n Jack's and getting one of those seafood buckets you always rave about."

She stopped, looked at me, and said, "Who are you talking to? You know I don't like seafood like that."

Laura did. I had to remember to write that down.

"Well, why don't we go to Sarducci's instead?" I suggested.

Okay, she was playing it close to the vest. I thought I could trip her up with the seafood thing, but clearly, she was playing her A game. But why the sudden change? Laura did like seafood, and usually, she would have jumped at the chance to go to Cap'n Jack's. This wasn't her at all. Let's see what she comes up with when we go to Sarducci's.

"That's good. It reminds me of Art's back home."

Again, when did she go to Sarducci's? Maybe for lunch, I thought.

"So you like Sarducci's, huh?"

She looked at me, annoyed at where this was probably going.

"You know I like Sarducci's, and you know I've *always* liked Sarducci's."

Really? Was *always* the three months we've been in California? At that moment, I wished I could have run upstairs to update my notes, but that would have looked too suspicious.

"What would make you think I didn't like Sarducci's?" she continued to question.

"I just never heard you talk about it like you're doing right now."

"And how is that?"

"Like it's the greatest thing ever. It's not like you grew up with it or anything."

"What do you mean by that?"

"I mean…nothing. Don't worry about it."

She closed her book, got up, and said, "I don't think I want to have lunch with you today."

I didn't know how to feel. On one hand, I didn't want to deal with her either. But on the other hand, I lost an opportunity for her to slip up again. And for me to find out who she really was. Although I had a good idea. Or did I?

She walked upstairs, and a few minutes later, she was coming back down to leave.

"Laura, I'm sorry baby." I said, trying to make amends.

She didn't say anything to me. She just put on her coat, grabbed her keys, and walked out the door.

"Where is she going?" I asked aloud.

I got up and walked to the window to watch her speed out of the driveway.

I walked to the front door and heard her phone ring before walking back over to pick it up. I ran toward the door, realizing I had no way to stop her.

*****

Kate ~ Twenty minutes later, I was in front of the house of Ivana Kosov, Peter's head programmer and marketing consultant.

I felt around my pocket for the bottle of chloroform and got out to knock on the door. When it opened, I stepped to the side.

"Hello?"

The door closed.

I knocked again.

This time, the door didn't open.

I looked around the porch and saw a newspaper. I grabbed it and threw it at the door, then knocked again.

A woman opened the door and walked out. She reached down and picked up the paper just before I pounced on her to press the chloroform-soaked rag across her face.

She backed into the house, slamming my back into the bannister to try to loosen my grip, if only momentarily. I tightened my grasp, eventually feeling her succumb and drop to the floor. I hurried to close the door, and in my haste, I forgot to see if she was alone. She had to be, right? I mean, with all the noise we made, and in the middle of the day, someone had to hear us, right? I walked around the first floor and saw that no doors or windows had been opened. Then I ran upstairs and discovered the same. I was relieved for the moment until I heard Ivana moan downstairs.

"Shit, is this real chloroform or what? People keep fucking waking up on me!"

I bounded down the stairs, simultaneously taking the bottle from my pocket to douse the rag once more.

"Phew!" I belted, sitting on the steps before I got up to drag her body into the kitchen.

I dropped her and walked over to the refrigerator to read the calendar.

"Aww, Anya, that's a pretty name."

The schedule hanging on the freezer told me just when she would be home. And that a lot of people had calendars.

"What's today's date?"

I looked at my watch, and I was surprised to find out that Anya would not be home tonight.

"Good, because she shouldn't have to come home to her mama being dead."

I walked out to the car and got the small black bag I had in the trunk before I hurried back into the house.

A couple of hours later, Ivana woke up groggy, with me still in her house staring at her.

"Who are you?"

I just sat there looking at her pathetic quivering.

"Hey, good evening. I was wondering when you were gonna wake up."

"What's all this about?" Ivana asked, trying to loosen her restraints.

"Well, you know how in chess you have the king, the queen, and the pawns, right? Well, you are the pawn in this game baby. And I hope you won't take this personal. Then again, why would you? You'll be dead soon. Forget I even said that."

"Dead, why? What did I ever do to you?"

"Baby, it's not what *you* did. It's what *I* need to do. And unfortunately, I need for you to die."

Now Ivana was really scared. She didn't want to die. What *was* I doing there? And why was I so *familiar* to her? If only slightly.

I could see my face racing through her mind while she tried to figure out where she had seen me before. Then it hit her.

"You're Peter's wife!"

I spun around and said, "Bingo! That's the answer to the twenty-five-thousand-dollar question!"

"What are you going to do with that?" she asked, looking at the knife in my hand.

"Oh, I think you know."

I walked over and straddled her, feeling her shaking between my legs. I jumped off and yelled, "DID YOU JUST PEE ON ME, YOU NASTY BITCH?"

"Please, I'm scared. I couldn't help it!"

I slapped her and said, "See, that's why men think we are sooo inferior to them. Because of timid bitches like you!"

"Please tell me what you want! I'll do anything!"

I slapped her again and said, "I want you to shut the fuck up! Can you do that?"

This was child's play, and so I decided to have a little fun. I would walk past her and thrust the tip of the blade toward her. And every time she jumped, it made me laugh.

Oh, and then I would cut her just a little bit to make her cry. But what really set her off was when I poured bleach into the cuts. That just drove her nuts.

"You see, this ain't personal honey. Sometimes we have to sacrifice ourselves for the greater good. And your sacrifice is all for my greater good."

"And what would that greater good be?" she said bravely, sniffling.

I stopped. I just wanted to stab her then and there. And actually, there was nothing stopping me. But I just needed her to understand.

"The greater good, my dear, is something you need not concern yourself with."

"Why do you have to kill me?"

"To make him understand. I need for *him* to understand."

"Make who understand what?"

"To make Peter understand who he really loves. And why he should love me!"

"Peter *does* love you! He talks about you all the time."

That statement infuriated me because I knew the woman she was talking about was not me. It was about the woman I was pretending to be. Plus, I knew that she was only stalling for time.

"Shut up! You don't know what you're talking about! If he loved me so much, he wouldn't have left me! If he *loved* me so much, I wouldn't have gotten this stupid-ass operation!"

I was all wrapped up in my emotions now, so I started to pace.

"What operation?"

I stopped and looked at her. She was trembling and barely able to control herself.

"The operation that made me look like...like this!"

She didn't see anything wrong because she had no idea what I was talking about. She was still trying to figure out why I was here terrorizing her.

"Like what? I don't know what you're talking about!"

"Like this bitch!!"

"I don't understand." She said confused.

"You know what? It doesn't matter."

I pushed the blade through Ivana's throat. She sat in the chair gagging while I combed my fingers through her hair, trying to keep her blood from it.

"We don't want to get blood into your lovely blond hair now do we? It's so soft and manageable."

She looked up at me before she died. Not with the frightened look of knowing she was dying. I think she had made peace with that. But with a look that said she felt sorry for me, as if she was sorry for the pain I was living with in my head. And in my heart. And she knew that after she was gone, I would still suffer. And through her blood, she gargled, "I forgive you." before she slouched to pass away.

"You? You forgive me? *What an arrogant fucking cow you are!* Do you actually think I need your forgiveness? You were just part of the plan, and all I needed from you was to die! So thank you very much!"

I sat on the floor next to her and said, "What the fuck does your opinion mean now? Huh, bitch? You feel sorry for me? Well, too bad nobody is here to feel sorry for you."

I started to cry because for the first time, I felt sorry—sorry that she had to die for her innocence and for the situation *I* was in, which made me feel really uncomfortable.

"Get the fuck up Kate, and straighten up bitch. You still have work to do." I ordered myself.

I wiped my nose and got up to rush out the house. But before I left, I stabbed her in the chest for good measure. Which made me feel a little better.

"When did you change?" Peter asked when I walked in.

I know he saw me when I left the house, and it was true. When I left, I had on a white blouse with gray slacks. And now I was wearing a T-shirt and sweats.

"At the gym." I offered.

My shirt was completely dry. I could tell he wanted to bring that to my attention before he decided to save that fight for another day. Good move. The look on my face must have made him think twice. So I guess he decided to follow his first mind and just keep quiet, which was fine with me because I was not in the mood for any of his bullshit right now.

CHAPTER 19

Peter ~ The next day, I went to work to see everybody crowding into Ivana's office. When I got there, Boris, her husband, was cleaning out her personal items.

"What's going on?" I asked, looking at all the sad faces.

"You haven't heard?" Tina asked, guiding me back out the office.

"Tina, what's going on? Where's Ivana, and why is Boris packing her shit?"

"Ivana's dead Peter."

My body went numb. I didn't know what to do, let alone what to say.

"Dead? How?"

"Somebody killed her yesterday. They found her tied up in her kitchen, stabbed to death."

"What the fuck is going on?" I asked, overwhelmed.

"That's exactly what I'd like to know." said the man behind me.

I turned toward the voice and said, "And who are you?"

"My name is Detective Ed Trask, Pasadena Police homicide."

"Let's talk in my office, Detective," I said before anybody could notice him.

We took the short walk, and once inside, I closed the door behind us.

"Have a seat, Detective," I offered.

"Thank you. Mr. Galvan, as you know, the death of Ivana Kosov makes it the second one of your employees' dead in under a month. Both women and both stabbed to death. Can you think of any reason why someone wanted them dead?"

I sat back in my chair and pondered his question, attempting to answer it without giving away my own thoughts. But I did have an idea of who it might have been though. But she was dead, wasn't she? Shit, this was just too overwhelming right now.

"No, Detective, I can't. I mean, they barely knew each other. So in my mind, I can't see the connection."

"Well, I can see at least one, Mr. Galvan. You see, in *my* mind, the only connection I see is *you*. Were you sleeping with either or both women Mr. Galvan?"

"What kind of a question is that?"

"A pertinent one. So could you please answer it?"

"No, of course not!"

"Of course you won't tell me? Or of course you're not going to answer the question?"

"I have never slept with either of them Detective." I said aggressively.

"Have you either heard of or seen the two women hanging out outside of work?"

"I really couldn't tell you."

"Well, what *can* you tell me?" he pressed.

"I can tell you that I've lost two very important people in my life that will be sorely missed."

The detective sat back in the chair.

"You know… I looked you up," he said.

"And I'm sure you know what I'm talking about. I'm also sure you know why both these women are dead."

"Are you fucking kidding me? You think I know who did this?"

"No, Mr. Galvan, I'm not kidding you, but I *am* watching you."

I sat in disbelief while the detective got up, dropped his card on the desk, and walked out. As slowly as he could of course.

Was I a suspect now? What happened to my life? It used to be so perfect. I had the perfect woman, the perfect job, the perfect house, and at no other time had I been the happiest than in that period of my life. Perfect. But somewhere along the line, something changed, and it had been hell ever since. And plus, I knew that Kate was possibly still out there. I also knew that she was smart as hell. But was she smart enough to have fooled the police and everyone else, including me, into thinking she was dead? Fuck, I hope not.

I had to move fast now. Whoever *was* killing people was doing it without regard, and I had to stop them before someone else got hurt. Or before I landed in jail. Because now I might be a suspect too. So that really put a fire under my ass to find out the truth.

I couldn't work because the phones had been ringing nonstop. Some of it was business, but the rest were cops and reporters grilling me about Janis and Ivana, to the point where I couldn't take it anymore.

"Tina, can you come in here please?"

She walked in and said, "Jesus Peter, you look like shit."

To which I replied, "Thank you."

"If you want to go home, I can hold down the fort until tomorrow."

"Thank you."

I got up, grabbed my keys and briefcase, and turned to Tina to say, "I really appreciate you. I'm going home to get some rest. If anybody important calls, forward them to my phone please."

"Are you sure? I don't think you should be disturbed."

"No, it's okay. I don't have anything to hide, and I don't want to leave that impression."

"Okay, you're the boss."

Again I said, "Thank you."

I was home in less than ten minutes, and the quiet of my house was a much-needed welcome.

I went into the kitchen and pulled a beer from the refrigerator before heading back into the den to turn on the television. Then my phone rang.

"Hello?"

"Hello, Mr. Galvan."

"Detective, I've already told you everything I know."

"And I understand that. I just need you to answer a couple of questions. Do you have time?"

"Do I have a choice?"

"Of course you do. You can either answer them now or later down at the station."

"So what do you need to know, Detective?" I asked, irritated.

"It says here that you were married before."

"Yes I was."

"And that was to a Kate Mulgrew, correct?"

"I'm sure you know that already, Detective, so let's stop screwing around and get down to it."

"Okay. It also says here that they found her dead. What happened?"

"Again, I'm sure you know that they found her near Bakersfield burned to death in her car."

"Yeah, I know that, but I mean, what happened between you and her? What would make a man move all the way across the country and start a new life while he was still married?"

I didn't know that Laura was already at home. When I drove up, her car was not in the driveway. And although I had not checked the garage, I had no reason to believe she would be home this early in the day. But she was, and now she was at the top of the stairs, listening.

"Hello?"

"I'm still here Detective. You wanna know the truth?"

"That would be nice."

"The truth is I was afraid."

"Afraid of what?"

"Of her. My mother and sister had just been murdered, and all the evidence pointed to my wife."

"Is that when she disappeared?"

"Yeah, or so I thought, until she killed Jose."

"And that would be Mr. Bernardo?"

"Yeah. And that's when I started to get scared. You see, she left just before I did, and I thought that moving would somehow flush her out."

"Why were you scared? And where did she go?"

"I was scared because…people were dying. People close to me. And so that's when I decided to leave, hoping that this whole thing would magically sort itself out. Plus I had no idea where *she* was, and that frightened me even more."

"Did you talk to Mr. Bernardo before he died?"

"Yes, just before I think he was killed."

"And what did you talk about?"

"Jose knew what I was trying to do, and we were discussing the next move when…"

"When what, Mr. Galvan?"

"When he saw Kate."

"And what happened after that?"

"He went after her, and I never spoke to him again. I told him not to, but he followed her anyway. And the next thing I knew was that he was dead."

"What do you mean?"

"I mean, I think Kate killed him. He rushed off the phone to follow her, and I tried to stop him. I tried to tell him…" I said, crying.

I started to sob.

Because now, after talking to the cop, the picture became even clearer to me.

*****

Kate ~ I could hardly contain myself. I killed Jose for him…*for us*. I killed everyone who stood in *our* way, and this was the gratitude I got?

Scared of me! I thought.

Well, I'll really give him something to be scared of now. Fucker.'

*****

Peter ~ *"Did you think Kate was going to hurt you?"*

"I didn't think so at the time, but I did suspect that she would hurt anyone who tried to get close to me, even if that person *was* me."

"So why do you think she killed your mother and sister?"

"Because my sister tried to warn me about her, but I didn't see it until after she was gone. And she and my mother never shared a

203

warm relationship anyway, so I think it was just convenient for Kate to get her out of the way."

"Was Kate with you when your mother died?"

"The police told me that she died between ten a.m. and four p.m. so, yeah, part of that time."

"Can you remember how long she was gone?"

"I don't know, maybe two hours, I think."

"Between?"

"Between what?"

"Between what times was she not with you?"

"I don't know, maybe between eleven and one."

"Are you sure?"

"No."

"Well then, I think that's all I have for now. Please be sure to call me if you think of anything else."

"Goodbye Detective."

I sat back and finished my beer, wondering where all of this was going when I heard a noise upstairs. I went to see what it was when I saw Laura walking down.

"Oh, baby, you scared me. When did you get home?" I asked.

"A little while ago."

"Who was that on the phone?"

"It was just business baby."

"Okay, then I'm going back upstairs and get some sleep."

She walked down and gave me a kiss before going back up to our bedroom. I didn't know if she had heard any of my conversation with the detective or not. But if she had, she knew exactly who I was talking to. And that was definitely *not* good for me.

After three more beers and a lot of thought, I fell asleep on the couch.

*****

Kate ~ "Baby?" I said, walking around to see his face.

"Are you asleep?"

His snoring told me exactly what I needed to know. So I walked back around the couch and saw that he had dropped his phone on the floor.

"Baby?" I said again softly.

I reached down and grabbed his big toe, which made him turn onto his side and snatch his foot away. That was when I reached down and picked up the phone.

I ran back upstairs, picked up my earbuds, and stuck them into the jack. Then I walked quietly back to the door to see if he was still asleep. I walked back over to the nightstand, pulled out the scotch tape, and ripped the pieces as quietly as I could so that I could place them over the face of his phone. And after a ten-piece patchwork, I was pulling it all off. And after all that I still had to go back downstairs to the kitchen to get the superglue. When I got there, I opened the junk drawer quietly, trying not to wake him up.

"There it is." I whispered.

I hurried back upstairs and ran into the bathroom to open the tube.

"Okay Axel Foley, let's see if what you said is true."

I turned on the heat lamp and held the tape up to it after generously spreading the superglue across the sticky side.

And just like magic, his fingerprints appeared.

I held it up to see the pattern, working the numbers backwards to try and crack the pass code.

I needed to know how often he was talking to the police because if he suspected me, then so did they, and I would have to start covering my tracks as soon as possible.

"8-3-9-7."

No luck.

"8-3-9-7."

Still no luck.

And then.

"8-1-7-9"

Fuck! The phone opened, and I went straight into the messages. I walked back toward the door to see if he was still sleep before I pressed last call.

"Homicide, Detective Trask speaking. Hello? Mr. Galvan, are you there?"

I hung up the phone, and when I did, it rang.

"Hello?"

"Did you just call me ma'am?"

"Oh I'm sorry Detective. I was moving my husband's phone, and I must have dialed you by mistake."

"Is this, Mrs. Galvan?"

I rolled my eyes.

"Yes."

"May I ask you a couple of questions?"

"Look, Detective, I really have to go. I have full faith in what my husband has told you, but I really…"

"Do you know, what he told me ma'am?"

There was silence.

"No, no I don't. But whatever it was, he can tell you better than me. Is there anything else Detective?"

"Yes, there is ma'am. Don't leave town because I'm going to bring you in for questioning real soon."

Click.

I walked back downstairs and tossed the phone on the floor just as Peter woke up.

"What are you doing?" he asked.

"Coming to see if you were hungry. I was about to start dinner."

He yawned and said, "Yeah, I think I can eat a little something."

I leaned over, kissed him, and said, "Good, then you'll be ready to eat when I'm done."

*****

Peter ~ Detective Trask had been a cop for eleven years and a homicide detective for the last three. He had two commendations for bravery and was an active member of the local chess club. But now he was sitting behind his desk, trying to piece together his most confusing murder mystery to date. He knew that the killer was always two moves ahead of him, or so it seemed. And although he was confident he would collar the murderer, the blatant brutality in which the kill-ings were carried out worried him.

And he hoped that nobody else would have to die like that, that was, if he had anything to do with it.

"Trask."

He didn't look up.

"Trask."

He looked up.

"I got something I think you might want to see."

He took the folder from the young detective and opened it. It was from Philadelphia, and inside was a letter.

Detective Trask,

My name is Dr. Patrick Krane, and in this letter, you will find all that you need to solve your case.

He looked inside the envelope and pulled out a picture of a young woman.

If you hadn't pulled out the picture by now, I think that you should take a look at it. That is Kate Galvan, who introduced herself to me as June. About three months ago, she kidnapped my daughter and black-mailed me to alter her appearance. I was unable to obtain a picture of my work because I feared for my daughter's safety at the time. I'm sure you can understand that. I also don't know the other wom-an's name whom she wanted to look like, but I will try to the best of my ability to describe her to you. Kate is about 5'4" or so, now with shoulder-length blond hair. The work I did for Mrs. Galvan will be evident. I sharpened her nose and filled in her lips before restructuring her chin to match the woman in the picture she provided. She also came back and asked for a cosmetic birthmark, which looked to me like the state of California, behind her left ear. I guess it's like her signature or something. I'm not really sure why she wanted that. But it should help you to identify her.

The reason I am writing this letter is because I fear for my daughter's safety now. This woman is dangerous, and I feel that in order to protect my daughter, I need to know that she is off the streets. You may be wondering how I found you. It wasn't hard. She had a California ID, and with the help of one of my friends in law enforcement, I was able to run it through the system. They belonged to a woman named June Walker from Bakersfield.

When I asked my daughter what happened while she was with this woman, she told me that she would sometimes call herself Kate. So I Googled Kate Galvan from California, and the first link that popped up was about a woman who died in an auto accident eight months ago. Her name was Kate Galvan, who just happened to look like the woman who kidnapped my daughter and forced me to change her face.

When I spoke with the Bakersfield police, they told me that she had a husband who lived in Connecticut. But when I looked him up, he was neither her husband nor living in Connecticut. And to my surprise, there he was on the national news under investigation by one Edward Raymond Trask. I think you know the rest.

I hope what I have given you would help in your investigation, and I hope you act on it quick. Because if you don't, we are all in danger. All of us!

"Well, this is interesting." the detective said, rocking back in his chair.

Tomorrow he would call the Bakersfield police to request their autopsy report to try to find the connection between June Walker and Kate Galvan. Because if Peter Galvan was not guilty of the murders, then could it be his wife? Tomorrow he would have the answers.

CHAPTER 20

Kate ~ I was furious because I knew that I couldn't trust anybody. And now that I knew Peter was possibly on to me, I needed to act fast to protect what I was trying to do. The first thing I did was look up Detective Trask to see what he looked like. Because *he* was a threat now. So I saved the image to my phone and altered my plan to include the detective.

"Some more reference material." I joked.

The next thing I had to find out was what else Peter was telling the police. I didn't know about the letter. But if I had at the time, his ass would've been dead too.

I walked downstairs and out the door.

"Baby, I'll be back I have some errands to run."

He said, "Okay," but I wondered what he would do if he *really* knew what I was up to.

I got into the car and looked at the picture of the detective again before I pulled off.

*****

Peter ~ I got up and turned on the television before I went into the kitchen to get a snack.

"I think I'll watch a movie." I told myself.

And twenty minutes later, I was ready to do just that.

With all these thoughts about Kate slash Laura running through my head, I really needed time to chill, just to take my mind off things, even if for a little while. At the time, it was impossible for me to think

210

of Kate being Laura, even though the evidence was starting to mount in that direction.

Someone knocked at the door.

I went to answer it.

"Detective, what are you doing here?"

"I have something to show you."

I was really trying to detox, so I was in no mood for Detective Trask and his cop bullshit. Plus Kate still might be somewhere still watching all this. And if she was, we would all be in danger.

"Detective, I'm really busy and…"

He looked at the bowl of popcorn I was holding, and then so did I.

"Mr. Galvan, I really think you're gonna want to see what's in this envelope."

I stepped to the side and let him in because I didn't want Kate to drive up and see him. Could you imagine that?

We both walked into the den.

"Take a seat Detective. Can I get you something to drink?"

"Yeah, a beer if you have it."

"Aren't you on duty?"

"Are you a cop?" he retorted.

I laughed at his taking exception to my question.

"I just thought cops didn't drink when they were on duty."

"A common misconception." he said, twisting the cap off the bottle.

"So what do you have to show me Detective?"

He slid the envelope across the table.

When I finished reading what was inside, I was blown away. This meant that Kate might in fact be Laura. And it took everything I had not to piss my pants.

"So what you're saying is my ex-wife *is,* my current wife?"

"It sure looks that way."

"So what do I do?"

"*You* don't do anything. You leave everything to us. Do you understand?"

"Yes." I responded.

Detective Trask had not talked to Laura yet about the murders, which gave me time to try to get her to admit who she *really* was before he did.

"Oh, and I'll need to speak with your wife too."

Shit.

"Okay Detective, I'll let her know when she gets home."

"Make sure you do."

He finished his beer and got up to leave, leaving *me* to wonder if Kate was out there killing someone right now or ducking behind a bush, watching the police leave our home.

"Detective, I believe this belongs to you."

He turned and said, "Oh no, that's your copy."

I looked at the envelope and watched him walk out of my house.

"What am I going to do with this?" I asked myself.

I got up and walked into the kitchen, about to tear it up, but then I thought about it.

I might need this.

I looked at the envelope again and put it in my pocket. I had an appointment, and I was late, so I had no time to think about it right now. I had to go.

*****

Kate ~ "Honey?" I said, walking in.

There was no answer.

"He must've left to go sign the papers for that new office complex in San Dimas." I said aloud.

I put the groceries away and walked upstairs.

"Why doesn't he just put his clothes in the hamper?"

I knew he left in a hurry because his shit was everywhere. It looked like he just threw off his clothes, showered, and left, which was what he probably did.

I picked up his shirt, shook it, and watched an envelope fall to the floor.

I opened it and sat on the edge of the bed.

"I should have killed you when I had the chance, fucker. So now I have to keep my promise, don't I?"

I dropped the rest of his clothes back on the floor and pulled my suitcase from under the bed.

*****

Peter ~ I got home close to an hour later and walked upstairs.

"Hey baby, where are you on your way to?"

"Hey honey," she said, walking over to give me the softest, most sensual kiss I had ever received.

"Margie called me and said that one of our donors wants me in Philly tomorrow."

"Why does it have to be you?"

"Because it's my nonprofit baby, and I'm the face of it. So when somebody requests to meet with me, I have to go and schmooze them."

Schmooze? I never heard her say that before? Was it a coincidence, or was I going crazy? Or was I just making mountains of molehills. Either way, just knowing Kate could be Laura caused me to think all kinds of ways. I didn't know what the hell was going on.

"Are you gonna be okay baby?" she asked.

"I don't know. How long will you be gone?" I joked.

"I don't know, a day or two I guess."

I looked at her, wondering if I could see any resemblance to Kate. There was none in looks or behavior, at least not now. I saw my shirt crumpled up next to the bed. *Fuck!* Did she find the letter?

"Can you do me a favor baby?"

"Sure." I said, trying to hide how nervous I was.

"Can you drop me off at the airport?"

"Sure. What time do you have to be there?"

"At five."

"What time is your flight?"

"At seven twenty."

"Okay."

"Can you take this down to the car please?"

I lifted the suitcase and said, "Damn, what do you have in here?"

"The usual baby. My briefs and proposals. Plus you know I need at least five outfits, complete with shoes and accessories." she said, like I was supposed to know that.

"Five outfits for two days?"

"Yes baby. Now can you take it to the car for me?"

*****

Kate ~ Friday 12:15 a.m. I was walking out of the terminal at Philly International.

"Need a cab ma'am?"

"Yes, I do. Can you take me to 15 Emerson Southwest please?"

"Sure thing." the cabby said, jumping out to open the door and load my bags. After the forty-minute ride, I was standing in front of the Hampton.

"Good morning ma'am." said the concierge.

"I have a reservation."

"Okay, do you have your credit card?"

"Yes, here you go."

While I was waiting for him to process my reservation, I turned to look out the door.

"Excuse me, what side of the building is this?"

"That's the west side ma'am."

"Do you think it will be too much trouble to get a room on this side? I really don't like the sun flooding my room in the morning."

"Well, we can pull the blinds for you ma'am."

"Can you please find me a room on the west side, please?"

He looked at the computer screen reluctantly and said, "We have a cancellation. Do you mind the second floor?"

"No, not at all, that's fine."

Really I was ecstatic about the change because it was the perfect vantage point for me to watch the entrance to the medical plaza across the park. And closer than where I was before.

"Okay, then I'll have someone take your bags up for you."

I reached into my purse and tipped the concierge before taking the key and walking to the elevator.

The next day, I sat in the window, waiting for the good doctor to leave.

"Is that it for today?" Dr. Krane asked, walking out of his office.

"Yes Doctor. Mrs. Salinger canceled, so you don't have any more appointments today."

"Okay good, then I'm leaving."

"Have a good evening Doctor. I'll see you tomorrow."

I was sitting in the window eating butter pecan ice cream, looking for the doctor when he walked out.

The sight of him made me so excited that the spoon fell out of my mouth.

"There you go, asshole."

I hopped up, grabbed the room key and my coat, and hurried out the door.

"Come on, come on." I said, looking at the illuminated numbers above.

The doors were barely open when I rushed into the compartment.

I ran out the elevator and bumped into a man who was getting on, almost knocking him over.

"Watch it bitch!"

I stopped and turned to look at him, reminding myself that I had more important things to do. So this asshole would be lucky. For now.

I rushed out the lobby, across the street, and into the park.

"Okay, there he is." I said, catching my breath.

If I was gonna keep killing people, I really had to start exercising.

The doctor thought he was safe. So he had no worries about me coming back for him. Stupid, stupid doctor.

I watched as he walked out of the small school with his daughter. I also noticed a considerable security presence.

"They did all this for me? They shouldn't have."

"How was school today baby?" the doctor asked, lifting his daughter.

"June?"

The doctor stopped, "What did you say baby?"

"I said there's June?"

He put the kid down and turned to see if I was there.

I stood as quiet as I could. And from behind the tree, I could hear the doctor tell his daughter, "Let's go."

"Daddy, why are we walking so fast?"

"Because Daddy has something to give you, and I'm anxious to show you."

"What about June?"

He stopped and turned around again, and again he saw no one.

"No one's there baby. Now let's go."

He disarmed the car alarm and rushed his daughter inside.

"Buckle up baby, because we're in a hurry."

I knew where he lived, so letting him go now was really no big deal. I just hated to waste an opportunity.

I also knew that I was up against time.

I had told Peter that I would only be gone a couple of days. So I had to kill him tonight. I turned casually to go back to the hotel and get my bag because it had just what I needed to get the job done.

Back in the room, I took a quick inventory of what I needed to kill the doctor, literally salivating at the thought.

"Good, I have everything. And now I'm going to kill that fucking liar."

I walked out the room dressed in all black and walked down to the lobby to ask the concierge to call me a cab.

After making sure he wasn't being followed, the doctor picked up the phone and dialed.

"911 emergency, how may I help you?"

"Yes, my name is Patrick Krane, and I think I'm being followed by a very dangerous woman."

"Who is this person sir?"

"Her name is Kate Galvan."

"Who is Kate Galvan sir?"

"I just told you she is a very dangerous person!"

"Well sir, I can send a car by your house. What's your address?"

"17 Clark Place."

"Okay sir, but let me advise you to just be aware of your surroundings and make sure all of your doors and windows are locked."

"Is that all you have to say?"

"Sir, I said I was sending a car, and that's all we can do for now. If you see her, call us back right away."

He hung up the phone and looked in the mirror, relieved that no one had followed them.

I had gotten to the doctor's house before he did. I paid the fare and got out, pulling my lockpick from my pocket as I walked around the house to the back door.

I stuck the tool in the lock and turned the knob.

"What's going on?"

The door didn't open, so I tried it again. I was starting to get frustrated, but then I just broke the glass with my elbow.

"That's better."

I reached in, unlocked the door, and walked in.

Soon after, the doctor pulled into his driveway, cautiously looking around.

"Come on baby."

"Daddy, are you okay?"

"Yes, baby, everything is fine. Why do you ask?"

"Because you're acting funny."

He chuckled nervously.

"Everything is fine baby. Now let's go inside."

He helped his daughter out of the car while he canvassed the neighborhood with his eyes, probably half expecting me to jump out from behind a car or something.

When he got inside, he locked the door and peeked back out before running upstairs to get his pistol.

"If this bitch wants problems, then I'll give them to her."

He loaded the handgun, then returned to attend to his daughter.

"Daddy?" she called out.

"I'm coming baby."

He hurried back down to the kitchen.

"Daddy look." she said, pointing at the broken glass.

"Baby, come here."

"What's happening Daddy?"

"Baby, come *here*," he said, slightly sterner.

He started to back into the dining room before he was stopped by the tip of my blade.

"Hello Doctor."

He froze, contemplating reaching for the gun.

"I'll take that."

I reached down and tried to free the pistol from his hand.

"I said I'll take that."

I pushed the blade further into his back, which made him squirm in pain and loosen his grip.

"Give me the fucking gun!" I ordered through clenched teeth.

"DON'T HURT MY DADDY!" Eliza screamed.

I looked around the taller man and said, "I won't hurt your daddy as long as he does what I ask. Isn't that right, Doctor?"

I pushed the blade into his back again to show him I meant business.

He dropped the gun on the floor and put his hands over his head.

I kneed him in the ass and said, "I said give *me* the goddamned gun! Not throw it on the floor! Now pick it up before I *shoot* you in the ass. I should've killed you before I left, but like my grandfather always said, common sense ain't common."

"I'm sorry. Please don't hurt me!"

"It's too late for that. Besides, how can I believe a fucking liar anyway?"

"Please, I'm sorry! I was just trying to protect my daughter!"

"How sorry were you when you put that letter in the mail? You even certified it to make sure it got there. So tell me again why I should believe your sorry ass."

"Look, I was just protecting my daughter. Wouldn't you have done the same?"

"No, you *fuck*! I would have kept my word!"

"How was I supposed to know that you wouldn't come back to kill us?"

"You're alive, aren't you?! But that won't be for long now."

"What can I do so that you won't hurt my daughter?"

"Oh, I could never hurt the kid, but you…you backstabbing douche, I'm going to cut you from your balls to your neck."

"Please don't hurt my daddy!" Eliza cried out again.

"Baby, you don't have anything to worry about. I'm just talking because I'm mad." I said, trying to keep the kid as calm as I could.

I put the knife in my pocket and replaced it with the pistol, directing everybody to sit down at the dining room table.

"Now we have a conundrum here, don't we?"

The doctor began to cry. "I'm sorry. I'm sooo sorry!"

He literally made me sick sitting there sniveling like a baby.

"*Shut up!* I don't want to hear that shit! You lied, you fuck! Now I'm here to keep my word. You told and…"

I looked over at the kid.

"Well, you know what's next." I said, walking up behind him. "You know, I think I've had a change of heart."

The doctor looked over his shoulder and asked, "What do you mean?"

"I mean I think I'll go easy on you."

"Oh, thank God!"

"Don't thank him yet. Save that for when you see him."

I reached into my pocket and pulled out the bottle of chloroform.

"Please don't hurt her!" he pleaded again.

"Hurt her? Hurt her? Now why would I hurt her? Did she make a promise she didn't keep?"

The doctor sat there, still sobbing through his tears.

I took the pistol from my pocket and said, "Get the fuck up!"

I hit him over the head with the butt of the gun and shouted, "I said get the fuck up!"

He fell to the floor, crying louder now.

"Put your hands out where I can see them!"

"Don't hurt my daddy!" Eliza yelled again.

"Baby, he won't be hurt as long as he does what I say. Do you think you can help him do that? So that he won't get hurt anymore?"

Eliza sobbed and agreed.

"Daddy, please get up and do what she says!"

I kicked him in the back.

"Did you hear what your daughter said? Get the fuck up!"

"Daddy, please get up! Please!"

He slowly climbed to his knees.

"Put your hands behind your back!" I ordered while reaching in my pocket to pull out the handcuffs.

"Please Daddy! Please, Daddy, get up!"

I put the pistol in my waistband and cuffed him.

"Now you just sit the fuck there."

I reached for the chloroform again.

"You don't have to do that!"

I looked down at Eliza with real sympathy in my eyes.

"I know baby, but me and your daddy have a lot to talk about, and we don't want you to hear it."

"She's lying baby. She's going to kill me!"

I got up and walked quickly over to him to whisper, "I was going to give you a chance to live. But now, now you've fucked that off so... I have to kill you and your daughter. I can't leave any witnesses now, can I? I can't believe you fucked it all up."

"Please don't hurt my daughter!" he pleaded, sniveling.

"Are you fucking kidding me? After what you just pulled? I *have* to kill her. I have to kill you both."

I walked back over to Eliza and screamed, "Look at me!"

The doctor straightened his back and looked over the chairs.

"Is this what you want?" I asked, putting the barrel of the gun against his daughter's head.

"No, please!" he cried out.

I pulled the hammer back.

"No!" he pleaded again.

I reached into my pocket, making sure to keep constant eye contact with him as I put the girl to sleep.

"Get up and sit in that chair, or I swear I'll shoot this little bitch in the head."

He did as I ordered immediately.

I put the gun back in my waistband so that I could lift Eliza and take her to the couch. But before I did that, I put the rag back across the girl's face again, just to make *sure* that she *would* stay asleep this time.

"Your ass ain't waking up on me again. Not tonight."

I took off my jacket and walked back over to the doctor.

"Now that the kid is asleep, we can have our own fun."

I stood in front of him and started to take off my clothes, stripping down to only my panties and bra.

"You see what you helped to create? Well, not the body of course. That was all me. But you did good on the face though. You know, sometimes I look at it, and I can't believe how good I look. And then I thought, that Dr. Krane is a real stand-up guy. And his daughter is just soooo sweet. But then I find out that you sold me out...to the *police*! So what should I do now? How can I trust you?"

I turned my back to him and bent over.

"Do you think a man can enjoy pleasure and pain at the same time Doctor?"

"Please don't hurt us."

"I asked...do you think a man can experience both pleasure and pain at the same time?"

"I... I...don't know."

I nodded repeatedly and said, "Well, there's a first time for everything, and I think we should find out."

I started to rub my body, caressing my breast before putting the tip of my finger in my mouth to rub between my legs.

I walked over seductively to the couch and picked up my jacket to pull the knife out.

"Don't worry. This won't hurt a bit."

I put the knife on the table and walked behind him.

"We don't want anybody to spoil our good time, now do we love?" I said, reaching around to place the ball gag in his mouth.

"And this will help to make sure you don't say anything you're not supposed to. Again."

I picked up the gun and hit him, sending him crashing to the floor, screaming through the gag.

"You see...? That's why I bought the gag."

I leaned over and pulled him into the bathroom.

"You're a heavy fucker, aren't you?" I grunted, helping him up.

Once in the bathroom, I ordered him to his knees and pushed him into the tub.

"Turn over!"

He did as I ordered clumsily.

I ran back into the dining room and got the knife.

"Now you just hold still because we have to get these clothes off of you."

I took the knife and began to cut the buttons from his shirt before I sliced open his tee.

"And now the fun part, the pants."

I put the knife down and unbuckled his belt before doing the same to his pants.

"Now let's get those shoes off."

I picked up the blade and cut the strings before slipping them from his feet.

"Lift your legs for me." I instructed calmly.

He had been crying the whole time, but now his eyes seemed to be extra teary, and he was starting to squirm.

"Aww, don't cry. Just help me get these pants off. Hold still for me now."

He reluctantly lifted his legs, allowing me to pull his pants down past his knees.

"Remember when I told you this wasn't going to hurt a bit? Well, I lied, this is going to hurt a whole lot. A whole fucking lot!"

He began to scream and flail. And in doing so, he hit me in the damn face with his head.

"Calm the fuck down!" I said, shoving the knife into his belly.

He screamed. And even though he was gagged, it seemed loud.

I climbed into the tub and shoved the knife further into his belly, causing him to pass out. I felt the warm thick blood gush between my legs as I began to push the sharp blade up his torso toward his chin. He woke up and started to flail wildly. And when he did, I pushed the knife further into his rib cage. His body started to convulse, which caused me to reach the edge of climax from the sight of his misery. I grunted while I wrestled with the blade that was now stuck in one of his ribs. When I released it, I felt his last gargled breaths bubble up before he passed away. He bled out fast, and the knife was becoming slippery, making it hard to grip.

"You stink!" I said as the knife cut through his intestines.

I needed stability, so I wedged my feet beneath the faucet and pushed as hard as I could to force the blade sloppily across his breast-plate. I was tired, but I had to sit up to finish the job. And after I sliced his throat, I turned around and joked, "Ooh, Doctor, I didn't know you knew how to reverse cowboy. But you *have* been bad, haven't you? So I guess this is no surprise."

I laughed as I reached between his legs and grabbed his scrotal sack.

"I don't think you'll need these. You never used them anyway."

I held up the loose skin and began to cut away his testicular pouch.

"I told you to keep your fucking half of the deal. So since you couldn't do that, I had to cut off your balls to show the world what a bitch you really are." I said with labored breath.

There was blood everywhere, but I wasn't worried about leaving any fingerprints. I had filed those off some time ago. Just another part of my plan, I guess. I walked across the floor and almost slipped twice before I heard.

"Daddy?"

What the fuck? Was the chloroform not working? Again?

"What's going on baby?" I asked through the door.

"Where's my daddy?"

"He had to leave. One of his patients called."

"I'm taking a shower. So sit there like a good girl, and I'll come out and make you something to eat. Okay?"

"Okay. Can I watch television?"

"Of course baby."

I turned on the faucet and took one of the washcloths from the towel rack to begin the cleanup. After thirty minutes or so, I came out with nothing on but a towel.

"Hey baby, I'm sorry for taking so long. I'll make you something to eat right now."

I rushed over and took the child's cuffs off before I remembered to lock the front door.

"Now don't move, and I'll be right back."

I went into the kitchen and fixed Eliza two peanut butter sandwiches and a glass of milk.

"Now sit right here and don't move."

Eliza looked up and agreed groggily.

I went back in and finished cleaning the bathroom. Everything except the tub of course, where the doctor was still lying, looking up at the ceiling with sheer terror on his face.

"You should have been a man of your word. If you had, we wouldn't be here right now."

After I was finished, I closed the curtain and turned off the lights.

"When will my daddy be home?"

"He'll be home late baby. That's why I'm here."

"What happened between you and daddy?"

I looked for the chloroform.

"We just had a disagreement, that's all. Everything is okay now. Don't worry about it. Eat your food."

"Were you arguing about me?"

"No, baby, not about you. Finish your sandwiches so we can watch a movie."

"Yay!" she rejoiced.

I was anxious to leave, but I couldn't take the child with me. How would I explain leaving for a business trip and coming back with an eight-year-old? I had to make sure that that would not be the case.

Two hours later, I was dressed and lifting Eliza to put her into bed. After tucking her in, I ran back downstairs to pack my bag. And when I was done with that, I ran back upstairs to say my final goodbye to the kid.

I opened the door and watched as she slept so peacefully. I couldn't deny it. I had feelings for the kid. But she would just get in the way if I brought her with me. So it had to be this way.

I sat at the edge of the bed and whispered, "Sorry kid. I know it was kinda fucked up what I did, but it had to be this way. I couldn't just let your father turn me in. I mean, why would I do all of this? So that some asshole could ruin it for me? And believe it or not, I do care for you…"

I paused. What in the hell was I saying? What in the hell was I doing?

And I found myself in *really* unfamiliar territory when I said, "I love you baby."

I started to tear up before I got up and turned back to look at her one last time. I wiped my eyes and ran out of the house.

I walked across the street and down three houses before I pulled out my phone to call the police.

"911 emergency."

"Yes, I live at 13 Clark Place, and I heard some disturbing noises coming from my neighbor's house down the street."

"What kind of noises?"

"It sounds like someone's in trouble. Can you please send a car right away? It's been going on for a while, and I think someone may be in danger."

"Okay ma'am, what did you say your name was?"

"I didn't."

I hung up the phone and started to walk down the street, hearing the sirens descend on the doctor's house just minutes later.

And for the first time in my life, I think I felt guilty. Not about what I did to the doctor, of course. He deserved everything he got. But about leaving the kid behind because I *really* did care for her.

"I hope you can forgive me baby. But it has to be this way." I said, trying to convince myself that what I had done was right and necessary.

I walked down the street crying. And I couldn't help but think of what might happen to the kid and what her life might be now after it had been so drastically damaged.

"Oh well, life goes on. And if *she* says anything, I'll just come back and kill her too."

CHAPTER 21

The cab pulled up to the hotel. I paid and hopped out.

"Thank you." I told the cabby.

As I walked through the lobby over to the elevator bank, I looked over, and who did I just happen to see? That same asshole who bumped me on the way out.

I wanted to go over and just stab him in the face right now, but I couldn't. I just held on tight to the knife in my pocket patiently.

I really hadn't thought about the man since he bumped into me. I was fresh off a kill and didn't mind doing it again, especially to this waste of life.

When I walked past the front desk, I tried to remain as inconspicuous as possible. I watched him walk into the bathroom and looked around before I followed him.

The lobby wasn't overly busy because it was Wednesday and almost 10:00 p.m. So this time of night was fairly quiet.

I wanted to case the lobby, so I went to the bar and ordered a drink.

I gulped half of it before leaving ten dollars for the bartender's trouble.

I wiped my mouth and got up to follow the man into the bathroom.

I really hadn't thought about killing him, but the circumstance now was just too perfect.

When I pushed the door open, I expected to see him standing there waiting for me. Instead, I heard him in one of the stalls, groaning. So I decided to wait. And after an excruciatingly nauseating twenty minutes had passed, I was ready to leave, almost letting him off the hook...almost.

I stood straight up, took a deep breath, and readied myself for the fight. It was just him and me now. And I was going to make sure he remembered me in hell.

I pulled the knife from my pocket and said, "Fuck it."

He opened the door, and I could see the unimaginable pain on his face as he felt the knife sink into his chest. He fell to this knees, trying to pull it out, before I slammed his head into the stall door and said, "Shut the fuck up, Mr. Big Shot. Look at me. Do you remember me? Well, if you don't, I think I can help you with that."

He fell to the floor, weak from his loss of blood and almost paralyzed by the pain.

"Look, I'm just here to teach you a lesson. I didn't *want* to kill you, but now...now I kinda do. I kinda *have* to now, if you think about it."

I pushed the knife deeper into his chest and looked at my watch.

"Shit, my flight leaves in a couple of hours."

I looked down at him.

"Sooo that means I can't have any fun with you. Man, I wish I could just kill you slowly. Good thing for you I have to do it fast, so you'll barely feel a thing."

I pulled the knife out, and he started to scream.

"Hey! Shut the fuck up!"

Now I *had* to gag him. I looked around and settled on a discarded cleaning rag that was left in the corner. Unfortunately, I had left my gag with the good doctor.

"You know, you really are a difficult fucker, aren't you? But I guess that's okay because after today, no one will ever have to deal with your bullshit again!"

I straddled him and pulled the knife out.

He screamed again, and I shoved the rag deeper into his mouth. Then I leaned over to whisper in his ear.

"You don't listen too well, do you? You fat bag of wind. So now I'm going to have to shut you up."

I sat back and raised the blade over my head. And with a quick snort, I plunged it into his neck and head.

"Good. Oh my god, I can't believe how good this feels."

I stood up and tried to remove the knife from his skull, trying not to get any more blood on me. I lifted his head and placed my foot on his face to help me free the weapon.

"I gotta get outta here."

I bent down and rolled up my pant legs before I put my foot across his head again. I pulled as hard as I could to release my favorite killing tool. And when it was free, it caused me to fall backwards and watch as his blood spurted out across the floor.

"What in the fuck?" I chuckled, getting up to check myself in the mirror.

There was a knock at the door.

"Who's in there?"

"Housekeeping."

"Who are you? And why are you cleaning this restroom?"

I grabbed the knife handle tight and decided then and there to kill anybody who tried to come through that door.

The man outside tried to push it open.

"DON'T COME IN HERE. THE FLOOR IS STILL WET!" I yelled. "I'LL BE OUT IN A SECOND. I JUST TRIED TO GET A JUMP ON IT WHILE WE WERE SLOW."

I squeezed the knife handle and waited for him to try me.

If he didn't believe I was housekeeping, he soon would wish he had.

"I don't know who you are. What's your name?"

I leaned against the door as he tried to push his way in again.

I looked at my watch, and even if I left now, I would still be cutting it close. I had to make a decision quick. So I decided to kill him.

He pushed on the door again and walked in.

"Hello?" he said before he discovered the dead man.

"Oh my god!" he said as the door swung close.

And when he turned to go and get help, he saw the devil standing there, holding a blood-soaked knife, ready to send him to hell for being, if nothing else, nosey.

"Who are you? And why did you do this?"

"You really wanna know?" I asked with an evil grin.

He backed up, shaking, before he slipped in the dead man's blood and fell.

"Please don't hurt me!" he begged.

"Why does everybody keep asking me that? Look I have to go. So first I have to make sure that you don't tell anyone that I was here. But before that happens, I wanted to answer your questions. First, who am I?"

I looked at his badge and said, "Well Gene, I think that you really don't need to know that. Second, why did I do this?"

I inhaled.

"Well, you're going to have to ask him." I said, pointing the knife at the dead man.

I walked toward him as began to scoot away in terror.

"Aww, don't do that. Come on now. Let's get this over with."

He tried to get up, futilely slipping in the other man's blood. There was only one way out, and I was standing in front of it. So I guess in his mind, he would make one last attempt at living. He inhaled, filling his chest with air, before he rushed at me, screaming.

I stepped toward him and said, "Would you please shut the fuck up?" before I stuck the knife deep into his gut. He fell backwards and hit his head on the sink basin, which knocked him out.

Seeing him unconscious almost changed my mind about killing him. Almost.

I walked over to him, grabbed his head, and broke his neck before I pulled out my knife and wiped it clean on his shirt.

"Phew! That was a close one." I said, talking to the dead men.

I noticed the blood beginning to pool around their bodies before I opened the door and peeked out. I cleaned up as best I could before I dashed out to make my escape.

I was covered in blood, and luckily for me, I was able to cross the lobby to the elevators virtually unseen. Once in the car, I had already made up my mind that I was going to kill anyone who got in my way. And luckily, no one did.

Less than an hour later, I was checking out, watching the police interview the staff, wondering if they would do the same to the guest. The thought made me anxious. But in just a couple of minutes, that would be something I no longer had to worry about. I would be on my way back to California, back to Peter.

*****

Peter ~ The house had been quiet while she was away, and I kinda liked it. Laura and I had been traveling a difficult road as of late. And in our particular case, I hoped that absence really *did* make the heart grow fonder.

"Baby, I'm home."

I walked downstairs to greet her.

"Hey baby, how was your trip?"

"It was good. I actually got a lot done." she boasted.

I think that she had been killing so long that she actually felt untouchable in her comfort. It was like getting away with murder in a mask you could do anything in.

"You know what I was thinking? You've been working so hard, and I think it's time you took a break. So I made reservations for Tony's."

Her eyes lit up when she hugged me and asked, "Peter, do you love me?"

I stepped back to look at her face and said, "Yes baby, you know I do."

"Good." she said seriously before kissing me.

"Let me get your bags." I offered.

"Thank you baby. I'm going to go and take a shower so that I can look and smell good for my man."

"You do that baby, and I'll take your bags upstairs and make me a drink."

I went into the kitchen after putting her bags away and fixed my usual concoction before going into the den to wait for my wife.

I sat down and turned on the television.

"In national news tonight, the police in Philadelphia are looking for the killer or killers who committed two heinous murders in the span of two days. Both in the Upper Darby section of the city. The first, Dr. Patrick Krane, was mutilated in his home while his daughter slept just upstairs..."

I damn near choked on my drink. I put it down and pulled the letter from my pocket.

"Fuck." I said, fumbling it open to read the signature at the bottom.

"Also murdered not too far away was hotel magnate Pierre Odenkirk along with a member of his maintenance personnel. They were found dead in the restroom of his flagship establishment. Both stabbed to death. Police say that the three were killed only hours apart and that security has been beefed up at all airports, train, and bus stations while the investigation is still open, saying now that they have no leads and no witnesses. If anyone has seen or heard anything, they are urged to contact the police immediately."

Was this a coincidence? Laura was just in Philly. And if she didn't kill the doctor, who did? Was I crazy? Maybe, because I basically *knew* the answers to all those questions. And I just sat there anyway like a dummy, hoping against hope that I was wrong.

I downed my drink and got up to make another one. What was I going to do now? Was I living with Kate all over again? And *why* did she kill the hotel guy?

I needed to find out what was going on. But first I had to speak with Detective Trask. I reached into my pocket and pulled out my phone to text him just as she came downstairs.

"Honey, have you seen those red pumps? The ones I wore for our wedding."

She wore all white to our wedding and reception.

"No baby, I haven't. Did you check the back of the closet?"

She snapped her fingers and ran back upstairs.

"I need to talk to you ASAP. Going to Tony's," I texted.

I pushed send and put the phone back in my pocket, just as she came back downstairs.

"You think I can I have a drink?" She laughed.

"Sure. Is wine fine?" I asked.

"Yes, white, please."

I poured her first drink, and after two more, we were on our way to Tony's.

Detective Trask was sitting at his desk when he received the text.

"Well, that's interesting." he said, finishing his coffee and grabbing his handcuffs from the desk.

"I always love to come to Tony's. It's so nice here. Remember when we came that night? We were the only two here when it was raining." she said.

What the fuck? How could she know that?

That happened with Kate years before I even met Laura. Right then, my suspicions were confirmed and on edge.

"Which night was that baby?" I asked, seeing if she would slip up again.

"You know, that night when…"

She caught herself.

"It must have been someplace else I was thinking about."

I took another drink. Things were so weird lately that drinking seemed to be my only solace. And I needed one now more than ever.

"Have you been here with somebody else?" I pressed.

"Don't be silly honey. I've only been here with you. Now."

"So why did you say that? That was something only Kate would know."

She got defensive.

"Well, I guess it was something you told me that got stuck in my head. Is that okay with you? I mean, lately that's all we've been talking about anyway, isn't it?"

I didn't remember telling her that. But I could have. So I let it go. And I didn't know why.

I took another drink and saw the detective walking toward us.

"Mr. Galvan."

"Detective."

"I don't mean to interrupt your dinner, but I needed to talk to you. Can we go somewhere in private?"

"No Detective, pull up a chair. Anything you say to me can be said in front of my wife."

I looked across the table and saw her getting jittery. Not enough to cause attention but just enough for me to know that she was bothered by his presence. She had just almost blown her cover, and now the *police* were here. I was sure it all hit her a like a ton of bricks.

"Okay, fine."

"Do you want a drink?" I asked.

"Don't mind if I do." he quipped.

"What are you drinking?"

"I'll just have a beer. I'm on duty."

I chuckled and called the server.

"Can I get a…"

"Sam Adams, thank you." the detective finished.

"So, Detective, what brings you on this side of town?"

"Well, I was going to call you. And imagine my surprise when I saw you coming in here."

I chuckled again. Thank God he was playing along because I really wanted to gauge her reaction to his questions.

"I'm sorry honey. Detective, this is my wife Ka… I mean, Laura."

Damn whiskey.

"It's a pleasure to make your acquaintance, ma'am."

"Likewise Detective." she said skeptically.

The server sat his beer on the table and asked, "Will these be separate checks?"

"No, just add whatever the detective drinks to mine. Thank you."

The detective took a small notepad from his pocket and said, "Okay sir. There are just a couple of things I need to be clear on."

"Okay shoot."

They both looked at me.

"That's just a figure of speech." I explained uncomfortably.

"I don't know if you saw the news tonight. But a doctor who recently contacted me was killed in Philly yesterday."

"Okay, what does that have to do with me Detective?"

I signaled the server for a refill.

"Well, when he contacted me, he said he knew your wife. Excuse me, I mean your ex-wife."

He pulled his copy of the letter from his jacket pocket, opened it, and gave it to me.

"Did you know she was seeing a plastic surgeon Mr. Galvan?"

"No, I had no idea. And how would I know that?"

"Well, according to this letter, he says that she came to him months ago. Did she try and contact you then?"

"That's absurd Detective. My wife's been *dead* for six months. Just ask the Bakersfield PD."

"And that's exactly what I did Mr. Galvan."

"You know what's funny? All the teeth in her mouth didn't match her DNA."

"What do you mean didn't match?"

"I mean the teeth they found on the ground near the wreck were from your wife. But the teeth in the back of the dead woman's mouth belonged to a… June Walker, who was the one, it turns out, was in your wife's car when it was found."

I saw her becoming more agitated as he continued to question me and as I continued to lie.

"What's wrong baby?" I asked, reaching for her hand.

"I have to use the restroom." she blurted as she got up.

"Okay." I said.

"Hurry back Mrs. Galvan. I have some questions for you too."

She looked down at him and left.

I made sure she was out of sight before I began.

"Detective, tell me the truth. Do you think my wife now is Kate?"

"I don't know, but we'll soon find out."

What I didn't know at the time, but kind of suspected, was that Kate didn't go to the bathroom. She walked just out of sight so that she could watch us.

"The body in the car was not your wife's. I do know that for sure. And I know the doctor was killed before I could get him to show me a picture of his finished work. Whoever is doing the killing is covering their tracks really well. We just have to catch them when they slip up."

His phone rang.

"Trask. Okay, thanks. That was the cops in Philly. It seems that all of the doctor's records and photos of your ex-wife have been destroyed."

"Are you serious? So what happens now?"

"Well, we do it the old-fashioned way. We try and get her to slip up and see if she really is your wife. Sorry, your ex-wife."

If Kate *was* pretending to be Laura, the one thing we had to figure out was what happened to Laura and if she was still alive.

Ten minutes later, she came back to the table.

"Are you okay baby?" I asked, standing up.

"Yeah, I think the fish I had for lunch disagreed with me, that's all."

"Mrs. Galvan, I noticed you just got back from Philly."

"Yes just tonight actually."

"May I ask what you were doing there?"

"Well, like my husband always says, I was schmoozing a client."

"Did it work?"

"We'll know if I get her check, won't we?"

"May I have her name, please?"

"Amanda Rothsdale Detective."

She was smarter than your average bear. She *did* go see Mrs. Rothsdale, and she *did* lobby for her support. Just before she killed the doctor.

"And where did you stay while you were in Philly?"

"Officer, is she under investigation? Because if she is, then I'd like to call my lawyer."

Why did I say that? Maybe because part of me wanted to find out on my own. And part of me still couldn't believe it. I just knew I had to play the part for now.

"No honey, it's okay," she said.

My wife leaned forward, looked the cop straight in the eye, and said, "The Hampton."

"Was there anybody there that could corroborate your where—"

"Detective, I am trying to have dinner with my husband. If you want to question me, you can do it when my lawyer is present. Otherwise, we don't have anything else to talk about."

He looked at me.

I looked at him.

He looked at her.

"Okay Mrs. Galvan. Just make sure you don't go out of town schmoozing anytime soon."

He got up and was about to walk away when she said, "Detective."

He stopped.

"Until I'm arrested or charged with a crime, I'll go anywhere I damn well please."

In hindsight, she was telling him that she was going to kill him soon because he was closer to knowing the truth than he knew. Than we *all* knew. And that was dangerous.

All the signs were pointing toward us though. And the reason I said us was because people around *us* were still dying. And I was sure from the outside it looked like we *were* the killers. But the only common denominator was me. They still hadn't found Kate. And what if they suspected *me* of doing the killing? I mean, here I was, remarried, and people were still dying. But I knew better, or at least I thought I did. Because there was *still* a chance that she had found the letter. And if she did, we were *all* in trouble.

CHAPTER 22

Kate ~ "Trask."

"Hello, Detective, it's Laura Galvan."

"Mrs. Galvan, what a surprise. What can I do for you?"

"First, I wanted to apologize to you for how I acted the other night. If Mrs. Rothsdale comes on board, it will jettison my nonprofit to national prominence. We could help even more people then. So you understand, the way I acted that night was totally due to my worrying about that. I was not in a good place. And that's why I've called you today. If you want me to, I'll answer any questions you have because right now, I really need to focus my attention on my business."

"Do you want to come down to the station? Only after contacting your lawyer of course."

Touché.

"No, I have a meeting at the Ridge. Can you meet me there around four?"

"Okay, I'll see you there."

"Perfect."

*****

Peter ~ You know by now that my head was spinning. It was like I was living with Kate and Laura at the same time. I mean, the woman I called my wife did everything my wife did, but then sometimes…sometimes she was Kate incarnate. I think deep down I knew that at that moment, both could be true. And with what Trask had told me, what I thought could have never happened could possibly be true now too. Laura just might be Kate.

And because of that, I would frequently work half days. Then go to a hotel to get some rest so that I could sleep with one eye open, as they say. I didn't know who this lady calling herself my wife was. But to find out, I had to be alive, right?

*****

Kate - The Ridge was an exclusive golf club nestled against the south side of the Angeles National Forest. And the seclusion that it provided made it the perfect spot to kill Trask.

"Detective, welcome."

"Thanks for having me Mrs. Galvan."

He sat down in the cart next to me and pulled out his notepad.

"I thought we could ride and talk. Do you mind?"

"That's fine. Do you play?" he asked.

"No, but whenever I'm here, I like to ride the course. I'm just thankful Charlie lets me do it."

"Charlie?"

"The club manager."

"Oh, okay."

I guided the cart down the hill toward the first hole, waiting for him to start the interrogation.

"So, Detective, what is it you would like to know?"

Looks like I needed to goad him a bit. I didn't have all day.

He flipped the pages in his notepad and wrote something down.

"So you said you stayed at the Hampton?"

"That's right."

"And did you happen to notice all the commotion going on? I mean, somebody did get murdered while you were there."

"You do know that people get killed in Philly all the time, right? But when I was leaving, I did see a lot of police there. But I never thought anything of it. Whatever they were there for, it didn't concern me, so I didn't worry about it. Why would I?"

"Did you see the deceased while you were there?"

"You mean the big guy? Yes, around. He would walk the lobby quite often. I really didn't think anything of it. I do remember him being rude to some of the guests though."

"Doesn't it seem funny that you were in the same hotel where someone was murdered? Considering your husband's past I mean."

"And what does that have to do with *me* Detective? There were a lot of people there. Are me and my husband going to be the suspects in every coincidental murder now?"

He looked at me like he expected me to confess all of my sins right there. But I might have been holding all the right cards. You see, I had just found out that the detective suspected Peter too. And that gave me the edge. Anything was possible now.

"Nothing, I guess. But don't you find it interesting? I mean, everywhere you guys go, death seems to follow. And now *you* go to Philadelphia, and guess what? There's a murder. There's three!" He chuckled.

"You're the detective, Detective. I trust you'll find out who's responsible, just like the fine officers in the great city of Philadelphia."

I pulled the cart just off the path to a secluded ridge that overlooked the club and parts of the city.

"I've always loved it up here. It's just a place where you can just come detox and get away from it all. You know?"

It was a lovely view, but the detective didn't look interested in that now at all.

"Ma'am, have you ever met Dr. Patrick Krane?"

"Should I have met him?"

"Well, according to the doctor, your husband's ex-wife came to him and blackmailed him into making her look like you. Do you know anything about that?"

I laughed vigorously, as if he had told the funniest joke I had ever heard.

"What is this, a movie detective? Or some kind of half-wit novel? Did I turn into the bride of Frankenstein too?"

He laughed.

"That I don't know. But you *can* say that I *am* trying to catch a monster."

"Well, for all you know, Detective, the monster may be trying to catch you too?"

"Well, what I *do* know is…there's a killer on the loose, and I'm going to bring whoever's out there doing this to justice. Monster or not."

I got out the cart and faced away from him.

"How can you be so sure?"

"Because of fact-finding, evidence, and to be honest, a little good luck. Mrs. Galvan, has anyone tried to contact you?"

"Anyone like who Detective?"

"Like Kate Galvan."

"No, Detective, Life has proceeded as usual." I said half-jokingly.

Trask got out the cart and joined me at the rail.

"Well, we have reason to believe that she might try soon. So I just suggest that you be vigilant."

I could feel him getting closer as I reached for my knife.

"If you ask me, I think that she *did* contact you, and you know *exactly* where she is."

He was standing right behind me now.

"It's cold out today. Don't you think Detective?" I said calmly.

He looked up at the sky and agreed.

"Getting back to your point now, Detective. She never had to contact me because I always knew where she was."

"Excuse me? What are you saying, Mrs. Galvan?"

"I'm saying that I can tell you exactly where Kate Galvan is."

"And where would that be?"

He stepped closer and leaned in.

"She's right here, Detective."

I turned quickly and shoved the knife into his neck, just beneath his chin and grabbed his gun.

"You see Detective? if that asshole in Philly would have kept his mouth shut, then none of this would have happened. And you probably wouldn't be here dying right now. Soooo when you die, don't be mad at me. Be mad at him."

I knelt down next to him and reached into my pocket.

"You see this? Well, this is nitroglycerine. By the time you feel it, your heart will be exploding. I just think this is the better way, neat and quiet. Don't you think?"

He looked up at me from his knees, gargling through the blood in his throat as I pushed the syringe into the bottle and pulled the plunger. I had taken to killing quite well, to the point of not caring now how I did it. Just the fact that they were dead became increasingly satisfying. You see, some killers bludgeon you for the thrill, whether it was psychological or sexual. I enjoyed it just as much as they did. But also for me, it was a means to an end. And so what I was doing had to be done, right? Well, at least in my mind. And I was gonna make sure that no one got in the way of that. *No one.*

The detective was writhing in pain and bleeding out. He knew that if he didn't try to get away, the pain would be the least of his worries.

"Oh no, where do you think you're going?"

I grabbed him and turned him faceup before I jammed the needle into his neck.

"Goodbye Detective."

The last thing he saw was me smiling at him.

*****

Peter ~ Two days later, the doorbell rang.

"Yes."

"Mr. Galvan?"

"Yes."

"I'm Detective Miriam Hernandez, Pasadena homicide."

"What can I do for you this morning Detective? Where's Trask?"

"May I come in?"

I stepped out of the way and invited her in.

"Um, can I get you some coffee or something to drink?"

"No, I'm fine. Thank you. Mr. Galvan, my friend and mentor went missing two days ago. And the last thing he said to me was that he was going to meet your wife at the Ridge."

"I don't know anything about that ma'am."

"Is she home now?"

"No."

"Do you know where she might be?"

"No, I was asleep when she left."

"Well, until we get to the bottom of this, we will consider her a person of interest."

"Is there anything else I can do for you Detective?" I said, gesturing toward the door.

"I'll be in touch." she said, walking out.

This was all too unreal. Did she really kill a cop? I didn't know what to believe now.

Did she really get to the doctor in Philly too? And was she *really* Laura or Kate in disguise? I had to find out because *now* I was resigned to the fact that Laura just might be Kate.

"Hello."

"Hey, do you know what happened to that detective you met at the Ridge a couple of days ago?"

I bet she was wondering how I knew that.

"Why would you call me and ask me something like that?"

Was she really going to make me work for it?

"Come on, Laura. The cops were just here looking for you!"

There was silence on the other end.

"Laura?"

"I'm sorry, it must have been bad reception. Honestly honey. I don't know. We met, I answered his questions, and he left."

"Do you know that they still don't know what happened to his body? He's still missing."

"And how would I know that? And if there is no body, how do they know he's dead?"

"I don't know. Anyway, they want to talk to you."

"Who wants to talk to me Peter?"

"The police, Laura!" I said impatiently.

"It seems like they couldn't wait."

"What did you say?"

"I'll call you in a bit honey. The police are here now."

"Do you want me to…"

Dial tone.

I grabbed my keys and rushed out the door, wondering what it was I was really rushing to.

This was the second time this week that my wife had been questioned by the police. And now a cop was missing. Was I rushing to protect her? I asked myself. And who in fuck was it that really needed the protection?

*****

Kate ~ "Margie, when the officers come up, send them straight in, please."

Five minutes later, Detective Hernandez and her partner, Joe Franks, were walking in.

"Good afternoon officers."

"Laura Galvan?"

"That would be me," I said, pointing to the nameplate on my desk.

"Do you mind if we ask you a couple of questions?"

"Only two?" I joked.

The cops were not amused.

"A couple of days ago, you met with Detective Trask out at the Ridge, is that correct?"

"Yes, he came to ask me questions regarding the murder of some doctor and hotel guy in Philly. Is everything okay?"

"And did he tell you why?"

"Yeah, he said that this was all part of some elaborate murder plot thought up by my husband's ex-wife to get him back. I find that quite laughable. Don't you?"

"And why would you find that laughable ma'am?" asked Detective Franks.

"Because my husband's ex-wife is dead, Detective. Do you think that she's murdering people from the grave or what? This is no dime-store detective novel. This is real life."

The two cops looked at each other. They didn't know what Trask had asked me during his interview. So to preserve the investigation, they did not offer any extra information.

"Did Detective Trask tell you where he was headed after he left you?"

"And why would he tell me that?"

"It might have come up during the course of conversation."

"Well, it did not."

Detective Hernandez walked closer to me and said, "What if we told you Kate Galvan was not dead?"

"I'd say you were crazy."

"Well, then I just might be a little crazy then."

"Why? Is Kate a little alive? Officers, what's going on here? What are you trying to tell me?"

"We'll let you know if anything else comes up." Hernandez said, handing me a card.

I sat and watched as they walked out. What was I going to do now? I just couldn't keep killing cops. Plus, I didn't know how much they knew. Any reaction now might be an overreaction. So I decided to wait them out and proceed as planned.

"Margie, I'm going home for the rest of the day. Can you reschedule my meeting with the planning commission for next Tuesday, please?"

"Sure thing. Laura, is everything okay?"

"Everything's fine. I just need to take care of some things, that's all."

One thing I knew I had to take care of was the cop's body. Peter wasn't going to be home for a while, and that gave me ample opportunity to prepare. And in less than an hour, I was leaving the house. I drove the forty-five minutes outside the city to the abandoned horse farm I had rented.

It was just after 6:00 p.m., and the sun would be setting soon, which would provide me the perfect cover of darkness.

I parked the car next to the barn, got out, and walked through a side door, past the detective and his cruiser.

"Good evening Detective. Don't worry. We're gonna have you outta there in just a sec."

I turned on the lights and walked back outside to get the shovel and lime I had in the trunk.

"I just wanted to keep this all quiet. I mean, who did it hurt?"

I looked at him, knowing the obvious answer to my question, and walked into the stall in the back of the barn to start digging his grave.

"I guess it hurt *you*, huh, Detective?" I chuckled.

I moved the hay and shit from a rear corner and started to dig.

Luckily, the dirt inside the barn was soft.

And although it was hard work, it didn't take as long as I expected.

I climbed out of the hole and walked over to the trough to splash the cool water on to my face, which made me long for the shower I would take when I got home.

But for now, I had to bury the detective.

I went to the car and opened the door to drag him to the hole.

"Come on big boy. I have to get you in the ground so that I can get home."

It's true what they say, "Dead weight *is* the heaviest."

"Shit, you didn't even feel this heavy when I killed you."

I was only a few feet away from the car and already gasping for air.

"What the fuck? You're just making it hard to fuck with me, huh?"

I took a deep breath and started again, this time making it half-way across the barn before I sat down next to him to rest.

I sat down next to him to rest.

"Now don't look at me like that. You and I both know it had to be this way. You were just getting too close, and I had to stop you before you went and fucked everything up. Look at it this way. You were killed for doing your job too well. At least take some pride in that."

I lay down next to him.

"You know, I never really noticed how cute you were. It's a shame that you're dead and I'm married because I really think we could've had something. But…"

I rubbed my fingers over the dried blood that stained his lips and said, "A damned shame."

I got up to finish the job, this time making it all the way to the hole. I was tired, and the only thing pushing me through was the life I was trying to preserve. And of course, a nice long hot bath. But first things first.

I got behind him and pushed him into the shallow grave with my feet.

I was still huffing and puffing when I went back to the car to get the two jugs of hydrofluoric acid.

I walked back and emptied both bottles over him. And before I could even cover him up good, he was already starting to decompose.

"A damn shame." I said, finishing the job so that I could get home.

*****

Peter ~ I made it home. And even though I *knew* I was there alone, I still expected Kate to jump out of some dark corner and yell, "SURPRISE, MUTHAFUCKA!"

I would lose my shit if that happened. But I couldn't run. I had to find out for myself who my wife really was. Or which one of them she really was.

What scared me the most was that I already knew the answer, I think.

CHAPTER 23

Kate ~ Over the next month or so, the cops had been watching us like hawks. And because I had not felt the need to kill, the time under surveillance actually freed me from my demon for the moment. That was not to say I wouldn't do it if I needed to. But for now, that was the last thing on my mind.

*****

Peter ~ You really had to marvel at her brilliance in hindsight. In between killing people, she still ran Laura's foundation, even winning a government grant to operate the nonprofit over the next five years. And now here she was standing in front of me, cooking dinner.

"You know the cops still think Kate's alive don't you?"

"That's what they say." she said with her back to me.

"Can you imagine if she was?" I asked.

No reaction. Not long ago, that news would have really bothered Laura. Today it didn't even seem to faze her.

"I think if she wasn't dead. She would have at least contacted you by now. Don't you think?" she offered to the conversation.

"I hope not!" I said.

I had to be careful because if this *was* Kate, I didn't want to upset her. And I think you know why.

"And why would you hope that?"

"Because she was crazy. You know that."

"The only thing I know is what you've told me Peter."

"Well, what I told you is exactly what it was."

"So why did you love her so much then?"

I didn't remember telling Laura that I loved Kate at all. In fact, I always tried my best to keep the affection for my ex at a minimum.

"I guess it was because I kinda hoped that she would turn back into the person she was when I first met her. But she never did. I guess she was just too far gone."

"What do you mean by *too far gone*?"

Laura had never been this interested in discussing Kate. I mean, sure, we would talk about her sometimes. But never like this.

"I mean, by the time I finally realized that she had a problem, it might have been too late to help her."

"What made you think she needed help? Or if she ever had a problem at all? And what made you think that *you* could help her?"

"What are you, her lawyer?" I asked.

She turned and looked at me.

"I'm just holding conversation. If you want to talk about something else, we can."

"Okay." I said.

"Okay what?"

"Let's talk about something else."

"Okay." she said, turning back around.

"What did you do with Laura?"

It was out there now, and there was no turning back.

She laughed.

"What kind of question is that?"

"A fair one."

"What do you mean? What did I do with Laura? I'm right here. Have you been drinking? I really don't understand you sometimes. What are you trying to say Peter?"

"You may be right there, but *you* certainly are not Laura."

There was a brief pause before she turned around again.

"Okay, well then, who am I?"

"Maybe you're Kate."

She laughed again in disbelief.

"Wow, she really did have you spooked, didn't she? So let me get this straight. You think that I'm Kate and that I thought up this elaborate scheme to get you back by killing your wife, *me*, and taking her place? You know what? I think you're giving yourself too much credit."

"Well…"

"Well what?"

"Is it true?"

There was more silence.

"Of course not! Do you really think I could have killed those people?"

"Kate could have."

"Not every woman you come across is crazy Peter!"

"True, but one of them was."

"Or maybe you're the crazy one!"

I nodded in agreement because she did have a valid point. Maybe it was crazy for me to think that I could save her. And maybe this *was* all in my head. The one thing I did know though, was this. There were real people dead now. And the trail, no matter how muddled, always led back to my wife Laura…or Kate or whoever the fuck she was.

"What did you do with Laura?" I asked again.

She removed the food from the flame and turned it off before coming to join me at the table.

Sitting across from me, she looked directly into my eyes. And for the first time, I saw her for who she really was. I couldn't believe it. Kate was here sitting across from me, and there was no doubt in my mind that it was her.

"How long have you known?" she asked, looking away.

"I just found out." I said.

"You know no one's gonna believe you."

"How can you be so sure?"

She leaned in like she did at the restaurant and said, "Do you see the cops knocking down the door to come and get me Peter?"

"They will when I turn you in, you sick psycho bitch!"

"Aww, now what a thing to say to your wife. I'd be very careful if I were you. You don't want to see what happens when you say too much, now do you?"

"Why? Are you going to kill me too?"

"Kill you? Naw, naw, I'm not going to kill you Peter. What sense would that make?"

"What are you going to do then?"

"Nothing, we're going to live our lives and grow old together. Or…*you* won't have a life to live. Then yes, I guess I would have to kill you then."

"Over my dead body!"

Why did I say that?

"Would you really want it that way?" she asked, smiling.

"Why did you have to hurt Laura? She was innocent."

"Innocent people get hurt every day! She…she was just collateral damage."

"And my mother and Lilly? Were they collateral too?"

"No, it was a pleasure to kill them." She smiled.

I wanted to slap the taste from her mouth. But after thinking about it for a second, I decided it better not to. No matter how I felt, Kate was still dangerous and willing to do whatever it took to have the life she wanted. With or without me. I could see that now.

"Do you remember when we got married? You promised to take care of me for better or for worse, in sickness and in health?"

She pounded her index finger on the table and said, "I intend to hold you to that!"

My mind was working overtime, trying to devise a way to get rid of this psycho once and for all. And the first step would be to call the police.

She got up and walked back over to the stove.

"If I were you, I would just sit back and be happy. I am kinda disappointed though. You didn't even appreciate all the hard work I put in just to be here. Just to be with you!"

"If you weren't so fucking crazy, the work would not have been so hard or necessary!"

"It wasn't so hard actually, but it *was* necessary."

She laughed again, but this time, it was boisterous and sinister.

"You know I can't let you get away with this, don't you?"

"Let me? Let me? You don't have the power to let me do anything, you poor excuse for a man. From this moment on, we are going to do things my way, or you won't be around to see how it all ends. Do you understand me?"

She sat back down as I got up from the table to walk out.

"Oh, Peter…"

I stopped to listen.

"If you're thinking about going to the cops, don't, because that would be a bad idea."

I walked out and jumped into my car.

Once inside, I exhaled deeply and lay back on the headrest. Then I pulled out my phone to call Detective Hernandez.

"Hey Peter." greeted the familiar voice.

"Kate, is this you?"

There was silence followed by a chuckle.

"All your calls will be forwarded to me now. Good thing, huh? Because now I see that I can't trust you."

I hung up the phone, stuck the keys in the ignition, and sped off.

I looked in my rearview mirror, talking to myself.

"That crazy bitch! If she thinks I'm going to play house with her demented ass, she has another thing coming!"

Minutes later, I was at the police station, looking for Detective Hernandez.

"May I help you sir?" asked the desk sergeant.

"Yes, I'd like to speak to Detective Hernandez, please."

"I'm afraid she's not in right now. Did you want to leave her a message?"

"No, I don't want to leave her a message. I need to talk to her!"

The cop behind the desk was not swayed in the least by my show of emotion.

"Look, I have some information about a case she's working on. Do you know when she'll be back?"

"You can come back tomorrow around eight, or…hear me out. You can leave her a message."

"I can't come back because my—"

"Your what, sir?"

"Nothing. Just tell her Peter Galvan needs to speak with her as soon as possible please."

He jotted down my name and what I said before looking at me to say, "I'll make sure she gets it."

"Please do." I said, walking out.

If Kate wanted war, then I had to be the one to give it to her. The next thing I needed to do was get another phone because I needed to find my wife, if she was still alive, before anything happened to her or anyone else.

I pulled into a nearby strip mall and went into an out-of-the-way wireless store. I put fifty dollars on a prepaid flip phone. And the first thing I did was call Detective Hernandez.

"Shit, answer the fucking phone! Detective, its Peter Galvan. Please call me back as soon as you get this!"

The one problem I did have was where I would hide the phone yet have it close enough to use when I needed it. Because if Kate found *this* phone, I would really be in a world of shit.

Before I pulled out of the parking lot, I made sure to dim the backlight and turn off the ringer. There would be no way to notify me if someone called. So I needed to keep it close, just in case Hernandez did. And then my other phone rang.

"Hello."

"Honey, where are you?"

"Wouldn't you like to know?"

"I know already. Did you have any luck with the police?"

What did she say?

"What did you say?"

"I said...did you have any luck with the police?"

"I didn't go to the police."

"Come on, honey. We both know you went to the police."

Okay, I wasn't going home tonight.

"And so what now?"

"Now? Nothing. All I want you to do is come and have dinner with your wife."

"You're not my wife! I don't know who you are!"

"I told you. I am her. Can't you accept that?"

"Come on Kate. She has nothing to do with this. If you let her go, I'll do whatever you want."

"I want you to come home. Can you do that?"

"Okay." I said reluctantly.

If there was a chance Laura was alive, I had to do everything in my power to ensure she stayed that way, and so... I went home... reluctantly.

"Okay, I'll just find out where Laura is, tell Hernandez, and be out of there" was what I told myself.

I put the phone in my pocket and drove home.

"Hey honey, I'll be done in a second. Why don't you make yourself a drink."

Just what I needed. I walked to the bar and poured a shot of scotch, and after the third one, I decided to get down to business.

I walked into the kitchen and got straight to it.

"Kate, where's Laura?"

"Sit down so you can eat. I'm almost finished."

"I don't want to sit down! And I don't want to eat!"

She stopped what she was doing and turned around.

"What do you want Peter? What's on your mind?"

"I want to know where Laura is!"

"Calm down. She's not going anywhere."

"Kate..."

"Shut the fuck up Peter! When you give me what I want, then I'll give you what you want. Now sit...the fuck *down*!"

She slammed her palms on the table before serving me.

"Well, go ahead. If I wanted to kill you, I wouldn't do it as boringly as poisoning you. Believe me, I'd have some fun first. Besides, how could I kill the only man I ever loved? Now eat."

I looked down at the plate and picked up my fork.

"That's better." she said, turning back around.

I can't lie, the food was good, and I had forgotten just how good she could cook. And with every forkful I took, surprisingly, the hungrier I got.

After a while, she joined me at the table.

"How is it?"

"Good." I said, stuffing my mouth with pasta.

"Well, enjoy because I made it especially for you."

I took a drink of whiskey and started to feel its effect, coupled with the shots I had downed earlier. It almost made me forget what I was really there for.

I *was* hungry, and I knew I had to keep Kate calm to find out where Laura was. So I continued to eat and act as normal as I could.

"I'm serious Kate. I need to know where Laura is. She has nothing to do with this." I said, finishing my drink.

"Why? Is it because you told the police you would get it out of me? And of course she does Peter. She has everything to do with it."

"I didn't tell the police anything."

"Sure you didn't. You must think I look stupid too, huh?"

I looked at her and picked up my glass.

"Can I get you a refill?"

She put her fork down and obliged.

"Why did you do all of this Kate? Did you really have to kill all of those people?"

"What do you mean? *Why* did I do this? I did this for you, for *us!*"

"What do you mean? You didn't do this for me! Do you think I wanted this? Do you think I wanted you to murder all those people, including my mother and sister?"

"A simple means to an end baby." she said, calmly sitting the glass on the table.

"The end of what?"

"Of whatever it is you think I've done."

"I know what you've done!"

"And is that what you told the cops?"

"Like I said, I didn't tell the cops anything. All I want to know is what you did with Laura."

"She's okay." she said, putting another forkful of pasta in her mouth.

"I don't know that."

She slammed the fork back on to the plate and said, "You know it because I told you so, you jag-off!"

She picked up her fork and started to eat again.

"I don't understand why you're so infatuated with her."

"It's not infatuation. I love her."

I saw the disgust in her eyes grow exponentially.

"You love her?"

Suddenly, I felt as though I had made a colossal mistake. But it was too late to turn back now.

"Yes, that's what I said. She's my wife."

"I'm your wife! I was your wife first, and I'll always be your fucking wife! Don't you forget that!"

"Do you think I want my wife killing anybody and everybody she sees fit?"

"Well, isn't that the *only* way?" She chuckled before starting to eat again.

"No, it's not! That's just crazy Kate!"

She stopped eating and looked at me long and hard.

"Well, then that's the way it is! And you can't change it!"

"You can't keep Laura hidden forever."

"Who says? You?"

"Sooner or later, you're gonna get caught Kate."

She looked over at the front door again.

"That's funny…still no cops."

Her sarcasm upset me to the point that I almost couldn't stand it anymore.

"What are you going to do Peter? Have you grown a pair since we've been sitting here?"

I wanted to lunge across the table and choke her ass to death. But I just couldn't take the chance of endangering Laura because I needed to know where she was.

"Just take me to my wife, please."

"Your wife is right here! After we eat, I'll tell you what happened to the substitute."

Substitute? Where did she get that from?

She laughed to herself and said, "I can't believe this shit."

"What can't you believe?"

"I said I can't believe you loved that skank."

"She's not a skank. And what do you mean by *loved*?"

She looked at me again and smiled.

"Okay…she's not a skank. She's a bitch!"

I got up, walked away from the table, and went back over to the bar to pour myself another drink.

"You know the reason I left in the first place is because I knew you were crazy."

She laughed out loud and said, "The reason you left is because you are a pussy. Simple as that. You're scared of me, and I know that now. And now I'm having second thoughts about what I did. I loved you, and you left me. I found you, and you treat me like trash? How am I supposed to act Peter? That *is* kind of funny though. You… scared of me. You've changed Peter. And not for the better."

That was true. But who wouldn't be scared of her crazy ass? Considering what she had done up to that point, I thought my reaction was totally warranted.

"I'm not scared of you!" I bluffed.

She laughed again and got up to clear the table.

I took another drink for courage because this was just too unbelievable.

"I should…"

She walked out of the kitchen with a knife in her hand.

"You should what? You pussy. What are you going to do? Be buried next to your substitute whore! That's what!"

"She's not a whore! She's my wife! Something you could never be again!"

"Sure I can." she said, waving the knife while smirking down at me.

I took another drink and immediately became braver.

"Just hurry up and take me to Laura!"

"Or what? What are you going to do?" she asked, wielding the blade through the air.

Seeing the way she waved the knife made me think better about challenging her further for now. So I stayed quiet and took another drink.

"That's what I thought, you fucking punk. Maybe I should have had the good doctor sew some balls on me. At least we'd have a pair between us."

She walked back in the kitchen and slammed the knife into the sink.

"Okay, I'll take you to the substitute. Are you ready?"

I stood there with the drink in my hand.

"HURRY UP AND FINISH SO WE CAN GO THEN!" she shouted.

I guzzled the last of what was in my glass and followed her out the door.

CHAPTER 24

Peter ~ All I could think about in the car was that she kept calling me a pussy. A pussy, really? I had no doubt I could beat her ass, but I was raised better than that. But still…a pussy? Who says that? And if being afraid of a psychopath made me a pussy, then so be it.

I really had no idea why that bothered me so much, but it did. Look, I might have been bigger and stronger than Kate, but let's face it. You had to give her kudos for planning and execution, something I could never do as well as she did. That was what made her so dangerous. And *that* was a good enough reason for me to be afraid and extremely cautious.

"Where are we going?"

"You wanted me to take you to her, and that's where we're going."

"And where would that be?"

"Where we're going." she said with deadpan sarcasm.

I saw then that I would have to wait and see where she was taking me.

"I just hope you didn't hurt Laura."

She looked at me and laughed.

"You suddenly have a great sense of humor, don't you?" I said.

"Well, you're a funny guy."

I wanted to reach into my pocket and call Hernandez then and there. I didn't care if she knew about the phone or not at that point because her ass would be in jail soon. But that would have to wait. I also didn't want to jeopardize Laura to hurt Kate. I just had to bide my time before I could turn *that* part into fruition.

Now I really wanted her dead. I know, I know. But after tonight, my mind and way of thinking were clear. I stared out the window and wondered, *Who will I buy a present for on Mother's Day? Or... What will I get my sister for Christmas?* Plus, who knew what she had done to Laura. Case closed. It all made sense to me now, and I wasn't going to make any more excuses for her in the name of love. Or for me. I knew who she was now. And after this was all over, I was going to make sure that she wouldn't hurt anybody again.

And although we hadn't spoken a word to each other in almost a half hour, it didn't seem awkward. It seemed...familiar. In a sense because I knew she really didn't want to hurt me, so that made me feel safe. I don't know. But what I did know was that during that time in the car, oddly, there was no tension between us.

We pulled into a secluded area just north of Sylmar.

"Where are we?"

"We're where you want to be baby." she said, reaching over to squeeze my thigh.

I grabbed her hand and squeezed it until I saw the pain in her face before I threw it back at her.

"Keep your fucking hands off me!" I demanded.

She nodded and smiled before mouthing to herself.

"For now."

"Excuse me?"

She looked at me, smiled, and said, "Funny guy."

I followed her out of the car and into what was soon to be a dilapidated barn.

Why was Trask's car here? She *did* kill him. Goddamn!

"Kate, where's Laura?"

"She's here. Calm down."

She walked into one of the stalls and picked up a pitchfork.

"Kate, what in the hell are you doing? And where's Trask?"

She stuck the fork deep into a pile of hay, and after two times, she stopped and said, "This is hard work. You do it."

I looked down at the pile and saw the makeshift grave.

"Laura!"

I ran into the stable and dove to claw away the loose dirt.

259

"Here you go."

She threw a shovel on the ground next to me.

"Dig her up." She scoffed.

I stood up and faced Kate with balled-up fists.

"Anytime you want to jump, here I am, little froggy." she warned, pointing the pitchfork at me.

"You are a cold and heartless bitch!"

She agreed with a cold wry smile.

In the next instant, something changed, and I saw something else in her eyes that I had never seen before: disdain for me, almost as if she felt sorry for me and was wondering how she had ever let herself fall so deeply in love with me.

"I loved your motherfucking ass! And now all you can do is whine and cry over *this* bitch! *This bitch!*"

"She was more of a woman than you could ever be."

"Oh yeah, I can see that." she said, smirking at the shallow grave.

"What was all this for Kate? I mean, all the killing, the surgery? What was it all for? It couldn't have been for love, I know that."

"IT WAS FOR *YOU*, ASSHOLE! HOW MANY TIMES DO I HAVE TO TELL YOU THAT?" she screamed with tears in her eyes.

She walked toward me with the pitchfork.

"What are you going to do with that?"

"I'm going to reunite you with your wife. Don't you want that? I mean, you've been whining for this bitch all night. This is the least I could do."

"Now Kate, don't do anything stupid."

"Stupid? Well, it looks like it's too late for that now, huh Peter?"

I put my hands out and backed away, trying to keep her as calm as I could.

"Kate, calm down! Think about what you're doing!"

"Calm down?"

The anger in her face grew into a twisted mask.

"All I ever tried to do is love you Peter! And this is what I get in return? You crying over this bitch and me crying over you? And now you want me to calm down?"

"Kate, calm down. You're in enough trouble as it is."

She laughed through her tears.

"Me? In trouble? No, no Peter. It seems to me like you're the one in trouble."

She stepped closer with the pitchfork to corner me.

"If you want to be with her, then this will be the day you're with her forever!"

She took the pitchfork and thrust it at me, missing by only inches. I grabbed the handle and tried to snatch it from her.

"Let it go!" she demanded.

I backhanded her, sending her flailing into the gate. And I have to say it felt good. *Real* good.

She tasted the blood from her lips and said, "That's good. That's good. Is that all you've got?"

She charged at me again, yelling, sending us both tumbling to the ground.

She was quicker than I expected. And in what seemed like less than a second, she was back on her feet, kicking me in the stomach and reaching for the shovel.

I rolled over on to my back and saw the shovel's spade coming toward my head.

"Kate!" I pleaded, moving out the way.

"It's too late baby! I'm so sorry it has to be done this way." she said, sobbing.

She hit me again, and I felt the horrible pain that shot through my arms as I tried to protect myself.

She started to cry more now.

"I'm sorry baby, but because you don't love me, it has to be this way. I'll make sure and tell the police you died trying to kill me because I found out about your little murder spree."

I rolled over on to my knees and tried to get up before she kicked me in the ribs. When I collapsed in pain, she came and knelt beside me.

"The best thing you can do is stay down, and this will be over real quick baby. I promise."

I lay on my side, gasping for air, waiting to see how she would actually kill me. But then I decided to plead and fight for my life.

"Don't kill me Kate. The cops will never believe you." I whispered through the pain.

"You know, I thought I could live with you and make you happy. But today I saw that that could never be. And so rather than live in pain, it has to be this way. Don't you understand?"

She hesitated for a moment, as if she were thinking of what life would be like in a perfect world, giving me the opportunity to reach out and grab her legs to make her fall backwards.

I got up and pounced on her, trying to dislodge the shovel from her hands, before she kicked me in the nuts.

I rolled off her as she got up, gripped the shovel, and hit me across the back, causing me to wail in tremendous pain.

"Please, Kate, don't do this!"

"I'm sorry baby, but I have to. I just want you to be happy. If it can't be with me, then…"

I put my hand up and pleaded.

"Wait! Wait. We *can* be happy again."

She lowered the shovel and asked, "Oh yeah? How would that happen? You've already proven to me how much you loved the substitute. So how can *we* be happy again?"

"I could… I do love you! And now that I know you're alive, we can start over!"

And just for a second, she believed me.

"No, it'll never work." she said, shaking her head.

She lifted the shovel again and hit me across the back of my neck and shoulders.

I had to get out of there, so I rose to my knees and tried to crawl away.

"Oh no, I can't have you disappearing on me again. Once was enough." She giggled.

She jumped in front me to block the gate, then she kicked me in the face.

"Kate, please don't do this. We can make it work! We can, baby!"

"Do what Peter? I didn't do anything. *You* did this! Was it me who left? I don't think so! Was it me who killed the detective? I don't think so. Was it me who killed your wife when she found out you were a murderous cocksucker? Nope, it was you. Or at least that's how I'll make it look. Do you think you can just come in here and tell me anything, and I'll just magically fall into your arms and forget everything that you've done? Are we just supposed to spend our lives happily ever after now, Peter? I don't think so."

"I didn't kill anybody! I left because *you* started killing people! Can't you see that?"

"Only because I wanted you to myself! But your selfish ass couldn't see that, could you?"

Selfish? Was she for real? Did she really just say that?

"I see it now." I said, gasping for breath.

"I bet you do Peter, but now it's too late. I mean, with you going to the police and all. It just won't work."

"It's not too late Kate. We can make it work. I promise I'll do whatever it takes to make you happy."

She turned her back to me and began to mumble to herself.

"Yeah, but will you love *me*, or is it her you love? I think we both know the answer to that, don't we? Especially since I look like the bitch now!"

Kate was conflicted. She couldn't discern the truth from a lie, and this gave me the window I needed to get up and call Hernandez.

She walked toward the barn door while I used the gate to lift myself.

"Kate, we can make this work baby. I never stopped loving you."

Why did I say that? She turned around furiously and said, "Is that why you went to the police? Because you love me? You fucking think I'm dumb, don't you Peter? First, you lied to me about the police. Then you lied about loving me. And now you're lying to save your life. You're pathetic, you piece of shit!"

I reached into my pocket and pulled out the prepaid phone and flipped it open to call Hernandez. I needed her help, and I realized that now.

"What's that in your hand?"

"Nothing." I said, slipping it back into my pocket.

She threw the shovel at me. I dove out the way, and before I knew it, she was on top of me, scratching at my face.

"Kate, stop it!" I demanded.

She was out of control at this point. And I came to the realization that I had to kill her to stop the nightmare.

"Give me the phone Peter!"

I rolled over on my side to try to make it more difficult for her to reach into my pocket. I got to my knees and tried to stand up.

"Give me the phone Peter!" she demanded again.

I pushed her up against the stable gate, which caused her to loosen her grip just slightly, before I pushed her back against it again. She fell to the floor, and I jumped just out of reach. Now it was my turn to kick her in the face. And I did. And it felt good.

She looked up at me and smiled again, tasting her own blood.

"YOUR CRAZY ASS IS GOING TO JAIL!" I screamed.

I pulled the phone from my pocket and called Hernandez.

"Peter, where are you?"

"I'm here with Kate, and you need to get here right away!"

"Where's here Peter?"

"I don't know. We're at some abandoned horse farm just outside—"

Before I could tell her where we were, Kate bit me in the leg.

"Oooouuuuuucccchhhh!"

"Peter, what's going on?"

I reached down and tried to push her head away, which caused her to bite me even harder.

"Stop, you fucking psycho!"

"Peter!"

I kicked her in the face again, which worked only for a second before she was back at it, trying to bite me.

"Hernandez, just get here!" I yelled into the phone.

I sat up and tried to kick her away, not realizing that she was reaching for the knife she had in her pocket.

She stabbed me in the leg, which caused me to drop the phone and reach for the knife. And no sooner than it hit the floor, she pounced on it.

"Peter! Peter!" Hernandez shouted into the phone.

Kate stood up and put the phone to her ear and said, "Who is this?"

"This is Detective Hernandez with..."

"Yeah, yeah, save your spiel for somebody who gives a fuck."

She hung up the phone and backed away from me.

"Was that the cavalry Peter? Here, let me help you with that."

She reached over and ripped the blade from my leg as I fell back in pain.

I still couldn't believe this was happening. I just knew I had to kill Kate before she killed me or anyone else. It *had* to end here today.

I grabbed my leg and looked around for the pitchfork.

"So you didn't go to the police huh? Then who the fuck was that on the phone Peter?"

She started to pace and cry again. She was really hurt, and until now, I had no idea of just how deep she loved me. You see, she didn't see that what she was doing was crazy. Because to her it wasn't. To her, everything she did deserved praise, not ridicule. And because of that, the emotional wound became massive. And at this point, it was too far gone to heal.

"I can't *believe* I loved you!" she cried out.

She ran back over and returned the favor of kicking me in the head.

"What else should I have done?" I said, rolling over to groan.

"*Be a man!* Have you tried that lately? God, I can't believe this shit!"

"Are you fucking crazy? You killed my family! Fuck you!" I said in defiance.

"*I was your family, Peter! I was...*your family."

"Oh my god, you are fucking crazy! Do you think I would ever forgive you for killing my mother and sister? And what about Jose? You wanted me to love you, but you took...you took everything that I loved. *Everything!*"

"They didn't want us to be together, and you knew that. You just laid back and let them treat me any way they wanted. That was as much your fault as it was theirs. So *fuck* them. They had to go. And now so do you. So fuck you too!"

I struggled to get to my feet. And I leaned against the gate to nurse my leg.

"So that gave you the right to kill them?"

"No. What gave me the right to kill them was the way you acted. The way you let them walk all over me. I was your wife, Peter!"

"So you're blaming all this on me?"

"Yeah, it seems that way." she said, nodding.

She was fucking crazy.

She looked down at the phone.

"And this betrayal? What about this Peter?"

"Betrayal?"

"Yes, Peter, betrayal! How stupid do you think I am? I knew you went to the police that night you left the house. And now you're calling them to save your life? You horrible waste of breath!"

I couldn't believe what I was hearing. But I guess I just had to hear it for myself to make it plausible in my mind.

"How do you think I betrayed you Kate?!"

"I was gone for what? Three months? And you're already out here making a life? *My life*, with another bitch?"

"After you killed my mother, my sister, and Jose, what was I supposed to do? Love you?"

Even though I still did.

"Tomato, tomato. It doesn't really matter now, does it? And now we just have to move forward with our lives, don't we?"

I propped myself up to try to gain my balance.

I looked around the barn for anything I could get my hands on to get this over with.

"It's a shame Peter, because I don't know what I'm going to do without you. My jealous husband," she quipped.

"It doesn't have to be this way, Kate. Please! We can work this out."

"Oh, but it does baby. It does. You see, you followed me here because you thought I was having an affair with the detective. And once your fears were realized, you just couldn't take it. So you killed him and tried to kill me. But I got you first."

She flipped the blade around and pointed it toward me.

"You're the missing link." she said.

I was confused.

"Missing link? What are you talking about?"

"You're the only one who knows what I've done and who I am. So to preserve my secret, I have to kill you. You killed Trask in a fit of rage, and I killed you to protect myself. So you see, *my* secret has to die with you."

I limped from the gate to brace for the attack.

"And where do you think you're going?" she said, blocking the way.

"This has to end Kate. Right here and right now! You can still stop this."

"That's precisely how I feel Peter. And I will stop this. Just as soon as you're dead."

She stepped toward me and felt the phone vibrate in her pocket. She took it out and looked at it.

"This bitch again?" she said, throwing the phone on the ground and stepping on it.

"Now there will be no more interruptions. Besides, I need to get up early tomorrow, so we'll need to hurry this up."

I hobbled back to the gate before I heard it: the whirling blades of a helicopter.

"You just stand right there, and don't you fucking move!" she ordered.

She ran to the door and peeked out, seemingly turning snow white when she looked up.

She closed the door and looked back toward me.

"The cavalry's here!" She laughed.

She waited until the helicopter flew into the distance before she closed the door and charged me.

She knew the police were close, and so she had to try to kill me before they got there, if they got there at all.

I dove toward the pitchfork, and she dove on top of me.

"Oh no you don't!"

I pulled myself closer to the pitchfork using all the strength I had to reach it. I felt my fingertips dance around the handle while she pulled my hair damn near from my skull.

She sat up and straddled my back as I turned over to catch her wrist, just in time to stop her from stabbing me again.

She leaned in and said, "*Peter*, just let me fucking kill you already! Come on! Just do this for me."

I moved her arm and threw her off me. But apparently not far enough because before I could catch my breath, she was back on top of me, screaming and trying to stab me in the face.

I reached up and grabbed both of her arms, trying to restrain her and loosen her grip on the knife.

"Let me go!" she demanded.

I thrust my hips into the air, attempting to throw her off me again. And after a couple of times, success came.

I rolled over, jumped up, and heard the helicopter again.

"HELP, I'M IN HERE!" I screamed.

I looked up toward the roof, ready to scream again, before I was hit in the head with the shovel.

Fuck!

I lay on the floor trying to stay conscious because I knew that if I passed out, I would never wake up.

I tried to crawl back to my knees before I was hit across the back again.

She started to cry before she said, "I'm going to miss you baby."

She went over to pick up the pitchfork. I rolled over to try to knock her off-balance before I got to my feet, and we squared off again. Before the helicopter flew back into the distance, I had to get their attention. So now it was my turn to be the aggressor.

I limped toward her as she backed away cautiously with the knife in her hand, preparing for *my* attack.

"That's it. Don't be a pussy anymore." she said, urging me on.

There was that word again. Did I really need to prove to her that I was no pussy?

At that point, I think I did. So I hit her in the nose. Not too hard but hard enough to let her know I meant business.

She wiped the blood from her face and laughed.

"Wow, is that all you got? I knew you were a pussy, but wow."

"I don't want to hurt you Kate."

"And I don't want to hurt you either. I just want to kill you Peter. So why won't you cooperate?"

I hit her again, this time knocking her to the ground.

She got up and screamed before she charged me again.

I stepped to the side, trying my best to stay away from the blade, before I hit her again. She didn't fall this time. Instead, she became even more ferocious, swinging the knife only inches from my face before slicing me across the forearm several times in the process.

I grabbed her arms again, and she kicked me in the nuts again. And I fell backwards into the stable...again.

"You hear that?" she asked.

We both listened.

"Nobody's coming for you Peter. Don't you see that now?"

She secured her grip on the knife and attacked me again. I put my feet up to fend her off so that I could get back up. Then I kicked her and watched her fall backwards into the watering trough.

I hurried over to her and said, "It's over Kate. It all ends here today."

She sat up, trying to get out of the trough, fighting the water to breathe.

"Nothing's over until I say it is!" she belted, spitting out water.

Before I could get to her, she was out and on her feet again, just in time for me to punch her in the face.

She fell back into the water and splashed around, trying to get out before I could hobble over to pick up the pitchfork.

"What are you going to do with that?" She chuckled and gasped as she wiped water from her eyes.

"Something I should have done a long time ago."

I limped toward her. This time, there was nowhere for her to go. And no hesitation from me.

I stuck the fork into her stomach, and she began to flail and fight. So I leaned on the handle using all my weight to hold her under. And after a short struggle, there was silence and stillness.

And when I saw her final breath expel as bubbles, I let go and fell to the ground to cry.

I had never killed anyone before, especially not someone I once claimed to love. This was all new to me. So I had to gather myself because I still had to bury her and find Laura.

I went to pick up the phone to call Hernandez. And just as I was about to push the button, Kate sprang from the water and wrapped a bridle around my neck.

"You see Peter, I'm not going anywhere! We'll be together forever! In this life or the next! You will be mine!"

I reached back and tried to stop her from pulling me under. But she had already tightened her grip. She pulled up on the bridle as I tried to wedge my fingers between it and my neck so that I could breathe.

"Just fucking die already Peter. Shit!" she grunted.

I could feel myself losing consciousness with every second that passed. And I began to black out when I dropped the phone. Water was starting to fill my mouth, and I could feel myself starting to choke.

She pushed me to the side and hopped out of the trough to try to get to the phone, which allowed me to catch my breath.

"Kate, no!" I pleaded before she dropped it in the water.

I dropped my head and inhaled deeply to try to fill my lungs as quickly as possible with lifesaving oxygen.

"This has to be handled between me and you Peter. No one else. This has to be settled in-house."

She wiped her hair from her face and looked around for the knife.

"You see Peter, it's time for me to start a new life. Just imagine me as the grieving widow, wondering what happened to my hubby. Why did he go so crazy and try to kill me? Never mind the poor detective over there. See Peter, you're a jealous abuser, and you tried to bury me in that grave over there. And there's the detective whom you killed and tried to bury with me. So by the time they find out what happened here, I'll be starting my new life. While you and the detective rot away together up here. Think about it Peter. Everybody gets what they want. I get to be happy, and you get to be with Laura…forever in hell! We both get a second chance. Isn't that wonderful?"

She grabbed her stomach and pressed her blood-soaked shirt against it. I knew she was hurt. So I began to walk toward her to act on my advantage.

"That's it. Come on over here." she said, backing away to look for something to protect herself with. And right now, the wound in my leg didn't hurt so much.

I reached into the water and pulled out the pitchfork while she stood there, trying to stop the bleeding.

Clearly, she thought she had the advantage because she really could have killed me anytime she wanted. I definitely gave her plenty of opportunities. But now I was determined to get out of here alive. So I decided to play my wild card, which was my own personal advantage.

I pleaded with her again.

"Just come back with me, and we'll explain all this to the police. Maybe they will say you're unfit to stand trial and give you a lighter sentence."

Her face contorted to hatred again. And suddenly, her stomach didn't seem to hurt so much.

"So you think I'm crazy?" she asked, standing straight up.

"No, I don't, but if the judge does—"

"*Judge?* What judge? I'm not going to see any fucking judge!"

"Kate, it's the only way. I'm trying to save your life!"

"Save my life? Really? By locking me up in some nuthouse for the rest of it? I'd rather be dead! Which is how one of us is leaving this barn today Peter!"

"Please Kate, I won't say anything, I promise!"

"Like you promised when you told me you hadn't talked to the cops?"

"I was scared Kate! What was I supposed to do?"

She shook her head in agreement. But the look on her face was that of disbelief.

"You see Peter, the only way two people can really keep a secret—I mean *really* keep a secret—is if one of them is dead. And since you have a penchant for squealing like a pig, I'm going to slaughter you like one."

She pulled another knife from behind her. Where did she get that from?

"Kate, stay back." I ordered as calmly as I could.

"Peter, make up your fucking mind! Do you want me to come with you or not?"

She had a point.

"Okay, drop the knife then." I said.

When I saw it hit the ground, I told her to get in front of me and walk toward the door. Just before she reached it, she turned around and tried to stab me again.

What the fuck? Where did she get *another* knife from?

She grabbed the end of the pitchfork and thrust the blade toward me while I wrestled to loosen her grip on the handle.

"I'M NOT GOING BACK WITH YOU! I'LL DIE FIRST!" she screamed.

"Okay, then so be it." I said.

With a quick jerking motion, I pulled back and pushed the handle into her stomach, this time driving her out of the stall onto her back.

I leaned in again before I turned the fork and tried to push it clear through to her spine. I watched her cough up blood in agony as she lay there, smiling up at me.

I started to cry again.

"I loved you Kate. Why did you make me do this? Why did you kill Laura?"

Smiling through bloodstained teeth, she almost looked like she wanted it this way, as if she actually preferred being killed by me.

Tears flooded my eyes as I lifted the handle to push the fork deeper into her stomach.

She cringed in pain, holding the handle, as her blood began to pour out in the dirt. I tried to remove the fork, but she just held on.

How did this all go wrong? I mean, we were in love once, weren't we? And now here I was trying to kill her. The woman who killed my mother and sister, and yep, you guessed it...*my wife*. And as she lay there dying, memories of her and I in better times flooded my mind. We were truly different back then, and I missed *that* Kate. Sincerely.

Because whoever *this* woman was dying in front of me was not the woman I fell in love with. This woman was a purely sadistic animal who had no remorse for anybody. And she was someone I could never ever love again.

She inhaled deeply and started to choke again, spewing blood into the cold air. And after she took what I thought was her last breath, I pulled the pitchfork out and started toward the stall to look for Laura.

I was relieved and thought that my nightmare had ended until I heard, "Going somewhere pussy?" She coughed.

I turned around, astonished to see her on her feet, holding her stomach, wearing a sinister and bloody grin.

She had lost a lot of blood and was becoming weaker by the second. But she was still dangerous to me.

"What's wrong Peter? Are you mad because you can't kill a woman?" she asked, swaying from side to side.

I picked up the pitchfork and took a firm grip. I swung it as hard as I could and hit her in the head, watching as her two front teeth flew from her mouth.

Kate was tough, tougher than I had ever imagined. And even after that powerful blow, she was still on her feet laughing at me. And so with hurt pride and all, I hit her again.

She spun around and fell to the ground, still smiling.

"Kate, stay down, please!" I begged.

She inched up to her knees, still holding her stomach while spitting out the excess blood that was streaming down her face into her mouth.

"Stay down Kate!"

She *still* tried to get up.

She fumbled through the dirt and picked up the knife before she dove at me to try to stab me in the foot.

I moved around her and stepped on her back before I jammed the pitchfork into her skull. And wouldn't you know it, *that* didn't kill her either.

She rolled over, a bloody mess. And as she reached up to clear her blood-soaked bangs from her face, she said, "Fuck you Peter! And fuck your whore of a mother and dumb, weak-ass sister! Oh, and don't go looking for the substitute because she's not here."

I looked at her. And through *her* expression, I could see that she saw something in *my* face this time, something that she had never seen before: hatred.

"No, fuck you, you psycho bitch! And I'm going to find Laura, no matter how long it takes. And you won't be able to stop that!"

I kicked her in the head and jammed the pitchfork through her throat, hoping to see her die...*finally*.

I pulled it out and jammed it into her neck again before stabbing her violently in the chest, stomach, and head repeatedly.

"You will *never* hurt another living soul again, you crazy bitch!"

I looked down on her while backing away, hoping she was dead this time. But if she wasn't, I would gladly try to kill her again. And after five or so minutes, I was convinced, but not totally. So I went back over and stabbed her in the chest, face, and neck again for good measure.

I would just have to rely on my own powers of deduction to find my wife. And whether here or back in Connecticut, I was going to make sure that she got a proper burial because I at least owed her that.

I limped back into the barn to grab the shovel. And when I came out I half expected her not to be there. But she was, still laying there, bleeding out.

I bent down and grabbed a handful of her hair, realizing at that moment how cold it was. I dragged her lifeless body across the pasture, through some trees to the top of a shallow ridge, and began to dig.

At first, the guilt of me killing her almost thwarted what I was doing. It almost caused me to alert the authorities and tell them everything. But I was hurting and cold, and all I wanted was to get this over with. So I kept digging, deciding that it was better not to tell the police.

At least not now.

What *was* I going to tell Hernandez though? That I found Kate, called her for help, but then she escaped into the mountains? That sounded good to me, and so that was what I would stick with when the time came. Only Kate and I would know the truth.

As I dug, I kept looking over at her lying there, staring at me through lifeless eyes, expecting her to get up and insult me again.

"Who's the pussy now, huh?" I said defiantly into the thin air.

Kate had killed multiple people, four of whom I loved beyond measure: my mother, my sister, my wife, and my best friend and brother, Jose. So at this point, remorse for her cursed soul was hard to come by for me.

Twenty-five minutes later, my six-foot-long, four-foot-deep hole was completed.

I walked over and grabbed her by the hair to drag her to her final resting place. And that was exactly what it would be. You see, now she truly *was* at rest.

And I would make sure that no one would ever disturb her again, for a long time.

I rested her body near the hole before kneeling to push her in. I had hoped she would land facedown. She didn't. She just lay there, judging me from the other side, as I began to throw dirt on top of her.

And so…after all this, had I truly known love? Yes, I had.

Did Kate love me? Yes, she did.

And was it in the name of love that she did what she did? I don't know.

But whatever made her do those horrible things would be buried with her today.

And *that* made me happy for us both. Our saga ended this cold, dreary day with her last breath. And I was relieved. And with that, I knew that it would be quite a while before I *ever* got married again. And that was fine with me.

THE END

ABOUT THE AUTHOR

This is the fourth work by Chris Rembert, who has been writing for twelve years now. His other works include *The Old India*; it' sequel, *Declaration of War*; along with his most gratifying work to date, *A Shattered Life*.

Kate, his latest endeavor, takes you on love's roller coaster, whipping you into a frenzy of emotions with his most compelling and complex character yet Kate, leaving you to wonder, *Can someone love or be loved too much?*

The author hopes that you will enjoy his work and many more to come and thanks you!

Good reading and good day.

CPSIA information can be obtained
at www.ICGtesting.com
Printed in the USA
LVHW010746200421
684992LV00006B/117

9 781662 410987